'What I know o   not attract.'

'One disastrous marriage,' said Nell drily, '
outs with his father ——'

'You are behind the times, Elinor — he is now
at ins, is learning to manage his father's
affairs.'

'Then he does not need to practise on mine,'
said Nell swiftly. 'An arrogant, ill-tempered
man such as Halstead is reported to be is the
last husband I could wish for. Thank you,
Uncle, but the answer is no.'

Dear Reader

Two of your favourite authors this month! After her 'faction', Paula Marshall has returned to the Regency period with MY LADY LOVE. Shad is horrendously insulting to Nell, and from then on nothing goes according to plan! Joanna Makepeace makes a very welcome reappearance with RELUCTANT REBEL, when all Isabel wants to do is settle down, but Adam still supports the deposed Plantagenets—and that results in adventures she could do without! Absorbing books, both—do enjoy them!

The Editor

Paula Marshall, married with three children, has had a varied life. She began her career in a large library and ended it as a senior academic in charge of history in a polytechnic. She has travelled widely, has been a swimming coach, and has appeared on *University Challenge* and *Mastermind*. She has always wanted to write, and likes her novels to be full of adventure and humour.

Recent titles by the same author:

AN UNEXPECTED PASSION
AN AMERICAN PRINCESS
WILD JUSTICE

MY LADY LOVE

Paula Marshall

First published in Great Britain 1993
by Mills & Boon Limited

© Paula Marshall 1993

Australian copyright 1993
Philippine copyright 1993
This edition 1993

ISBN 0 263 78061 9

Masquerade is a trademark published by
Mills & Boon Limited, Eton House,
18–24 Paradise Road, Richmond, Surrey, TW9 1SR.

Set in 10 on 12 pt Linotron Baskerville
04-9309-74704

Typeset in Great Britain by Centracet, Cambridge
Made and printed in Great Britain

CHAPTER ONE

'WHAT can have possessed you, Shad, to behave as you did? So unlike yourself! Last night's excesses at Watier's were the outside of enough. And in front of Cousin Trenchard, too. Shad! Are you listening to me, Shad? You can't still be drunk at four in the afternoon!'

Charles Augustus Shadwell, Viscount Halstead, heir to the third Earl Clermont, always known as Shad since he had been a captain in the cavalry in Wellington's Army — now, in 1818, five years out of it — tried to sit up. He failed. His head, and the room, were still spinning round. His mouth tasted like the bottom of a parrot's cage, and his stomach. . .!

'Do you have to make so much noise?' he groaned at his younger brother Guy.

'Noise!' said Guy indignantly. 'And I thought you never drank, not since the army anyway. What on earth possessed you?' he repeated. 'It's all round the town this morning, and Cousin Trenchard, trust him, has already been to Faa and spun him the yarn.'

'What yarn?' ground out Shad, who had sat up on the bed, to discover that he had fallen into a drunken stupor, still clad in last night's clothes. 'And why are you ringing such a peal over me? And, for God's sake, Guy, as you love me, don't draw the curtains. I feel bad enough in the dark, but the light——'

'Oh, damn that,' roared Guy, and pulled the curtains violently open, to reveal the elder brother whom he had always worshipped, haggard and drawn, his clothes

5

disgustingly soiled, sitting on the edge of the bed, his head in his hands.

Guy's disillusionment was complete. He said so.

Shad tried to remember what he had said or done the night before to cause Guy to behave in such an uncharacteristic fashion—he was usually respectful to his brother. The last thing that he remembered was flinging out of Julia Merton's home in Albemarle Street, yesterday afternoon, head on fire, anger and disgust choking him to such a degree that he was almost outside of himself.

And then he must have got blind drunk, and done something appalling to justify the brouhaha which Guy said that he had created. Only. . .he could not remember anything. All that had passed since he had banged Julia's drawing-room door behind him had vanished from his memory as though it had never happened.

Guy, his frank young face drawn with grief and disappointment, was still ranting on, 'And Faa wants to see you immediately. Good God, Shad, why did you have to do this, just as you and the old man had started to get on reasonably well together? And what about Julia? What will she think when the news reaches her?'

'I don't give a good Goddam what Julia thinks about anything,' said Shad inelegantly, rising to his feet and staggering towards the long pier-glass which stood in the corner of his bedroom.

He shuddered at the figure which he saw there. His face was a harsh one, strong and craggy, but it was not normally tinged principally with yellow and purple. His jet-black hair fell in wildly disarranged ringlets, and his deep blue eyes were red-rimmed and bloodshot. A face to frighten women and children.

Well, the more women he frightened the better. He

had attracted too many of them over the years, and all of them whores at heart — Julia, God help him, being the latest.

Guy was still reproaching him. 'Oh, do give over,' he said at last, and reeled to the washstand, plunging his head into the bowl of cold water which stood there — it might help — and with his head under water he could avoid hearing Guy.

He surfaced, water dripping from him, and turned to face his brother.

'At least have the goodness to tell me what it is I did, or am said to have done.'

'Oh, you said it, no doubt of that,' announced Guy bitterly. 'I was there. Who was it who hauled you home, do you think, and stopped Nell Tallboys's cousin from killing you on the spot?'

'Well, thank you for that,' ground out Shad, and, face wicked, he launched his full thirteen and a half stone, six-foot-one frame at Guy, and seized him by the throat. 'Now, will you tell me what I did? Or do I have to beat it out of you? If I am to be so madly abused, at least let me know what for.'

'You mean you really don't know?' gasped Guy, as Shad released him. 'Oh, pax, pax,' he began hurriedly. 'You came into Watier's, half-foxed already, barely on your feet, began to gamble like a madman, and then. . .'

'Oh, God,' groaned Shad, collapsing on to the bed. 'Enough, Guy. I remember everything. Would that I didn't.'

'Well, that's a relief,' said Guy sturdily. He walked over to the jug on the washstand, poured water into a glass and handed it to his brother. 'Here, drink this. It will make you feel better.'

'Nothing will ever make me feel better,' muttered

Shad, looking up at Guy, and feeling sorry for causing
his brother's evident distress. Guy at nineteen was
eleven years younger than Shad and had always hero-
worshipped him. Perhaps, Shad had often thought,
because they were so different, Guy being blond, slim
and rather diffident; he took after his dead mother, and
Shad after their father.

'Here, let me ring for Carter,' said Guy. 'If you're
going to visit Faa, you'd better spruce yourself up. You
look like an unmade bed at the minute.'

Shad let Guy order him about. It seemed the least
that he could do for the brother who, whatever else, had
always loved him and stood up for him.

Later, he waited outside his father's suite of rooms in
Clermont House, the Shadwell family's London home.
Colquhoun, his father's secretary, had told him, a
grieving look on his old face, 'My lord will see you
shortly; he is at his business at the moment.'

The business of making Viscount Halstead wait, no
doubt, thought Shad bitterly. Well, closing his eyes, and
remembering yesterday, he thought it was no less than
he deserved. Nor was he surprised, when Mr Colquhoun
finally summoned him in, to discover his father, standing stern and tall before his desk, over which hung
Romney's famous portrait of Shad's dead mother.

'So, you are at last up, Halstead. Is this true, what
Cousin Trenchard tells me?'

'Seeing that I don't know what Cousin Trenchard
told you, sir, it is difficult to say.'

'Come, Halstead, don't chop logic with me — this
scene at Watier's. Making shameful bets and brawling
with the cousin of the subject of them is hardly the
conduct of the man who is my heir.'

Shad's control, insecure since yesterday, broke. He

made no effort to defend himself—he could not—merely replied bitterly, 'I have never ceased to regret, sir, the day that I became your heir. Oh, I have tried, God knows how hard, to fill Frederick's place for you, but in your eyes I shall never be Frederick's equal. He was your. . .nonpareil.'

'Which you, sir, are most definitely not!'

'Yes,' said Shad, feeling that he must defend himself a little, after all. 'His untimely death deprived me not only of a brother whom I had no wish to succeed, but also of a career in the army, which I not only loved, but in which I was beginning to excel. Remember that.'

'Come, come, sir,' snapped the Earl. 'My heir could not remain in the army, and, in any case, the wars are over now. You were needed to learn to run the estate, to take over from Frederick in every way.'

'Which I have tried to do,' retorted Shad steadily. 'You can have no grounds for complaint on that score. Green has told you not only of my application, but of my innovations at Pinfold. Only I can never be Frederick, and that is the true ground of the division between us. The only time, sir, when we were not at odds was when I was away at the wars.'

If the Earl thought that there was any truth in this bitter statement, he gave no sign of it. His dislike for his second son was plain on his face.

'You were always a wild boy, Halstead, and became a wild man. Your marriage to Isabella French, against all my wishes—and look what that led to! Your——'

'Spare me,' said Shad, his face white beneath the jaundiced shadow of his last night's debauch, 'I paid for that, God knows, and in the five years since Frederick's death I have lived an exemplary life, and done your bidding faithfully. Why should last night's work, which

I regret more than you can ever do, cause you to cut me up so severely? One failure after so long. . .'

'Because, sir, I have been in the country discussing with her uncle, Chesney Beaumont, her mother's brother, an alliance with the very lady, Elinor Tallboys, Countess of Malplaquet, whose name you soiled last night in your drunken folly. We had reached terms. He is to broach your marriage with her today, in her Yorkshire fastness, and I was to speak to you this very morning, when, instead, you lay in your drunken stupor.'

Shad, composure gone for once, gaped at him. 'Do I hear you aright, sir? You were arranging for me to offer for Nell Tallboys — Nell Tallboys! — without so much as a word to me beforehand. You expected me to marry *her*, at your simple word of command!'

'My mistake,' replied his father coldly. 'I had thought you almost Frederick, who saw my wishes as his command. I cannot imagine him refusing such a noble prize, so suitable an alliance. You would be. . .would have been. . .the richest man in England.'

Shad's laugh was almost a shriek, or a curse. 'And that's it, sir? That is to be my end? No arguing, agree, or cut line, is it? You knew that I was involved with Julia Merton, intended to marry her. . .until yesterday, that is,' he amended with a shudder.

'Oh, that was never on, sir, never on,' shrugged his father. 'One more proof that you have not yet rid yourself of your youthful follies. A steady marriage with a steady woman is what you require to settle you, but now. . . I wonder what the Countess of Malplaquet would think of a proposal from a man who threw her name about in a gaming house? Why did you choose that woman to slight, sir, why?'

What could he say that would not make matters worse than they already were? Only, in his chagrin and, yes, shame, at his conduct yesterday, the more because he had always prided himself on his iron self-control, he muttered stiffly, 'But Nell Tallboys, a plain bluestocking, past her last prayers, with a face to frighten horses, they say, and a virtue so rigid that any man is rendered ice by it, and her very reputation caused me to lose mine last night.'

He stopped at last; his mixed anger and shame had caused him to make matters worse, not better.

'Yes,' said his father glacially. 'Cousin Trenchard said that you bet an enormous sum — twenty thousand pounds, was it not? — that no woman was virtuous, and that even that paragon would succumb to your wishes without marriage, should you care to try her.'

Oh, God forgive him that he had said any such thing. Was it her cousin Bobus Beaumont's high-minded praise of her which, while he was smarting from his second cruel betrayal by a woman whom he thought had loved him, had caused his drunken self to behave so badly?

'Lightskirts all,' he remembered roaring. 'Damned mermaids, even the best of them.'

'You may well look ashamed, Halstead.' His father's voice was so distant, so cold, the dislike which he had always felt for this second son, unworthy successor — as he saw it — to his beloved Frederick, was so plain in his voice that Shad's shuddering, brought on partly by last night's drinking after years of abstinence, increased.

'And now you have the task of trying to mend matters. All may not be lost. Before this news reaches her, I shall use my influence to suppress this latest folly, while you, sir, must go north, to offer for her. An honourable proposal must wipe out what was said. Idle and jealous gossip will explain all.'

Shad stared dumbly at his father. 'Are you light in the head, sir? What can wipe that out? And besides I have no wish to marry Nell Tallboys, would never offer for her, would never have her if she was handed me on a plate. Nor do I wish to marry again, ever.'

'You will do your duty by me, Halstead,' was his father's only reply to that. 'Or I shall disinherit you. The estate is not entailed, as you well know. I was minded to pass you over and put Guy in your place when poor Frederick died. But my honour would not allow it. If you refuse me now, I shall——'

'You shall, and need do nothing,' flashed Shad. 'I have worked for five years like the trooper I once was to clear up the mess which Frederick made of running your estates. No, do not shake your head; Green will confirm the truth of what I say. Yes, Father, I tell you that now, what I would not tell you before, and my reward is to be disposed of in marriage, without my consent, and be insulted into the bargain, and what's more. . .' He stopped on seeing his father's stricken expression — he could not tell him the truth about Frederick; it would break him — and said instead, 'You may have your way. I shall leave for my mother's small estate in Scotland, and live there. You cannot take that away from me and you may do as you please with the Clermont lands.'

'Glen Ruadh will not finance a luxurious life in London for you,' snarled his father.

'Nor do I want it,' said Shad wearily. 'You do not know me, sir. I shall consider returning to the army. At least I was happy there. I should never have left it.'

'Leave this room, sir, without obliging me over the

Countess of Malplaquet, and you may go to the devil for all I care,' was his father's only reply to that.

'Willingly, sir, willingly. And since Nell Tallboys enchants you so much, may I recommend that you marry the lady yourself?' ground out his son, and almost reeled from the room. He had thought that five years of hard work and dedication had reconciled his father to the loss of Frederick and his own succession, but the secretly arranged marriage, and his father's response to one night's folly after such devotion, had shown him his error, for nothing had changed.

His only regret was the loss of Guy, who met him at the bottom of the great staircase, and stood back in dismay at the sight of his brother's face, his own white.

'Oh, no, Shad! You are hopelessly at outs with him still, I see.'

'So hopelessly that he has disinherited me. He wants me to marry Nell Tallboys, God help me. Has arranged the marriage behind my back, without so much as a by-your-leave. I'm off to Scotland, immediately. For good. I'll keep in touch, Guy. Do what you can for him; he does not live in the world as it is, but as he thinks it is. Frederick's shadow hangs over me still.'

'Then I shall tell him the truth about Frederick, Shad, seeing that you will not.'

Shad caught his brother by the shoulders. 'Indeed, you won't — it would break him. Be a mortal blow.'

'And he is not giving you one?' riposted Guy. 'Do you still love him, Shad, after thirty years of curses and dislike — still hope that he may care for you a little? To hand you Nell Tallboys!'

'No,' said Shad steadily. 'I have long surrendered any hope on that score. I should never have left the army,

but I thought. . . Oh, to the devil with what I thought.
It's over at last, and I'm not sorry.'

But, as he left the room, and shouted for Vinnie, his
late sergeant and now his groom, valet and man of all
work, to be ready to accompany him north, on the
double, he was. For so long he had hoped to be
reconciled with his father, and now all was ashes.

'No,' said Elinor Tallboys, Countess of Malplaquet,
Viscountess Wroxton, Baroness Sheveborough, all in
her own right, mistress of all she surveyed here in
Yorkshire, châtelaine of so many properties that even
she could not remember them all, wealthy beyond the
dreams of man, and woman, too. 'No, no, not at all,
never. That is my first and last word, Uncle.'

'But only consider, my dear,' said her uncle, Sir
Chesney Beaumont, her mother's brother, closing his
eyes against her obstinacy, 'only consider.'

They were standing in the Turkish parlour at
Campions, the Malplaquets' great house on the edge of
the Yorkshire moors, a house over three hundred years
old, huge, dominating the landscape and the lives of all
those who lived near it. The Turkish room was so called
because it was filled with rare *objets d'art* from that
country, brought home by a former earl of Malplaquet
who had been ambassador there. Over the fireplace,
carved on a ribbon of stone, was the family's motto, 'As
the beginning, so the end'.

Nell Tallboys sometimes thought that she was the
only thing in the whole house which could not by any
judgement be considered a work of art. She was plainly
dressed in a prim grey gown, high-waisted, a small pie
frill around its neck being her only concession to any

form of decoration. She wore no jewellery, and her hair was tied in a simple knot at the back of her head.

'No,' she said, firm again. 'I will not consider — nor reconsider, either. I have no wish to marry — let alone consider a proposal from the father of a man whom I have never met and do not wish to meet.'

'But you must marry, my dear Elinor——' This was met again with his niece's smiling refusal, laced with a touch of the steel which made her the resolute character she was.

'"Must. . .must. . .?" as good Queen Bess said of a similar suggestion. Not a word to use to me, Uncle, I think.' Her smile and her gentle tones took away the sting of her words a little, but her steadfastness, her determination always shone through even her lightest utterances.

He smiled, a little painfully. 'No "must"s then, my dear. But you are already twenty-seven years old; you need a husband and the estate and the title need an heir. You do not wish all this——' and he waved a hand to encompass the sumptuous room and the landscape outside '— to go to your cousin Ulric.'

'God forbid!' exclaimed Nell, shuddering, thinking of Ulric's debauchery, his wasting-away of his own good estate, and what he would do if he got his hands on the Malplaquet fortune.

'Well, Elinor,' said her uncle eagerly. 'What constrains you?' And then he added unluckily, 'The land needs a master.'

'It does?' said Nell, suddenly savagely satiric. 'Tell me, Uncle, have you asked Henson how we are faring here since I took over, compared with what we did before I inherited from Grandfather? If his running of

Malplaquet's lands is typical of what a master might do, then I am content to remain merely its mistress!'

There was nothing Chesney Beaumont could say to that. He knew only too well that since Nell had inherited at barely twenty-one, and had taken control of the management of her lands, with the help of Henson, whom she had appointed, the Malplaquet estates had multiplied their returns and their efficiency tenfold.

'Nevertheless, I ask you to consider most carefully this offer from Lord Clermont on behalf of his son Charles, Viscount Halstead. A most noble offer, nobly made.'

'Nobly made to acquire Malplaquet's lands,' said Nell drily. 'What I know of Halstead does not attract. One disastrous marriage, after which he killed his wife's lover in a duel, at outs with his father——'

'You are behind the times, Elinor—he is now at ins, is learning to manage his father's affairs.'

'Then he does not need to practise on mine,' said Nell swiftly. 'An arrogant, ill-tempered man such as Halstead is reported to be is the last husband I could wish for. Thank you for attempting to take care of me, Uncle, but the answer is no.'

'At least see him,' returned her uncle desperately. 'Clermont proposes that you meet with Halstead, either here, or elsewhere, wherever you please, to see if you might suit.'

'Nowhere is where I please,' responded Nell, finality in her voice, 'and that must be that. Halstead is the last man I should wish to marry. I would not have him if he brought me a dukedom—nay, if he were a royal prince, on his knees before me,' and, as her uncle groaned and shook his head at her implacability, she added, 'Come, Uncle, admit it. Even you are acknowledging by what you say that the only reason why any man would wish to marry me is Malplaquet's fortune. What man of sense could wish for a plain woman past her last prayers otherwise? Never once, in all our talks on this subject, have you ever suggested that I should marry other than to secure the estate and the succession.'

'Now that is unfair, my dear,' he said quickly.

'Unfair?' Nell's eyebrows rose. She could see herself reflected in the beautiful Venetian glass above the hearth. A plain woman, plainly dressed, too tall, her features too harsh, too definite, she thought; only the glossy dark chestnut of her hair, and her large grey eyes, softened the severity of her appearance.

That she wronged herself she was not aware. But in a society which preferred pink and white prettiness, Nell's face, full of strength and character, was not the sort to be enshrined in a *Book of Beauty*, and, because she had long since resigned herself to that, she dressed for practical use, not to attract.

'Come, Uncle,' she said gently, 'I have long known that any marriage I make will be one of convenience, but at least allow me to choose the man I make it with.'

'And how will you ever do that, madam, tell me,' said her uncle, at last angry with her obduracy, 'when you never meet a man other than estate servants, old Challenor, your librarian, even older Payne, your secretary, middle-aged Henson, and assorted stablehands and flunkeys, led by that ageing warrior Aisgill, of whom you are so fond?'

He snorted, and then was off again, hallooing himself on, thought Nell with wry amusement, as though he were out with the Quorn Hunt and racing for the kill. 'You are grown a hermit, if a female can be such. How can you choose a man to marry you, unless you consent

to go out into the world, or allow them to visit you here?
At least let Halstead come to Campions. Talk to him.
You might deal well with him. My information is that
he is a man of sense, who was a good soldier, underval-
ued by the world and his father.'

'I am content as I am,' said Nell, turning away, tears
springing unwanted to her eyes. 'And I do not wish for
visitors, male or female. You forget that I have Aunt
Conybeare, and all the care of the estate to keep me
busy.'

She remembered her one dreadful season in town,
nine years ago, when she was eighteen, and the muttered
laughs and comments which had followed her tall,
gauche person. 'Such a great gawk,' Emily Cowper had
drawled in her spiteful way, 'that, were she not to be
Malplaquet's Countess, the season would be a waste.
But, be sure, whatever she looks like, she will have offers
aplenty.'

Nell was sure that the comment had been meant to
be overheard — as were others, equally mocking.
Nothing, but nothing, could comfort her after hearing
that, and social disaster seemed to follow social disaster.

She had grown more clumsy by the moment, felt
everything about her to be too big, too raw, and, once
the season was over, and half a dozen suitors repelled,
their insincerity so patent that it hurt, she had retired to
Yorkshire and happiness in seclusion, and refused to
return.

Her grandfather's long illness, and then his death —
her father and mother had died in a boating accident
years before — had assisted her wish never to visit
London again, and, once she was her own mistress,
Yorkshire had sufficed.

That the years had greatly improved her looks, given

her a poise and command that came from dealing competently with those around her, she had never found out — nor had society — for there was none to see, or tell her, and she would not have believed them if they had.

Her companion, gentle Aunt Conybeare, also hated town, and the two women lived comfortably in their isolation.

'You will regret this, Elinor, my dear,' said her uncle as he took his leave. 'I do believe it might have been better for you to have accepted Ulric, rather than live like this.'

'And there's no amen to that,' said Nell lightly, 'and you know that you don't mean it, Uncle. I shall see Halstead if he arrives here, but I warn you, he won't like what I have to say.'

And that was that. Only to her horror, this time Aunt Conybeare hemmed and hesitated, and finally said in her gentle voice, 'I think that your uncle has a point, my dear Nell, and, if you cannot bring yourself to accept Halstead, perhaps we ought to try the season again.'

'Well, you may,' said Nell, harsh, for once, to her aunt. 'But I shan't and that's flat. I shall marry when I'm nearly thirty, someone old and feeble, just able to give me my heir, and too fond of comfort to want to interfere with my life.'

And then, when she saw her aunt's face crumple a little at her severity, she went quickly over to her, fell on to her knees by her chair, and embraced her.

'No, my dear Aunt Honey-bear ——' which had long been Nell's pet name for her '— I must not tease you, who have been so good to me, but you, of all people, know how I feel about men and women and marriage.'

'And I,' said her aunt, a little reproving for once, 'know what a good marriage can mean to a woman, and can do for her. I have never ceased to regret that poor George was taken from me before his time. No, Nell, do not make faces at me. I know what you must endure, which I never did, but believe, as I do, that one day you will meet someone whom you can love and care for, and who will love and care for you.'

Nell grimaced. 'Oh, I thank you for that, Aunt, but it is Cloud-cuckoo-land of which you speak. For I am not you, and Malplaquet stands in everyone's way, and blinds them to me, and what I am.'

Now what could Aunt Conybeare say to that? And the look which followed Nell, as she walked away, tall and graceful, was a sad one, for where would Nell find a man to whom Malplaquet meant nothing, and Nell everything?

CHAPTER TWO

SHAD drove himself and Vinnie hard on the way to
Scotland. The weather was poor, but that meant
nothing to him. He had begun to see Glen Ruadh as
sanctuary, and could hardly wait to be there. Behind
him lay his old life and his old self, which he was
beginning to dislike.

The nights were the worst, the worst since Isabella,
and he had Julia Merton to thank for them.

How could he have been so blind to fall again into
the same trap, and this time with, as he had wrongly
thought, his eyes open, and himself armoured against
betraying women?

Julia had been so lovely and so clever, quite different
from Isabella and her dusky charms. Oh, he had
thought that, at last, he had found the one woman.
From the moment he had met her he had been in a
dream of love. He could see now that he had been as
infatuated as a green boy.

For she had sought him out, and day by day had
bound him with her magics, and he had worshipped the
unattainable and hoped to attain her by marriage. He
had laughed at those who had suggested that Julia
Merton, still unmarried at twenty-four, might be so for
reasons not altogether respectable — not that there were
any blots on her reputation, simply the lack of response
to the many who had offered for her.

'I was waiting for the right man,' she had whispered
once, in a scented ballroom, when he had gently posed

that very question. And then she had looked at him, wide-eyed. 'And — do you know? — I think I've found him.'

Oh, she had, she had! Her modesty, her gentle wit, the way in which she drew back from him if she thought him over-bold. And then, when he had proposed, on his knees, as though the ten years since Isabella had never happened, she had, ever modest, drawn back, said, 'All must be proper. I know you are of age, but speak to your father, and then, Halstead, then —— ' for she refused to call him Shad; that was for his old, rowdy army life ' — I will accept you.'

Unknowing of his father's other plans for him, he had thought that the asking would be easy, and on that happy morning he had promised her that he would see his father on the next day, when he arrived from the country — where he now knew that he had been conferring with Chesney Beaumont about Nell Tallboys.

She had told him that she would be resting in the afternoon, but he had been to Bond Street, and seen a ring there, an exquisite thing, as delicate as she was, diamonds and sapphires to enhance her blonde loveliness, and he had rushed to Albemarle Street, his head on fire, to give it to her — surely she would see him.

He burned, he absolutely burned, when he thought of how her maid had tried to put him off, of how he had said so complacently, 'Oh, tell her I am here; she will rise for me, I am sure of it,' and he had pushed his way so confidently into the little private sitting-room where she usually received him.

He remembered the maid, pulling at him, babbling, 'No, my lord, wait in the French drawing-room, rather,' but he had hardly heard her, heard anything until he had thrown the door open, and seen the reason for her dismay.

For Julia, his Julia, lay naked beneath Jack Broughton, that noted lecher, married — but his marriage had never stopped that — and a thousand things, half-heard, half-seen, came together, and when she pushed Jack off, and stared at Shad, face white, whispering, 'No,' as her world collapsed, too, he saw something else which told him why she had pursued him, netted him in her toils.

By her breasts and body she was pregnant, and how she could have hoped to deceive him after marriage, he could not think. Except, of course, once safely married, there would have been nothing he could do without making himself a laughing-stock.

Jack pulled away, and laughed at him, and at the woman both.

'What's this?' he remembered saying in a hoarse voice, and Jack shrugged, even as the woman on the sofa improbably tried to protest innocence.

'Why, Shad, truth will out, I see. She has been my whore these five years, since after I married Nancy. Oh, quiet, Julia,' he drawled. 'Too late to pretend now. And Shad won't talk, you know. Too full of honour — to say nothing of his pride. He won't tell the world what he so nearly did!'

Shad was not proud of what he did do next. For he seized Broughton and beat him nearly senseless, and then had the privilege of watching Julia wail over his battered form.

'You devil,' she spat at him. 'Do you think that I could have borne your ugly face, if it weren't that I needed you, or any man, to hide the proof of my love for him?'

'Love?' he said. 'What's that?' and walked from the room, but not before throwing the ring at her. 'And here's your payment from me,' he said. 'Sell it to buy baby clothes for your bastard.'

And then he had drunk himself stupid and gone to Watier's and attacked another woman's good name and ended, possibly forever, the fragile *rapprochement* he had achieved with his father.

So much for that. And it was to exorcise these demons that he drove himself and Vinnie on through the bad weather of that dismal autumn.

At what point he was sure that they were being tracked he did not know. They had stopped overnight at a dirty inn, and after a bad night and a poor breakfast, Vinnie grumbling over his flat ale that it was worse than campaigning, they had set out across the moors, north of Bradford on a poor road which grew worse.

The feeling of being watched grew stronger in him, and Vinnie felt it too. But mile after mile as he drove the carriage north, wishing that he had not brought it, but had travelled on horseback, however hard the journey, nothing untoward happened, so that he began to think that his imagination, fevered with the memory of Julia's betrayal was working overtime, was deceiving him.

They stopped at midday to eat bread, cheese and apples and to drink the bottle of ale which Vinnie had brought with him from the inn, and then water from the spring by the roadside.

He remembered that Nell Tallboys's great house stood near by, and he wondered briefly what she might think if told that her uncle's choice of a husband was passing her by without as much as a how do you do.

Well, judging by reports, she probably wanted him as little as he wanted her. He grimaced, wiped his mouth, and they set off again into the teeth of a wind more suited to November than late September.

And then, just after they had reached the moor's highest point, and the road, now little more than a track along which the carraige lurched, descended before them, all his forebodings came true. His instincts for danger, honed by his army career, had not played him false.

Two bullets whined at them. One missed him, the other took poor Vinnie, riding by the carriage, in the chest, and dropped him dead from his horse. The French had not been able to kill him, but a group of Yorkshire banditti had done for him.

Shad never did know who or what they were, whether common footpads or poor devils without work, perhaps even old soldiers lost without a war to fight, but whoever they were they knew their business. They came across the moor at him, on horseback, rode over poor dead Vinnie, and, firing a second shot at him, demanded his valuables on pain of his life.

'You'll have to fight me for them, then,' he yelled in feeble defiance, and, another shot catching him across the shoulder, he lost control of the horses, and one of the cut-throats launched himself at him, and struck him such a blow with a bludgeon that he was felled — to lie half in the carriage, and half out of it.

Stunned, but still with some shreds of consciousness, he felt rather than saw them drag his bags out and begin to plunder them. They were particularly excited by his fine pistols, and the Baker rifle which he had bought from a friend in the Rifle Brigade who had later died at Waterloo.

Then they pulled him from the carriage, he struggling, weakly and futilely, consciousness coming and going. Once they had him stretched on the ground, blood from his gashed shoulder staining his fine coat, they stripped him of his clothing and his possessions, so that he lay naked and shivering on the hard earth.

The leader, a grimy ginger-headed bravo, a man as big as himself, discarded his own filthy rags, put on Shad's, including his top hat, and then, half in malice, half in jest, told his fellows to dress Shad in his discarded clothing.

He struggled with them, was struck again, hard, for his pains, and knew no more until they mounted their own horses, with one of them driving his carriage, with dead Vinnie propped up by his own half-concious self, bumping and rattling across the moor towards a quarry, earlier glimpsed in the distance.

Shad's last thoughts as they pushed the carriage over the quarry's edge — they had kept his horses as plunder — was that perhaps it was fitting that everything should end here so ignominiously, after he had survived a dozen battles, guerrilla war, and his father's dislike. He'll never know what happened to me — nor will he care, was his last conscious thought.

'And that's the end of my fine gentleman,' grinned the man who was now wearing Shad's clothes, watching the carriage break into pieces as it fell towards the water in the quarry's bottom. What he did not know was that Shad, thrown out almost immediately, was caught, a third of the way down, in some bushes, unconscious, but still breathing, and still blindly, instinctively determined somehow to survive.

* * *

For Nell Tallboys that day began like any other. There was little to show that, after it, nothing was ever going to be the same again. She had spent the morning going over her correspondence with old Payne, and she had been compelled to admit that her uncle's criticism of him had been just. He was past his best, and she would need to pension him off soon and find someone younger, which would be a nuisance, for she would have to train him — with Henson's help.

She had then gone over accounts with Henson; he had told her of some discontent, not Luddite — that seemed dead, these days — but something similar, over towards Bradford. He hoped that it would not affect Nell's people, but thought not.

The day was fine and sunny, and after luncheon — cold meat and fruit — she had decided on a ride to blow the cobwebs away, and, instead of sending one of the footmen to the stables, she had decided to walk there herself, once she had changed into her riding habit. She liked to come upon the men unawares, see how they behaved when their betters were not about.

Again, she was later to ponder on the might-have-beens, if Nell, Countess of Malplaquet, had not walked into the altercation going on in the stable yard.

The stables themselves were beautiful buildings, large, in the Renaissance style, fine things, with better homes for horses than most men had, she sometimes thought, and the yard was reached by a triumphal arch, with a centaur — half-man, half-horse — galloping across its top.

Beneath, the human centaurs were all gathered, arguing. Aisgill's voice, its broad Yorkshire even broader than usual, was the loudest.

He was railing at Henson, who stood civilised and

stolid in his fine black suit, his thin, clever face at odds with the craggy ones around him.

Aisgill stopping to draw breath, Henson began to speak in cold measured tones. Originally a countryman himself, he had adopted the manners and dress of those whom he served.

'Campions cannot,' he said, 'be the refuge for every wandering derelict plucked from the highway or the moors.'

Aisgill began again, 'Common humanity——' to be addressed by Nell.

'What is it,' she asked, seeing that all the stable lads, the grooms and gardeners, together with some of the house's indoor servants, were clustered around one of the doorways to the stable lads' quarters, 'that is worth all this brouhaha?'

Henson and Aisgill began to talk together, and for once Nell spoke with some of the hauteur of the great lady she was.

'One at a time, if you please, and some of you stand back a little. I wish to see what exercises you so.' For she had become aware that the cause of the argument was half sitting, half lying on the steps before them.

'To your work, lads,' roared Aisgill, suddenly aware of the crowd that had gathered while he disputed with Henson, and then on Nell beckoning him, rather than Henson, to speak, said, 'This poor creature was brought in today by Gilbert Outhwaite from Overbeck. He found him wandering on the moor on the way of here. By the looks of him, he had been crawling on his hands and knees,' and he indicated the figure on the steps, visible now that all the servants had reluctantly dispersed, leaving their betters to argue.

'Outhwaite knew that you, Lady Elinor——' for

Nell was still Lady Elinor to them, as she had been for many years seeing that she had been merely heir presumptive to Malplaquet until her grandfather died, and disliked being called m'lady, or Lady Malplaquet ' — were giving charity to such unfortunates, in exchange for casual labour, and thought that we might help this one.'

Nell looked at the man on the steps. He was bigger, much bigger than all the stocky moors men who had surrounded him. He had a heavy growth of black stubble on his face, and his hair was a mass of shaggy black ringlets. His clothing was so torn and exiguous that Outhwaite had thrown an old blanket from his cart around his broad shoulders. He was shivering beneath it, his feet were bare and bleeding, and his eyes, suddenly raised to stare at Nell, were a brilliant, feverish blue. They held hers almost challengingly.

'Henson will be after telling me that we cannot take in every vagrant in the Riding,' said Aisgill grimly, 'but we cannot turn such a poor thing away. He's starving, ate one of the turnips in Aisgill's cart as though he were a wolf, is perhaps simple, for he hardly knows his own name.'

'Not true,' muttered the man suddenly, his eyes still on Nell. 'It's, it's. . .' He seemed to struggle a moment with himself, then growled something which sounded like 'Chad'.

'Is that all?' said Nell. 'Chad? Ask him what his other name is.'

Aisgill spoke to the vagrant, who shook his head, looked puzzled; then, as he stared again at Nell, his face seemed to lighten.

'That he doesn't know,' said Aisgill ruefully. 'Only that he's Chad. Nor does he know where he comes from,

Outhwaite said, nor even where he is. That is why Mr Henson here wishes to turn him away. Says he'll only be a belly to feed, won't bring hands to work with him.'

'That is so, Lady Elinor,' said Henson severely. 'Charity is well enough, but Campions cannot support every useless half-wit who roams the countryside. Either the parish supports him, or he finds work on some farm — but who would employ a simpleton?'

Nell looked doubtfully at the man. Beneath his growth of curling black hair she thought she saw a harsh and craggy face, and his body, what she could see of it, seemed a strong one, well made.

'He does not look a simpleton,' and then, decisively, 'Show me his hands.'

The man looked at her again, held out his hands with a smile which showed excellent white teeth, said, 'Will they do?' in a tone which was almost provocative, sharp and sure, quite unlike his confusion of a moment before — and then doubt and puzzlement crossed his face again, and he hung his head.

His big hands were torn and bleeding, bruised, the nails broken, the hands of a manual worker, Nell thought, although his speech, what there was of it, hinted that he was more than that. Nell caught his brilliant blue stare again, and something there, something powerful, almost feral, had a strange effect on her. She shivered, and as she did so he dropped his gaze, and when he looked at her again his face was dull, expressionless.

'He's had a blow on the head recently, or a fall,' announced Aisgill suddenly. 'There's a half-healed gash on his shoulder. He's been sleeping rough, by the state of him. But he doesn't look a regular idiot to me.'

'An irregular one, then,' snorted Henson. 'He stinks like one. Begging your pardon, Lady Elinor.'

'Be quiet, both of you,' said Nell sharply, seeing Aisgill bridle and prepare to answer Henson angrily. Both men stared at her; she rarely came the fine lady with them. 'We can at least give him a trial, find out what work he can do. Take him in, Aisgill. Feed him, see he's washed, give him some clean clothes. If you think that he might not be well, let Dr Ramsden look at him, and then, when he's fit again, try him as a stable hand. You were saying you had not enough lads only yesterday.'

Henson opened his mouth, saw Nell's expression, said wearily, 'Begging your pardon, *my lady*,' and he stressed the title. 'If he don't suit, and won't work, as many simpletons won't, then he may go to the parish when he's had his chance.'

'He doesn't look a simpleton,' said Nell again, but best to make concessions to them both, seeming to favour neither the one nor the other. 'But yes. A fair trial with Aisgill first, and, if that fails, as you say.'

The man of whom they were speaking had fallen into a daze, his eyes on the horizon, apparently unaware of Nell, Aisgill and Henson, and that they were concerned with him.

'Chad,' said Nell sharply. 'You heard what I said — that you are to be given a trial here?'

He nodded, looked up at Nell, his eyes clearing again. He took her in, standing tall and graceful before him, in her bottle-green habit, elegant boots, and her tiny top hat, a very Diana. Elusive memory, running before him, stirred in Chad. He spoke without thinking, and the words were almost a command.

'Who are you?' he said, blunt.

'Respect due from you,' snapped Henson, annoyed, but Nell said,

'No, he means nothing by it. Natural for him to wish to know — especially if his memory has gone. You may call me Lady Elinor, as the rest of my people do here,' she told him gently. 'But you must do as Mr Aisgill here bids you, or be turned away. You understand?'

The man nodded. His puzzled look, so different from the one of a moment ago, had returned. 'Do as Mr Aisgill bids me. I understand,' and then, almost as an afterthought, with a slight bow in her direction, 'Lady Elinor.'

Once more those strange blue eyes were on her, and were doing their work, holding her, trying to tell her something, causing her to be patient with him, affecting her in the oddest fashion. And then he turned to look at Aisgill, for instructions, presumably.

Henson sighed noisily, turned away himself. 'Good,' said Nell, 'then we all understand one another. Now, Aisgill, tell one of the grooms to attend me; I wish to ride on the moor this afternoon,' and then as Aisgill nodded, and the man, helped up by one of the hands, for, despite his size, he seemed weak — probably from hunger — was led away, she said, 'His voice is educated, Aisgill, I wonder how he came to be a vagrant, wandering the moor half clothed, his memory gone?'

Henson, still standing there, and now suddenly a little ashamed of his harshness before the hands' gentleness with the derelict, said, 'Many a man ruined these days, Lady Elinor, with the wars over and business failing. Soldiers ruined, too, their occupation gone.'

All three of them watched their new acquisition walk into the men's quarters.

'Well, I don't like us getting a reputation for saving

half the riff-raff in Yorkshire, but perhaps one more won't do us harm — if he is willing and able to work, that is, which seems unlikely. Another worthless mouth to feed, no doubt, and throw out after a few weeks.'

Later, Henson's words came back, if not to haunt him, but to remind him that even the cleverest of us could make the grossest of misjudgements.

CHAPTER THREE

'I WONDER how the vagabond Aisgill rescued is getting on?' said Nell idly to Aunt Conybeare, who sat stitching at her canvas work before a roaring fire. Early October was colder than usual that autumn.

Nell had been poring over a thick book, not a lady's mindless and agreeable novel, but a report from the Board of Agriculture on hill farming. All her reading seemed to be functional these days, and Lord Byron's latest — and naughty — work, *Manfred: a Drama*, discreetly hidden from public view by the *Quarterly Review* on the occasional table by her chair, sat waiting for her to find time to pick it up.

Nell knew it was naughty because Aunt Conybeare, sighing and deploring it as she did so, had eagerly read every word, before telling Nell that, as an unmarried girl, she really ought not to open it.

Nell privately wondered whether an unmarried girl who ran England's biggest and most successful stud could be unaware of anything to do with reproduction, human or otherwise, but discreetly said nothing.

For no good reason, ever since she had seen the vagabond on the steps, and he had raised those amazing eyes to look into hers, the derelict she had taken in had haunted Nell's memory.

Really, this is absurd, she told herself. Whatever had she thought that she had seen there? It had disturbed her so much that she had privately determined to avoid meeting him again, and apart from asking Aisgill once if he was still at Campions, to which Aisgill had said, Yes, and he was putting him to work in the yard, she had not spoken of him again, and had avoided the stables.

Restlessness gripped her, a feeling that life was passing her by — probably the result of Chesney Beaumont's doomings about her unmarried condition. She rose, put down her book, said, 'I need air. I think I will go for a walk. No, Aunt,' as her aunt raised agonised eyes to her, for the air was keen outside, 'I shall take John with me, for protection, if not company, and you may enjoy the fire in peace.'

Did her feet take her stablewards consciously or unconsciously? She was interested in the horses, of course. She was a skilful horsewoman, and the Campions stables were nationally famous, particularly the stud, where horses bred by the Malplaquets constantly won the great classic races.

John, the footman, walking behind her, carrying a large green umbrella — although how he was to keep it up in the wind should he need to open it, Nell could not think — she passed through the great arch to stand in the yard.

She was wearing a heavy mannish coat over her light dress, and had put on little black boots against the mud of what appeared to be an early winter.

One of the stable hands stopped currycombing a horse, came up respectfully to take her orders. 'Lady Elinor?'

'Where is Aisgill?' she said. 'I wish to speak with him.'

About what? she thought. What odd compulsion has brought me here?

She looked around the busy scene, at the blacksmith in his forge at the end of the row, the lads mending tack, another lad forking feed into a barrow. She could not see Chad anywhere.

'Maister Aisgill's in the riding school, Lady Elinor. Shall I fetch him for you?'

'Thank you, no.' Nell was always polite to those who served her. 'I'll go there myself,' and she set off towards it.

The riding school had been built by the second Earl, a noted horseman, after he had seen the famous one in Vienna on his Grand Tour. Designed to school horses, not only in the elaborate ritual of dressage, but also in their general management, it had fallen into disrepair until Nell, early in her running of the estate, had had it renovated, and had encouraged Aisgill, who needed no encouragement, to bring it into use again.

In the round building, open at the sides, beneath a slightly domed roof, the work of the stable was going on briskly.

Aisgill, suddenly seeing her, came over, his ruddy face welcoming. Dismayed at first by the thought of a woman taking charge, he had found that Nell was his closest ally in restoring Malplaquet's racing pride, and he was now her most fervent supporter.

'Good to see you here, Lady Elinor. We've missed you lately. You wanted me?'

Nell made a vague motion with her hands, her eyes were busy. 'Nothing, really. Just to see that all's going well,' and then, offered as an afterthought, 'What have you been doing with the vagabond you rescued a fortnight gone?'

'What have *I* done?' he said, with an odd grin. 'You might well ask what *he's* done and doing. He's on Rajah, as you see,' and he pointed at the rider and horse

completing a neat trotting circle, and coming to rest not
far from them.

In the gloom of the arena Nell had not seen him, but
she saw him now. He was straight-backed, in perfect
control of the giant stallion. She saw his head turn, and
the blue gaze fell on her again.

'On Rajah! You mean you have let him ride Rajah!
And he can control him like that?'

'Oh, he's amazing with the horses, Lady Elinor. He
says he can remember nothing, but even on his first day
at work when Rajah broke loose he stopped him and
quieted him when no one else could.'

Aware that the man on the horse was watching them,
some delicacy made Aisgill bend his head to speak low
to his mistress.

'It's my belief, madam, that he's been in the army, a
trooper, possibly. He rides like a trained cavalryman,
and he has the scar of a great wound on his chest. Some
poor devil turned away because of the peace, fallen on
hard times since. He asked to ride Rajah, and, seeing
how he gentled him, I gave him permission, and look at
him now. It was a good day when we took him in.'

So it was, thought Nell, for Rajah, a great black, the
most beautiful horse in the stud, had always possessed
a vile, unmanageable temper, and most were frightened
to lead him, let alone ride him.

Chad, for so she must think of him now, for he was
one of her people, had trotted the horse into the centre
of the circle and was teaching him to walk on the spot.
Rajah was showing his dislike of the restraint put upon
him, but his rider was using his voice, as well as his
body, to force his will on him. Nell watched him,
fascinated by such power, such control.

'And such patience,' she said at last to Aisgill.

'Yes,' he replied; he was a little surprised, for Nell, although usually interested in the work of the stable, was seldom so particularly interested. Her whole body had gone quite still, her attention given completely to what she was seeing.

'But it's time he stopped. Rajah is growing impatient.'

As though Chad had heard him, he turned the horse towards Nell and Aisgill. He trotted him over, the strength of both horse and rider plainly visible as he controlled the only half-willing beast. Slipping from his back, to hold Rajah firm where he stood, he touched his forehead to Nell, as he had been taught, said briefly to Aisgill, 'He's had enough, sir. Best let him rest.'

The words and the actions were servile, those of a good, obedient servant, but despite that there was nothing servile about him, Nell thought.

Now that she could see him plain, it appeared that the vagabond had been tamed and groomed. His crisp black hair had been trimmed, so that it clustered in loose ringlets about his harsh and craggy face, which was now clean-shaven, although a dark shadow shaded his mouth and jaw.

The face was strong, and there was nothing handsome in it, but it was strangely compelling, and not that of a wastrel. His eyes shone bluer than she had remembered them, and they were surveying her, not insolently, but coolly, as though they were simply man and woman together — a strange experience for Nell.

The rest of him, clad in the smart but serviceable green uniform of the stable hand not engaged in dirty work, with his once bleeding and naked feet in bright black boots, was remarkable as well, broad-shouldered, beautifully proportioned, and looking at him Nell felt

the strangest stirrings rising in her, stirrings which she
had never felt before.

He was so large that he dwarfed her, another pleasant
sensation for Nell, who was usually as tall as, if not
taller than, many of the men around her.

Allied to all these odd stirrings and throbbings, which
grew stronger not weaker the longer she looked at him,
Nell was experiencing a strange breathlessness which
she had never felt before, and her heart began to beat
wildly. She mentally shook her head, reprimanded
herself. In God's name, what was coming over her that
the sight of a strong stable hand who had been plucked
half-naked from the moors should cause her to behave
like a green girl confronted by her first lover?

For, inexperienced though she was, Nell had no doubt
about what was the cause of these strange and involun-
tary reactions. Desperately she tried to compose herself,
for now he was speaking to her in that deep, almost
gravel voice, which added to her inward confusion.

'I have to thank you, Lady Elinor, for taking me in. I
think I should have died else, my wits were so addled.'

Nell inclined her head, fought for control, was surprised how calm and measured her voice was. 'If you
can tame Rajah,' she managed, 'it was a good day for
Campions, as well as for you.'

He smiled, showing his strong white teeth again.
Whatever and whoever he was, he had been well fed,
and decently educated, and Aisgill's guess that he had
been a soldier was probably a good one.

'Oh, no one will tame Rajah,' he said confidently.
'Only if you show him who's master, he might choose to
do your bidding occasionally.'

And you too, thought Nell, looking at him. For like
Rajah, there was something wild about him, something

which, like it or not, called to Nell, who, if not wild, seldom did what was expected of her.

'Aisgill tells me that you might have been a soldier. Have you no memories which might help you to recall who you are, or where you came from?'

His eyes were suddenly shadowed. 'No, madam,' he said, almost painfully. 'But I bear a scar of what I think must be a wartime wound and I have. . .bad dreams.'

'Bad dreams?' Nell was aware that she was spending far too much time talking to one poor stable hand, but he intrigued her. 'What sort of bad dreams?'

'Of noise, and fighting, and men dying,' he said simply. 'So yes, I was probably a trooper. I remember riding a horse.' He thought a moment. 'He was white and splendid. . .and then he fell beneath me. . .'

He paused. 'And then?' said Nell encouragingly.

'And then, nothing. The other lads say I wake up shouting, but they cannot tell me what I say.'

'You may remember in time, I hope,' said Nell, only to hear him reply strangely,

'I may not like what I remember, madam.'

She let him go, turned to Aisgill, who had been listening to them, wondering at Lady Nell's interest — but then, she had always been unpredictable.

'Chad,' she said slowly. 'What name do you use for him on the books?'

'Young Peel said that he should be called Newcome, because that is what he is—new come among us,' replied Aisgill with a smile, 'and he agreed, so that is how he is styled.'

Nell was still watching Chad walk Rajah away, watched him until he left the arena, drawn by she knew not what.

'A corporal or a sergeant, you think,' she hazarded.

'By the way he speaks, his sureness, he has given orders in the past — and taken them, too. He has had some education — he knew how to speak to me.'

'Oh, aye,' said Aisgill, who had been a cavalryman when he was a boy, before injury had sent him back to civil life with a permanent limp. 'It's passing strange. He cannot remember who he is, nor anything about himself, but he knows how to school a horse, and a dozen other things. He told Seth Hutton off for being careless with a fowling piece. Said that it was no way to treat a weapon!'

'A useful man, then,' commented Nell. 'And the mare you had in foal — Bluebell — how does she do, these days?' For she thought that it was time that she stopped showing an interest in Chad Newcome, or Aisgill would be wondering what was coming over her — not that she did not make a point of showing an interest in all her people!

Chad Newcome sat on the same steps where Nell Tallboys had first seen him, mending tack. The October day was grey and gloomy, and, to some extent, so were his thoughts.

And yet, in an odd way, he was strangely content. He began to whistle an old song — and where did that come from? he wondered, and how remarkable that he, who could remember nothing about himself, could remember that, and how to school a horse, load and use a gun, and perform a hundred other tasks. Day by day he recovered a little more of what he knew, but, of himself, nothing.

The words of the song ran through his head, and when he came to the phrase, 'One is one and all alone,' there came the unbidden thought, And shall I always be alone, as I have been in the past?

He frowned, and stopped working, busy hands still. Now, how do I know that? Had he no chick nor child, wife nor father and mother to love and care for him? Had he always been a vagrant wanderer?

No, that could not be true. His good body, and the growing realisation, as his powers slowly returned, that he had been an educated man, told him that once he must have had a settled life, and he knew beyond a doubt that he had had women, and more than one, although how he knew he could not say.

To think of women was to think of Lady Elinor, or Lady Nell, or even 'Our Nell', as the men affectionately called her behind her back.

'God send she never marries,' he had heard Aisgill say once, 'for we should never get a master as good as she is, and I never thought to say that of any woman.'

Perhaps it was because his first conscious memory in this new strange life was of her, standing straight and tall before him, that she haunted him a little. He remembered how foolishly pleased he had been that day at the riding school when he had first seen her again, and she had spoken to him kindly about his schooling of Rajah.

It had been difficult not to keep his eyes hard on her the whole time he was with her, and he had frequently looked away because he had not wished to seem insolent, but she drew him in some fashion he could not define.

Or was it, after all, simply that before he had seen her everything had been blurred, a fog through which he had walked unknowing of himself, or his circumstances, uncaring almost, as though he was at one with the few animals which roved the moors?

He shrugged as the song in his head reached the betraying phrase again, and then, as the word 'alone' rang out, she was before him, in his mind's eye, and this time he inspected her closely, as he could not inspect the living and breathing woman, the Countess who held all their lives in the hollow of her hand.

She was tall for a woman, but beautifully proportioned, moving with an easy athletic grace. A grace confirmed when he had seen her ride off on horseback, in perfect control of her mount.

And her face! It was neither pretty nor beautiful, but somehow better than either. Beneath the glossy wealth of her dark chestnut hair, it was as strong and powerful as the face of Diana in an old painting. The high-bridged nose, the full and generous mouth with its humorous set, the grey eyes beneath high-arched black brows, the whole poised on the proud column of a shapely neck.

But best of all was the compassion he had seen there when she had bent that proud head to examine the poor wretch who had been decanted on her very doorstep.

Well, a cat might look at a king, so surely a homeless vagrant, for vagrant he must have been, from his clothes and his condition, might look at a queen — for Nell Tallboys was a queen in Yorkshire.

He rose and stretched. There was a growing pride in him as his faculties returned which Aisgill had noticed, a pride in his ability to control Rajah and to do the menial tasks around the yard well. 'He's been a man under orders,' Aisgill said to Henson when the agent had enquired how Newcome was faring, 'and he's given orders as well. I'd bet my life on his being a sergeant in

the army, and a good one. Wonder why they let him
go?'

Henson had shrugged. Newcome might be a bit of a
mystery, but not one on which he cared to spend time.

Aisgill came towards Chad now, said briefly, 'Lady
Elinor needs a groom to escort her on her daily ride this
afternoon. You know the lie of the land now, Newcome.
Saddle Vulcan, the big gelding, for her, and you may
take Rajah, if you think he will behave himself. Without
his daily run, he'll be a devil to handle.'

So, later, smartly dressed, wearing a jockey cap with
a green and silver cockade at the side—Malplaquet's
colours—he helped his Countess into the saddle, word-
less, and then mounted an impatient Rajah, to ride with
her across the moors, already clad in their winter
colours.

Nell thought that Newcome, riding by her side, looked
better than he had done since he had arrived at
Campions. The drawn, rather haunted look he had
worn in the early days had vanished, and like Aisgill
she recognised the pride he was displaying in his work.

And his control over Rajah was greater than ever.
That proud beast was suddenly willing to serve an even
prouder master. What a strange thought, that one of
her stable hands could be proud! She took a covert look
at Newcome's harsh profile, and when they reached the
usual end of her ride, for she always took the same
route—safer so, Aisgill said, if they always knew exactly
where she went—a pile of stones known as the Cairn,
and they dismounted, she signalled for him to sit by her,
on one of the large boulders scattered about the Cairn.

Chad hesitated; he had been prepared to stand by
Rajah whom he had tethered to a broken tree, and he
knew what the proper place of a groom was, and it was

not sitting by his mistress. But orders were orders, and Nell, amused, watched him struggle with his sense of what was fitting, and her command.

She had dressed herself more carefully than usual; indeed, for the last week she had chosen to wear turn-outs far more *à la mode* than she usually did, so that when she was about to leave for her ride Aunt Conybeare had stared at her, and said, 'Gracious, Nell, we are fine these days!'

Nell had blushed. She had put on a deep blue riding habit, adorned with silver buttons, and had wound a fine white linen cravat, edged with lace, around her throat and had secured it with a silver and sapphire pin.

Her boots had a polish on them so high that Aunt Conybeare had asked if they had been prepared with champagne; she had heard that the great London dandies did that! And her deep blue top hat had ribbons of pale blue silk wreathed around it, falling in long streamers down her back. Even her whip was a fine thing, decorated with silver trimmings; it had belonged to the third Earl, a noted fop in his time.

As a final concession to vanity, she had had her maid, Annie Thorpe, brush and brush her dark chestnut hair, and then Annie had dressed it for her, far more elaborately and carefully than usual, so that the top hat sat proudly on it.

'A pity you're not going to meet your lover — dressed like that,' had been Aunt Conybeare's final contribution, and one that had had her going hot all over. Because she had asked Aisgill to assign Newcome to her for the ride, and it was Newcome she was dressing like this for, if she told the truth.

And what would Aunt Conybeare say to that? Or

Aisgill, or Henson, or. . .? Well, to the devil with them
all!

But she was not thinking of this when Newcome
finally sat down, and she said in the most bored,
Countess-like voice she could assume, 'Tell me,
Newcome, have you recovered your memory yet?'

Chad looked at her, and thought that he had never
seen anything so superb. Not, of course, that his conscious memory was more than a month old! But Nell
Tallboys, who usually walked round the yard looking
more like one of the stable lad's girls, shabby clothing
pulled on any-old-how, and her hair falling down and
blowing in the wind, was truly Lady Malplaquet this
afternoon, and he hardly knew how to address her.

Except that his tongue did it for him. 'No, Lady
Elinor. I still know nothing of myself, and Maister
Aisgill——' he pronounced the name as the tykes
did; his own speech was accentless '—tells me that
Blackwell, your tenant on the Home Farm, found me
sleeping by the haystack two nights before Outhwaite
brought me to Campions, refused to feed me—apparently I begged for food, although I have no memory of
doing so—and moved me on.'

'Blackwell is a good tenant but a mean man,' said
Nell reflectively. 'He should have sent you to Campions,
but he doesn't approve of Campions charity.'

'Well, I approve of it,' said Chad sturdily. 'Or I
should likely be dead on the moor by now.'

Nell's laugh at that was not one that any past
Countess of Malplaquet would have approved of. 'Well,
that is true enough,' she said appreciatively. 'Aisgill
tells me that you are a good worker and not only with
the horses.'

'But I like working with the horses best,' said Chad,

seeing that Lady Elinor was determined to talk to him. 'I have a strange feeling that, while I have often worked with horses, it was not as a groom or a stable lad.'

'Which would support Aisgill's belief that you were a trooper. But you don't object to doing the hard work round the yard?'

'It would be a mean soul who would not work for those who had given him his life back, and who were prepared to take him on without knowing of his past.'

Seeing Nell look a little puzzled, he added, somewhat stiffly, 'A man without a past must be a suspect man, Lady Elinor. Who knows what I have done, or may be fleeing from? It sometimes worries me at night, when I cannot sleep.'

Nell looked at Chad's strong face, the face which she hardly dared inspect too closely, it had such an effect on her.

'You do not look like a criminal, Newcome, nor do you behave like one.'

Chad shrugged. He did not tell lady Elinor that in the long night watches his efforts to recall who and what he was often served only to confuse him. Once, when he had been unable to rest at all, and had finally fallen asleep from very exhuastion, he had had a nightmare in which she had figured.

Something about her and himself which had made him cry out so strongly, and throw himself from his bed. His behaviour had been so violent that he had awoken several of the lads and they had been compelled to restrain him because he was not properly awake and he had tried to fight them off. When he had woken up he could not remember what in the dream had distressed him so.

Seeing that he could never have met her before the

day on which she had ordered him taken in, and had shown him nothing but kindness, it seemed a strange dream to have.

To take his mind away from unhappy things he did something he knew no good servant should do; he initiated a topic of conversation with his mistress, for the pleasure of seeing her lively face turned towards him, and hearing her beautiful voice.

'These stones, Lady Elinor. Were they put here of a purpose, or did Nature simply pile them up at random?'

Nell looked sharply at him. More and more Newcome was beginning to demonstrate that he had been given a good education.

'The people round here believe that the gods threw them down in play, the old Norse gods, that is. This part of the North was never properly Christianised, they say, until long after the South. There is a book in the library — Challenor showed it to me — which says that people lived in the Cairn long ago, although I find that hard to believe. Think how cold they must have been in winter!'

Unconsciously she had spoken to him as an equal, and he answered her in kind. 'If that were true, there must be an entrance.'

'And so there is,' said Nell. 'Look, I will show you.' She rose and walked to the side away from the one where they had been sitting, and, pointing to a gap in the stones, said, 'Follow me,' turned sideways and wriggled through.

With difficulty, Chad followed her, to find himself in a small low chamber, so low that Nell, as well as he, had to bow herself to stand in it.

'They must have been dwarfs!' he exclaimed.

'So Challenor believes,' answered Nell, turning to go,

but as she did so her foot slipped and she felt Chad catch her, to break her fall.

Nell was suddenly hard against him, could feel the heat from his body, his male strength, and was held there, face to face, her head level with his chin, tall man and tall woman, bowed — then he tried to avoid standing up, so as not to bang their heads, lost his footing as well, and they were on the ground.

It was the first time that he had touched her, other than to hold her foot as she mounted Vulcan, and the sensations Nell experienced were extraordinary. She remembered being in a man's arms, dancing a waltz, being lifted by a boatman, Aisgill picking her up once, when she had been thrown from her horse, and in not one of these encounters had she felt what she now did when Chad Newcome touched and held her.

I am going mad, running a fever, loneliness is making me prey to a disgraceful lust; I should never have brought him in here; whatever would Aunt Conybeare — Aisgill, Uncle Beaumont, Henson — think if they knew how wanton I am grown? ran through Nell's head, before he released her, and they crouched, face to face, in the gloom of the confined space.

Chad was suffering, if suffering was the right word, the same experience as Nell. Loss of memory, he was finding, was leading to some loss of control. He had a mad desire to kiss the woman half kneeling before him. He repressed it, the refrain 'And lose your place to be thrown out to starve' running through his mind and stopping him from following his natural inclinations.

Whatever would she think if he assaulted her so? Worst of all, his strongest instinct was to do much more than that to her; it was to bear her to the ground and take his pleasure with her.

Still half crouched, he turned, and pushed his way
into the open again, to lean on the biggest stone, fighting
for self-control before she came after him.

Once outside, Nell was Countess of Malplaquet
again; she said in a voice so false that it frightened her,
'I think, Newcome, it's time we went home. I feel
strangely tired.' She was pleased to see that Newcome
appeared his usual stern self, that he merely bowed his
head silently, and silently helped her back on to Vulcan
before mounting Rajah and waiting for her to lead them
home.

Still silent, they rode back to Campions. What neither
of them understood was that both of them had reacted
in the same way to the other, and each thought that he
or she was the only one to experience such savagely
strong feelings that rank, decorum, climate, and rules of
conduct had meant nothing to them. Had they followed
their natural inclinations they would have mated inside
the Cairn as though they were at one with the birds and
the beasts around them!

CHAPTER FOUR

'NELL,' said Aunt Conybeare reprovingly — they were sitting in Nell's private room, overlooking the park, 'your wits are wandering today. This is the second time that I have asked you the same question, and you have not answered me on either occasion. Most unlike you. What can you be thinking of?'

Nell flushed. In her wild and wicked thoughts she had been on the moors again, with Newcome, and then in the Cairn, on her knees before him. How to inform her aunt that she was trying to tell herself that she must have dreamed her reactions to him? An elderly female of twenty-seven, untouched and past her last prayers, could not possibly have felt as she did about a stable hand, a nobody who had arrived at Campions half-naked — and why did she have to think of him in that state? Her whole body flushed hot at the thought.

Of course she had imagined the whole thing, including the way in which Newcome had looked at her when they had been crouched in the Cairn together, as though he wanted to eat her, whole. On the ride home, and afterwards, he had been stiffly proper, had helped her down without so much as looking at her, and had led Vulcan and Rajah away, still with his eyes averted. Which, now she came to think about it, told its own story!

Well, she would not look at him, and would try to avoid his company — but, on the other hand, not too much so; unfair to him, to let Aisgill think that he had

offended her, when the offence was hers, not his. He had
done nothing.

Nell was almost too distracted to read her private
correspondence — sorted for her by old Payne, who had
looked more decrepit than ever this morning. One badly
scrawled missive was from Cousin Ulric Tallboys,
informing her that he intended to visit her on his way
north to the Borders, and would arrive some time in the
next fortnight, he did not know when. He was staying
with the Staffords at Trentham.

'Who probably wanted him as little as I do,' said Nell
drily to Aunt Conybeare, 'but are too polite to say so.
I'll tell Mrs Orgreave to make a suite of rooms ready for
him — he is the heir, after all.'

Work seemed a way to drive out improper thoughts
about Newcome. She also considered a visit to High
Harrogate. Perhaps more company was what she
needed, to meet some young and sleek gentlemen whose
smooth and civilised charms would compare well with
Newcome's austere, straightforward manner.

Newcome again! Nell rose smartly to her feet, said
abruptly, 'I'm going to work in the library. Challenor
said that he'd found some old folios, stuffed away in a
cupboard, and I ought to look at them.'

'Yes, do, dear,' said Aunt Conybeare comfortably. 'It
might settle you. Your bibliomania is nearly as bad as
his, although the stables seem to have seen more of you
lately than the library.'

That did it! Nell almost bolted from the room. Oh,
dear, is it as bad as that, that Aunt Conybeare is
noticing something? Humour touched the corner of her
mouth at the thought. Well, some fusty old books, dry
as dust, perhaps containing woodcuts of men and
women who looked more like Mr and Mrs Noah in a

child's version of the ark which her grandfather had once given her than the people she saw around her, might cool her down and drive away these feverish fantasies which were filling her errant mind.

Pushing open the library door, registering old Challenor's pleasure at the sight of her, she said firmly to herself, I will forgo my usual afternoon ride for a time, come here instead. Say I don't feel quite the thing — God forgive me for the lie, I feel too much the thing — and then I needn't go to the stables at all, and shan't see. . .him.

She did not even want to think of his name, for that seemed to have nearly as strong an effect on her as seeing him.

These splendid resolutions lasted exactly forty-eight hours. . .

Nell awoke early, restless. She could not remember her dreams, only that her sleep had been disturbed and that they were vaguely disgraceful. She remembered crying out once, then sitting up, sweat streaming from her, although the air in the room was cold once she had pushed back the bedding.

Indoors seemed oppressive. She did not ring for Annie, but did what she often did, although Aunt Conybeare as well as Annie disapproved of the habit; she pulled on her clothes rapidly, finishing with her old grey woollen thing, which she wore to work with Challenor, and then a shabby overcoat over that — it had been worn by a young male Tallboys in the last century, and she had rescued it from the bottom of an old press to wear when she visited the stables.

She would, she told herself firmly, go for a walk in the

grounds immediately round the house, so she would not
need John or Annie to accompany her.

The day was grey and cold, but dry, and the walk
exhilarated her. She made a circuit of the house, quite
alone; it was so early that the house still slept, all the
windows close-curtained, and, at the end, instead of
going in again, her wandering feet led her to the stables
as though they were leading her home.

Well, Aunt Conybeare, she thought afterwards,
wryly, always did say that if I wandered into the stable
yard without warning I should end up regretting it, and
at last I did.

But did I? Regret it, that was.

As she walked through the arch the place seemed, at
first, deserted. And then she turned the corner, into the
flat paved area before the stable hands' quarters, a place
she rarely visited, but which seemed safe at this hour.

And there, in the morning's half-light, standing in
front of the pump, a bucket of water at his feet, and
water all about him, was Chad.

He had evidently, despite the cold, taken an
impromptu outdoor bath, and his face was hidden by
the towel with which he was drying his hair, so that he
could neither see nor hear her coming.

But that was not it at all, not at all. What was *it*, was
that he was stark naked, and facing her. Nell was
paralysed, except that at the sight of him her body was
suddenly prey to the strangest feelings.

The worst was in the pit of her stomach — no, be
honest, Nell, lower down altogether — where a most
strange ache, exacerbated by throbbing and tickling,
suddenly began, and her breasts, also, had begun to
ache, and feel sensitive, and it was exactly as though
she, too, were stark naked before him!

For he had lowered the towel to reveal those brilliant and disturbing bright blue eyes, and he was staring at her, as she, dreadfully, was staring at him.

Nell had never seen a naked man before, but she knew at once, without being told, that she had in front of her just about the most superb specimen of the male sex that she could hope to encounter. Almost against her will her eyes drank him in, from the powerful column of his neck, his broad and splendid shoulders, deep chest, covered in fine, curling black hair, a triangle which narrowed into an arrow, and then into another inverted triangular fleece above his. . .sex. . .which hung proud and magnificent before her, so that she hurriedly transferred her gaze to his long and splendid legs, muscular thighs, calves and feet, all perfectly proportioned, as though the giant statue of Mars, god of war, in the entrance hall of Campions had come to sudden and inconvenient life.

She also took in the great scar below his shoulder of which Aisgill had spoken, but most shaming of all was that she registered that he had seen her fascinated interest in the figure he presented, and was staring back at her, before he slowly dropped the towel to cover his loins, and began to turn away.

But not before saying in that deep, gravelly voice which so matched his harsh and powerful face, 'My apologies, Lady Elinor, I did not know that you were here.'

'Not — not at all,' she stammered inanely, as though she was addressing a fellow aristocrat, fully dressed in a polite drawing-room. 'My fault; I know that I should not have come here without warning.'

He half turned back, to speak again, she thought, except that he did not, merely gave her his rare and brilliant white smile, the smile that softened his face, and which, although Nell did not know it, had already won the heart of every female servant at Campions— only Chad had not cared to do anything with or to them, despite its power to seduce.

The paralysis that had gripped Nell left her as suddenly as it had come. She walked briskly away, still dreadfully aware of her own body and its primitive reactions. She had never experienced such a thing before when with any man.

It was a sensation so strong that it frightened her. For she knew, beyond a doubt, that if Chad Newcome had walked over, taken her into his arms and begun to. . . to. . .she would have been unable to stop him; nay, more, would have collaborated with him, stable hand though he was, and Countess in her own right though she was!

The primitive call of man to woman which she had always denied had any meaning for her—had denied, indeed, her very sex, and even that a man could ever rouse her—had her in its thrall.

Nell was compelled to face the fact that it had merely been sufficient for her to see him naked, for the pull of him which she had improbably felt the very first time on which she had seen him, which she had felt again in the Cairn, to be revealed in its purest and most passionate form, to tell her that merely to see him thus was enough to rouse her completely.

Pure! What a word to describe the sensations that coursed through her, and which gripped her still. Nell, unbelieving, shook herself as she walked blindly back through the arch.

It is being on my own so much, and seeing so little of

anyone but old Challenor and Aunt Conybeare and the rest, old and middle-aged men, all of them. I really must order my mind a little. It cannot be him, it cannot!

But she could not forget what she had seen, and for the rest of the day, every time her mind strayed, Nell saw before her the form and physique of the perfect athlete that Chad Newcome had revealed to her, accidentally, that morning.

Aisgill was working in his little office when Chad came in for his day's orders. He was struggling with his paperwork, the stud book, the accounts of the hands' wages, the expenditure on the stud, everything connected with the stables, and for which he was responsible.

He waved an irritated quill at Newcombe, 'Wait, man, wait. I'll deal with you in a moment,' for the details of his work were refusing to sort themselves out on paper, however clear they were in his head.

He was aware of Newcome, standing there, quiet, and when his pen dropped ink on the paper for the second time, so that he screwed it up and flung it across the room, he saw Chad begin to speak, and then stop, hesitant.

'Yes, man, spit it out, what is it?'

Chad looked at Aisgill, who had been consistently kind to him, if stern, as he was with all the lads; he reminded Chad of someone — who? A vague figure in the mists of lost memory who had given Chad orders which he felt, rather than knew, he wanted to carry out efficiently. He also wanted to be of use.

He decided to speak; after all, Aisgill could always rebuff him.

'Maister Aisgill, sir. I have recovered a little more of my memory, not much, but it might be useful to you. . .'

He stopped. Something told him that in his old life, whatever that was, he had given orders, and men had jumped to them, but here he was a menial, and must know his place.

'If you have something to say,' barked Aisgill, 'then say it. Time is valuable.'

Chad threw caution to the winds. 'I remember that I know how to keep books, write letters, and, if you wish, I could be your clerk; I know. . .' he hesitated again, but in for a penny, in for a pound '. . .that Henson chases you about the paperwork, and if you used me, he could not.'

Aisgill was minded to roar at him, but something in Newcome's humility, a humility which he sensed was not natural to the man, but which told him that his servant did not wish to offend, but to help, stopped him. Stupid not to use a man's talents. More and more it was becoming plain to him that Newcome was other than a feckless fool who had ended up walking the roads because of his folly. Bad luck had probably done for him, as for others. What he actually had been was difficult to gauge.

'I took you in,' he said slowly, 'at my and Lady Elinor's wish, because we thought that you might be of service. You have proved yourself a hard worker, and, more than that, your skill with horses and around the stables is exceptional. If you think that you could be helpful to me in other ways, then why not? A man would be a fool not to take up such an offer.'

He rose, said with a wry smile, 'If you can write without blots, do so. Do you think you can copy out in fair what I have writ there in rough?'

Chad picked up the quill and sat in Aisgill's chair, looked at the pile of odd and grimy pieces of paper and scrap on which Aisgill kept his daily records, said cheerfully, 'I think I have a memory of working with worse than this,' and he let Aisgill instruct him in what was needful, before beginning to transcribe, in a fair copper-plate hand, and swiftly, what was before him.

'I was not,' he said, raising his head, to see Aisgill watching him intently, 'used to doing much figuring, I think.' He frowned; he could not tell Aisgill, for it appeared improbable, that he seemed to remember that other men had done that for him, and that he had inspected their work. 'But I do have a little grasp of the matter, enough to keep these simple accounts.'

When he had gone, the work done, and some letters written, still in the same fair hand, with a number of suggestions, diffidently made, which improved their sense, Aisgill walked over to the table which served as his desk, picked up the papers, and frowned.

The work before him was meticulous, and he laughed a little to himself at Henson's probable reaction. There'll be no grumbling this week, that's for sure, about my careless undecipherable hand, for he meant to go on using Newcome as his clerk — and then he frowned again. Every new talent which Newcome uncovered only served to demonstrate that he had been a man of more than common affairs.

Which made his arrival here at Campions, a nameless, memoryless vagabond, more than passing strange.

Aisgill was not the only person Chad Newcome troubled. His mistress hardly knew what to do with herself for thinking about him. She had always prided herself on her downright stability — what the late Dr Johnson had robustly called bottom. That, she knew, was a quality which denied fiddle-faddle, hemmings and hawings, acknowledged the truth of what was, as another philosopher, Hume, had said, and not what ought to be.

Men—and women—were naked, forked animals, she knew that well enough, and she should not have been so shocked to be reminded of what he, and she, so essentially were.

Be truthful, Nell, she said to herself, severely. You know perfectly well that what is shocking you is not having seen him, but what the sight of him did to you! You can no longer pretend complete indifference to the opposite sex, which you have done since you were nineteen. That is gone forever, along with your innocence. For what happened in the Garden of Eden to Adam and Eve has just happened to you. Be truthful again; you desired him, your stable hand and groom, a nameless nobody, and nothing that you can say or do will alter that one simple and undeniable fact.

And his own cool acceptance of what had happened, there in the yard, no mark of shame about him, at having been so found—what did that tell her about him?

Restlessly, Nell put down the book which she was reading in the library. One of the giant folios which Challenor had found—her predecessors, apart from the fourth Earl, had been careless of their books.

They had been careless of everything, and she had seen it as her duty to put matters in order, and since her succession six years ago order was what she brought to her great possessions.

And inside them her own life had been the most orderly thing of all—but no longer. Outwardly, all was the same, but inwardly—oh, inwardly, was a different matter, and cool Nell Tallboys had gone forever.

CHAPTER FIVE

'WELL,' said Henson, 'here's a turn-up!' It was a week later, and the Countess of Malplaquet and her advisers, Henson, Aisgill, Challenor and old Payne, her secretary, whom she had privately nicknamed her Privy Council, were having their Friday meeting in her study.

It was a vast room, with windows running from the floor to the ceiling, looking towards the park, which sloped away before them, and then across to the moors, a view so splendid that Nell was thinking of commissioning Turner to come and paint it. One wall was covered with bookshelves containing everything which Nell had thought it necessary to read in order to run Campions and her other properties correctly.

Over the hearth was a portrait of her grandfather, Patricius Tallboys, in all the glory of his youth, painted by Gainsborough, a lovely feathery thing, with the blue of his Garter ribbon glowing like a jewel across his white court dress. Two Canalettos, depicting views of London, were mounted on each side of the hearth above cabinets full of precious porcelain from China, Japan and Germany.

Nell's desk was a work of art, walnut, with inlays showing elaborate flowers, and had a little gilt rail at its back. But its use was practical, not decorative, and she and her cohorts had been doing their weekly examination of the estate's books.

Henson's exclamation had been provoked by the sight of Aisgill's books, which usually evoked either derision or criticism from him. 'You've been learning,' he accused. 'Who taught you?'

The two men had a running battle, half friendly, half not, for Nell's favour. Aisgill, hesitant, decided to tell the truth. Better so.

'Not me,' he offered. 'Newcome. He offered to be my clerk, and it is his work you are admiring.'

Payne picked up the letter written out for him to approve, amend and send out in Aisgill's name. 'I need make no alterations or additions to this,' he said in his cracked old voice. 'I take it that he did not copy it, but wrote it for you.'

'Wrong to deny it.' Aisgill was brief. 'Credit where credit is due. Yes, I told him what to say, and he did the rest.'

'A man of parts,' commented Henson, the comment grudging. They were all a little surprised by these further revelations of Newcome's abilities, including Nell. She did not let them see how much this news pleased her.

At the end of the meeting Nell made a decision. 'Stay behind, Aisgill. I would have a word with you.'

Henson looked sharply at them as he left. Nell walked over to the windows, looked out, spoke to Aisgill, uncharacteristically, without turning her head. 'I have not taken my daily ride lately. Pray see that Vulcan is saddled for me at two of the clock.'

She turned as she finished, to see Aisgill bob his head. 'It shall be done,' and then, for no conscious reason he could think of, he said, 'Will Newcome do as your groom, Lady Elinor?'

'If you can spare him from his clerkly duties, yes,' replied Nell lightly, and then, as though idly, 'I take it that he has recovered more of his memory — but still has no idea of who he is, or where he came from?'

'That is true, Lady Elinor.' Aisgill was hesitant. 'It is strange, is it not, how much has come back to him, and yet he does not know himself? I am an ignorant old man, but I sometimes wonder——' And he paused again.

'Yes,' said Nell encouragingly. 'What do you wonder, Aisgill? You know that I value your opinion.' Which was true, she thought. He might not be educated, like Henson and Payne, but he had an earthy and unsentimental shrewdness which was sometimes better than book learning.

'I wonder, which is stupid, I know, whether he does not wish to remember himself. He has such bad dreams, madam.'

'You think that he may have done something dreadful, perhaps,' said Nell, a little anxious.

'No, not that. I think he may have been unhappy, but is happy now, except when he sleeps.'

Nell was glad that she had said and done nothing — such as asking for another escort — to make Aisgill suspicious of Newcome; he seemed to trust him, not only to do his work well, but to protect her. Originally, when he had assigned him to ride wth her, he had said, 'What better than an old soldier to look after you? If he cannot protect you, no one can.'

She was thinking of that, and what had passed in the morning, when she waited that afternoon for Newcome to bring her horse round to the steps before the grand entrance, and when he appeared, leading Rajah, young Peel behind him with Vulcan, there was nothing in the behaviour of either of them to suggest that anything untoward might have happened on their last two meetings.

Nell mounted Vulcan, and they rode off together, Peel watching, in silence, my lady and her respectful groom, riding slightly behind her as though nothing had ever passed between them.

What nonsense! Of course nothing had happened. A couple of mischances, that was all. She had stumbled, and he had saved her, and then they had met... somewhat unfortunately.... And not a word of that was true. She had been strongly affected, and, trying to look behind at him without him realising it and failing, she could sense without knowing how that he, too, had been affected, but how, she could not tell.

If Chad had told her the truth, which he had no intention of doing, he wondered how shocked Lady Elinor Tallboys would be. Would she recoil from him, have him thrown back on to the moor from which he had emerged? For what he had felt when she had come upon him, naked, and had felt so strongly that his body had almost betrayed him before her, was a desire for her that, although he did not know it, was no stronger than Nell's for him.

No difference of rank or circumstance had meant anything. Simply, he was a man, and she was a woman, and the accident of their meeting thus, even more than the encounter at the Cairn, had finally told him that what he felt for Elinor Tallboys, Countess of Malplaquet, Viscountess Wroxton, Baroness Sheveborough, all in her own right, was more than simple lust. It was a longing for her as his partner as well as his love!

Which, look at it how you would, was preposterous. For how should he, poor Chad, nobody from nowhere,

lucky to have a coat on his back, dare to raise his eyes
to that?

No, he must go carefully. Give no hint of his true
feelings, be surly, even, and his dour expression made
his harsh face so much harsher that Nell, looking at
him, felt her heart sink. Was he annoyed with her that
she had disturbed his privacy that morning?

Before they left Aisgill, as usual, had seen that they
were properly equipped to protect themselves. There
were dangerous men about, he had said, and, although
he doubted that there might be any on Lady Elinor's
land, the moor must not be considered perfectly safe. So
each rider had a horse pistol in a holster on their saddle,
and Chad had orders to guard his mistress with his life.

Nell always refused to ride with more than one escort,
'For who would attack me?' she had said. 'And I do not
wish to ride out in a procession, and besides I never go
far.'

But that afternoon, instead of turning for home at the
usual point, fairly low on the moor by the Cairn,
restlessness overcame her. She swung off her horse, and,
turning, said to Newcome, 'Tell me, have you ever
ridden to the Throne of God?'

To her amusement, the strong face broke up a little
as he replied. 'No, Lady Elinor. I have not had that
privilege.'

Nell laughed; she could not prevent herself. With one
light sentence he had diffused the tense atmosphere
between them.

'Not the real one,' she said. 'I mean the great pile of
rocks there.' And she pointed with her whip to the far
distance, where a massive cluster of giant rocks and
boulders reared, high on the moor. 'That is what we
Yorkshire tykes call the Throne of God, and, being good

Yorkshiremen, we think it natural that God should have
made his home on the moors.'

It was Chad's turn to laugh even as, standing, he
tried to hold the impatient Rajah.

'You surely don't intend to ride there this afternoon,
madam,' he ventured. 'It is hardly wise. The hour is
late, and by the looks of it the journey is not a short
one.'

For whatever reasons, Nell suddenly became skittish,
she who was always so full of common sense — and, yes,
bottom.

'Are you giving the orders, Newcome? Or is it your
Countess's commands that you must, and should, obey?
I wish to ride there now, immediately, and you shall
accompany me, unless, of course, you prefer to return
on your own, and explain to Aisgill why I am not with
you!'

Afterwards, she was to curse her light-headed folly,
and the behaviour that was so out of character for her.
Perhaps it was being with Newcome; perhaps, in some
fashion, she wished to tease, to provoke him. She never
knew.

Chad was uneasy. While they were standing there,
talking, he had been overcome by the oddest feeling. A
feeling of being watched, secretly observed. It was a
feeling which he knew that he had experienced before,
but of the where and when he had no notion. Only that
it might be unwise to ignore it.

He tried again. 'I cannot,' he said, voice grave, 'advise
your ladyship,' and he used her correct title deliberately,
'to do any such thing. I have a. . .bad feeling about such
a journey.'

'Well, I have not,' averred Nell gaily, feeling delight-
fully irresponsible for once in her oh, so serious life. 'So

spurs to horse, Newcome, and take *my ladyship* —' and she trod on her title comically '—where she commands you to go.'

No help for it; against all his instincts and the raised hair on the back of his neck, there was nothing for it but to obey, and they set out again, riding through the withered heather and bracken, dull after the flaming reds, golds and mauves of autumn.

And now, he thought, the dark was threatening to be on them early, well before they saw Campions again, and the other threat was Aisgill's anger with him if anything happened to the suddenly wilful woman who was now riding alongside him, and if he fell back as a good groom should she reined back so that alongside he was compelled to remain, unless they were to lose even more time.

The feeling of danger grew stronger and stronger as they approached the Throne itself. Nearer to, he saw that several piles of rock were heaped together, some at quite a distance from the main grouping of stones and boulders which stood in the middle, and which with a little imagination could be seen as a throne of sorts.

Nell, having got her way, was a little ashamed, but not so ashamed that she was above playing games with Chad over riding level with him. But, like Chad, she was beginning to realise that an early dusk would be on them before their return, that they were in a lonely and isolated spot, and she had no business undertaking this mad expedition, just to contradict her groom, and to impress on him who was master—or, rather, mistress!

Master, she thought, was better; mistress had unfortunate associations!

They had reached the Throne itself, and were on level ground. She was preparing to dismount, and Chad was dismounting before her — she had difficulty in thinking of him as Newcome — when disaster struck. There was the whine of a bullet coming from the direction of the far group of rocks, and Nell's horse dropped wounded, and probably dying, beneath her.

Fortunately she was thrown clear, to land, stunned and shocked, on the bare earth. Chad, who was still in the act of dismounting, holding Rajah only loosely, was also thrown down, as Rajah, on hearing the shot, flung back his head with a great whinny, and bolted, running at speed across the moor.

Chad rolled away in the direction of the Throne, instinctively protecting himself from a possible further shot, if more than one man was firing at them — he had no doubt that the bullet had been meant for Nell.

Silence had fallen; with both on the ground there was no target for a sniper — if sniper it were — for him to aim at. Chad, memories stirring in him, crawled over to Nell, to find her living and apparently unharmed, only winded by her fall, but shocked, her face grey. On seeing him, apparently unharmed, she gave a little cry and tried to rise.

'No,' he said urgently, pushing her down again. 'Not yet. Do not make yourself a target.' Words, ideas, memories were roaring through his head.

Being shot at from ambush was not a new experience, and he knew how to deal with it. Words of command unthinkingly streamed from him.

'Come,' said Nell, a little fiercely, 'you cannot believe that the bullet was meant for me. A sportsman's accident, surely.'

'At this hour, on the moor, with little on it, from someone who I am sure has been tracking us all afternoon, staying to windward, out of sight,' rasped

Chad. 'Best take no chances. Crawl with me to the Throne, or, even better, wriggle like a snake. Now!'

Nell took one look at his face, hard and set. His tone had been so authoritative, that of a man ordering other men, and expecting to be obeyed.

She shivered. Supposing that the bullet had been meant for her! Prudence dictated that she obey him, and she wriggled away from the screams of her horse on her hands and knees. She reached the shelter of the Throne, turned, to find that Chad had not immediately followed her, had detoured to poor Vulcan, and was pulling her pistol from its holster.

Foolishly, her first thought was that he meant to put Vulcan out of his misery, but no such thing. The pistol once in his possession, he was crawling after her, to push her further beneath the seat of the great Throne, so that she could not be easily seen, or even shot at.

'That's my brave girl,' he whispered, as though she were a wench from the village, and not his Countess. 'Do as I say, and you may yet be safe.'

'And what do you say?' Nell asked of this new man, who seemed to know what to do in a tight corner.

'I say that you will stay here, hidden, and I shall leave you to smoke out who shot at us and why. It may be that I am imagining ghosts, that you were right, a sportsman's accident, that he took himself off when he saw what he had done, but I think not.'

'You would leave me?' panted Nell.

'What else to do?' answered Chad, with indisputable logic; a habit of his she and others were to find in the coming months. 'If we stay here, we are his sitting targets sooner or later, for we cannot stay hidden forever. I assume that he is better armed than we are. If I track him—and he will not be expecting me to do that — I might. . .dispose of him. . .otherwise, he will surely do for us.'

He did not add and nobody knows where we are, as you, in your wilfulness, have decreed, but the thought was there, unexpressed, and Nell swallowed at it.

'I'm sorry,' she said ruefully. 'I broke all Aisgill's rules. . .'

'No,' he said, and then, perhaps not strictly truthfully, for he wanted her to maintain her brave spirit, and not repine at her folly, 'If he meant to shoot you, and God knows why, he might have done it at any time, and there are more dangerous places to be than this — at least we have cover. Enough of talking. I must go.'

'And if you do not return?' she asked steadily, although her heart was hammering, for his danger as well as her own.

'You are still in no worse case than you are now — for at least if I go there is the chance of my scotching the snake,' he replied, 'and that is the best I can offer you, for our case, yours and mine, is desperate. Stay here, do not come out, and if I am lost, pray, lady, pray, for only your god can save you.'

Nell had to be content with that for he was impatient to be off. She pushed herself further under the seat, nothing of her to be seen, and he was gone, silently, like the snake of which he had spoken. She remembered what Aisgill had said of him, that he thought that Chad had been a soldier, and almost certainly a good one. She thought by his manner, and what he had said, that he had stalked men like this before, and that after all the outcome might not be too terrible.

Oh, she must hold on to that while she lay hidden beneath God's seat, and time passed with infinite slowness. She prayed a little that he might be safe, and, shocked, realised that she had prayed for him before she had prayed for herself.

Dear God, he must not suffer for my folly. I could not bear that. I might deserve to pay for a moment's light-mindedness, but Chad does not.

And then suddenly, shockingly, there was the sound of two shots, and, after that, silence.

CHAPTER SIX

CHAD remembered that he had, as Nell suspected, done this before: that was, stalked a sniper who was ambushing him and his men — although when and where this had happened he had no idea, only knowing that he had done it.

Warily, like a serpent, belly to the ground, he worked his way forward as silently as he could, making a wide detour through the bracken to a point slightly below that from which the shot had come, and where there had been no movement, no action, since.

Above him, he suspected, was a man with a rifle, who had carefully stalked himself and Nell, raising Chad's own hackles in the process. He should have listened harder to what his instincts told him, and, if necessary, have thrown her wilful ladyship over Rajah's saddle, and hauled her home, before he had ignored what some kind god was trying to tell him.

And now, with one ball in a horse pistol, he must try to overcome a man armed with a rifle, and probably a pair of loaded pistols as well.

Suddenly, there was the man himself, and his horse, loosely tethered to a dead tree, ready for a quick getaway. He could not have moved since he had loosed his shot at Nell, and yes, he had a rifle, like the ones he had seen in. . .in. . . His tortured mind gave up the useless struggle. Suffice it that he knew what he was seeing.

Chad worked his way silently, silently as a guerrilla —

what guerrilla? Where?—towards his enemy, who was lying prone, his rifle propped on a stone, to hold it steady. He had evidently done this kind of thing before. There was a brace of pistols by him, on the same stone. He was waiting for him and Nell to emerge from their fastness, as sooner or later they must.

He could not shoot the man from where he was, as there was no target to aim at—the prone position protected him—as it was meant to. If he could get nearer. . .he wriggled another few yards, and then, his hand closing around one of the small stones which littered the ground, he threw it, to hit the man on the back.

Cursing, the man above him rose, turned, snatching up a pistol to fire at where the stone had come from, probably judging that to raise the rifle and sight would take too long. He was sharp against the skyline, a perfect target, even in the gathering gloom, and Chad, who had leapt to his own feet the moment the stone had left his hand, ran forward, and shot him at point-blank range, in the chest—nothing for it; it was kill, or be killed.

As he fell forward, dying, the assassin's finger clenched on the trigger. The second shot, which Nell heard, rang out, and at its sound the dead man's horse broke from the rope which held him, and, like Rajah, bolted across the moor.

Chad waited. His adversary might not be quite dead, might be shamming, might even have accomplices close by, although Chad thought not, but best take no chances.

And then, when nothing stirred, he went over, rolled the man into a position where he could see his shattered chest and grimy face, fringed with a ginger beard.

Something about him and his clothes was almost familiar. Chad shrugged, damned his lost memory, and examined the rifle on the stone with a professional eye.

It was a beauty, a fine thing, delicately engraved, its cost, he would have thought, far beyond what the dead ruffian could have paid for it. Something odd about the rifle, too. He shook his head again to clear it. Trying to remember always troubled him.

Thoughtfully, he put it down, and, no need to be cautious now, he ran back to where he had left Nell, as he had begun to think of her. She would be imagining him dead, and wondering when her turn would come.

Nell, hearing the sound of a man running towards her, cringed a little, and then, when Chad's voice came, 'Do not be frightened, Lady Nell, there is no one left to do you harm,' she gave a little cry of relief.

'And you are safe?' she called.

'Quite safe. You may come out of hiding now.'

Nell, clothes filthy, her whole body one ache from the combined effects of her fall and lying cramped for so long, crawled out, tried to stand, needed Chad to steady her.

For a moment they stood, locked together, for her to feel the strength of him, to murmur fervently, 'Thank God you are unharmed. My fault, my fault.'

Even in this last desperate strait, for they were now abandoned on the moor, their mortal enemy dead, but left to the night and the elements, with none knowing where they were, Chad could not help registering what a vital armful he held.

And then he loosed her from him.

'What happened?' she asked. 'I heard two shots. You are not wounded, and he? Where is he?' And she made as if to go look for him.

Nell felt him restrain her. 'No,' he said. 'Best not. He's dead, I fear.'

'Dead,' she half moaned, and then fiercely, 'He meant to kill you, so you shot him.'

'No alternative,' said this new grave Chad, who had killed to save her, and oh, she honoured him for it. 'And a pity, Lady Nell, a great pity.'

'Oh, your wish to have spared him honours you.'

'No,' said Chad, his face hard. 'Not that. Dead, we cannot question him, you see, discover why he did it, perhaps who paid him.'

'But some Luddite malcontent, surely,' said Nell, 'who shot at me because he sees me as his enemy.'

'Perhaps.' Chad was grave. The devious mind which he had recently discovered he possessed was working hard. He thought of the splendid rifle again, and wondered why it troubled him. He also wondered what enemies Lady Elinor might possess. Who, for instance, stood to benefit by her death? He shivered at the thought, and said no more. He did not wish to disturb her.

For they were not yet out of the wood, or, more properly, off the moor!

Aisgill was beginning to grow anxious. Lady Elinor and Newcome should have returned long since. He was debating what to do when he saw Henson coming across the yard, struggling against the bitter wind which had sprung up.

'What's this?' Henson said, almost angry. 'I was due to meet her ladyship an hour ago, and Mrs Conybeare tell me that she is not yet back from her ride, and it is almost dark. Where has she gone, and who rode with her?'

He was determined to prove to Aisgill, whom he thought Lady Nell gave far too long a rope, that in the last analysis he, the agent, was master here.

Aisgill regarded him sourly. 'You cannot be more worried than I am,' he announced. 'Yes, she should be back, but Newcome is with her. She should be safe enough.'

'Newcome with her!' ejaculated Henson. 'You've gone light in the attic, man, to send her out with him. You know nothing of him, and that loss of memory could be all a pretence. Ten to one, he's made off with her.'

'That I do not believe,' said Aisgill, although he was beginning to have qualms himself about letting the mistress go off in the company of one so dubious, when all was said and done. 'I am about to be sending search parties to look for them. Lady Elinor usually rides only to the Cairn.'

'And if that were where she has gone,' said Henson sharply, 'she would have been back long since, and I should not be troubling you.'

It was while Aisgill was drawing up and instructing search parties, every face worried, for Lady Nell was loved, and Newcome was beginning to be liked, that one of the lads ran up, face alarmed.

'It's Rajah,' he blurted. 'He's running on the moor, riderless, and none can get near him to bring him in.'

'And Vulcan?' said Aisgill, desperately, sure now that something was badly wrong.

'No sign of Vulcan, nor either of their riders. Rajah's in a fair old lather, looks to have come a long way.'

It took some time to corner Rajah, his weariness letting them catch him rather than any acts of theirs, and while this was going on the first party of lads, carrying lanterns, and with orders to halloo when they reached Lady Nell's usual turning-point, had set off on their mission.

Foam flying about him, Rajah, who bucked and snorted at every hand laid on him, was inspected.

'No sign of hurt,' reported Aisgill to the worried Henson, 'the pistol still in its holster. No reins broken. All his lines intact. Nothing to explain why he lost his rider, and was parted from Vulcan.'

Rajah continued to show his dislike of everyone who was not Chad Newcome before he was finally wrestled into his stall. Both of Nell's senior servants were beginning to be seriously worried, and Aunt Conybeare finally appeared in the yard, shawl about her shoulders, to voice her distress that her darling was missing. Nell was a daughter to her, the daughter she had never borne.

'More search parties,' ordered Aisgill, and then, decisively, 'and I shall lead one to the Throne of God.'

'The Throne of God,' snorted Henson, 'why there? It's miles away.'

'Because Lady Nell loves the place, and think, she might have wanted Newcome to see it. He's never been so far afield to my certain knowledge.'

Henson stared at Aisgill. Something odd there. Something both men instinctively felt.

'Lady Nell to take Newcome to see something! *Newcome*! The vagabond hauled half-naked off the moor. Why should she do that?'

'They deal well together,' said Aisgill, almost uncomfortably.

Henson stared again. 'What are you saying, man?'

'Nothing,' growled Aisgill angrily. 'What are you saying? Lady Nell is kind. The man is good with her horses. She might think the Throne of God a good place

to show him — and why am I gossiping here with you?
The more I think of it, the more likely it seems. The
night is drawing on, and if they are unprotected out
there in the open. . .' And he ran off, shouting to round
up the horses, to order yet another group of Nell's
people on to the moor, himself leading it.

Behind him, Henson stared at nothing. 'Rainbows,'
he said finally to himself. 'Whimwhams, and dammit,
since that man arrived here, nothing has been the same.'

That man sat with his mistress in the lee of the rocks
around the Throne of God. The night was bitterly cold,
and a fine rain had succeeded a strong wind. Beside
him, Nell, wrapped in the warm green coat from his
livery, shivered, and tried to prevent herself from shivering further. Shock as well as the bitter night held her
prisoner.

And, to keep her warm, Chad had stripped to his
shirt, and must be feeling the cold dreadfully. What was
worst of all was that it was her silly irresponsible fault.
Without the journey to the Throne, they would have
been home and dry hours ago.

She said as much to Chad, who grunted, 'Nonsense,'
at her. 'He could as well have tried to shoot you on the
journey back from the Cairn, as he did later, when we
pressed on.'

Nell had suggested that they try to walk towards
Campions, but he had said, 'Nonsense,' to that as well.
Since the attempt on her life, and his killing of the
would-be assassin, ladyships and stable hands seemed
to have flown away; they were man and woman
together, struggling for survival.

'There's no shelter on the way should we need it,'
Chad said, 'and its cloudy tonight, with little moon to

help us. God knows where we should end up. Rest here, and we may try to walk at first light. Aisgill will surely be sending search parties after us, and with luck Rajah might have run in, to warn them that something is very wrong.'

Nell thought of poor dead Vulcan, whose screams had stopped long ago, and of the other body, lost among the rocks where Chad had left it, beside all the incriminating evidence of guilt and murder.

'Newcome. . .' she said suddenly — she really must not be thinking of him as Chad.

'Lady Nell?' For Chad had begun to call her by the affectionate name the hands always used of her in her absence.

'You might as well have your coat back,' she said, teeth chattering. 'It might warm you. I think that nothing is going to warm me.'

Chad became quite still, turned towards her where she sat by him, took her small frozen hand in his large one.

'I have been remiss,' he said abruptly, memory stirring in him again, for his hand, although he wore less than she, was warmer than hers. 'We must do something to warm you. . .or. . .'

Nell knew what the 'or' meant. Men and women had died of exposure on the moors in temperatures similar to this. There was, fortunately, no frost, but the wind and rain were working against her instead.

'Come,' he said, slipping his coat from her shoulders. 'There's no help for it. Forgive me, my lady,' he said, all formality, which was ironic enough in the face of what he was about to do.

For he wrapped his coat closely about the two of them, but not before he had drawn Nell into his arms, against his broad chest, to hold her in order to warm her, and then he began to chafe her cold hands, to restore them to life.

Oh, thought Nell dreamily, how comfortable this is, to be sure. She could feel the living warmth of him, the clean male scent of Chad and stables mixed, the latter a smell Nell had known and loved all her life. She could feel the steady beat of his heart, and she turned her head further into his chest, so that its rhythm began to affect her strongly, and as heat passed from him to her another heat began, slowly and stealthily, not outside her, but inside, as though flames were being ignited in her.

What was happening to her? For this new feeling was not only powerful, but was making strange demands of her. For she wanted to burrow further and further into Chad, to put her arms about him, to. . .

Chad knew quite well what was happening to Nell— and to him. He felt her breathing change, took a deep breath, and began to speak, to take both their minds off their errant bodies.

'A strange thing happened out there, Lady Elinor,' he said, speaking with exquisite formality to keep his voice steady and his own breathing easy.

'Oh, Chad, what was that?' murmured Nell drowsily, forgetting her resolution to address him as Newcome, the strongest sense of well-being beginning to take her over, repressing a little her desire to seize hold of Chad and stroke him as he was stroking her hands and arms.

'I recovered a little of my memory,' he answered. . . and paused for her to say warmly,

'Oh, how splendid. You know who you are?'

He shook his head, as much to clear it as to deny what she had said. The woman in his arms, so warm

and soft. . . He started to speak again. 'Not that, but I
had glimpses of my past, which tell me that Aisgill's
guess that I was once a trooper is correct. Flashes only,
but I know that I was once in Spain, with the guerrillas
there. I must have been cut off from the army and my
officer, because I was giving orders, so Aisgill was right
that I was a sergeant.'

He stopped again. 'Which would explain my clerkly
abilities a little, except. . .' How to say that somehow
none of these deductions seemed correct to him, there
was something missing, but what, he did not know?

And in the meantime, however much he tried to
distract himself, Nell's proximity was beginning to affect
him so powerfully that it was all that he could do not to
begin to make love to her on the spot.

And what he felt for her was not simple lust. The
woman he held was not just any woman, she was. . .she
was. . .the one woman, the woman the memoryless
wanderer had wanted all his life — and never found,
until now. And how did he know that? But he did.

It was the Countess Nell, hard-working, proud, com-
passionate, careful of those who served her, whom he
held and wished to pleasure. Countess Nell of the strong,
sweet face, whose presence lit up every corner of
Campions. Countess Nell who had taken pity on him,
and, Oh, God, I want to make love to her, not fiercely,
but slowly and gently, to see her fulfilled beneath me,
her pleasure more to me than mine, for Countess Nell
gives, never takes, and I must give, to her.

And temptation was too much, at last, for he was only
a man, and not a saint, and he bent his head, to cup her
chin in his hand, and tip her face towards him. To do —
what?

Nell, lost in a dream of happiness, hardly aware of

where she was, obediently turned her head to help him as she felt his big hand cup her face so gently, and as he tipped it up towards him, before she knew what she was doing, she kissed the palm that cherished her.

For Chad as for Nell, time stood still. Propinquity, the growing warmth spreading between them, was doing its work. After she had kissed him, he returned her kiss, gently, on the cheek, and then, since she showed no sign of distress at what he was doing, kissed her again, on the other, turning her head slightly, and her response was to make a little noise, almost like a cat purring. For, thought Nell light-headedly, he saved my life at the risk of his, and he surely deserves some reward.

Besides, I like what he is doing!

She was now fully in his arms, body as well as face offered to him, and Chad was desperate. Honour said that he must not take advantage of her, reason said that he would suffer for it if he seduced her, as he now so easily might, but something deep and strong was telling him that what he wanted she wanted too, and that was all that mattered.

His right hand now cupped her breast, stroking it through the cloth, and she purred again, said indistinctly, 'Oh, thank you, Chad, thank you,' and her right hand stole up around his neck to stroke him in return.

He kissed her again, and this time not on the cheek, for as he bent to do so she turned her own head hungrily towards him, and the kiss found her mouth, and they were suddenly drowning in passion.

From the depths of the memory he no longer possessed, something called, No! so loudly that Chad pulled away for very honour, for it was honour that was calling, and said in a voice husky with desire, 'No.'

And then still holding her, to keep her warm against

him, he said, even more formally than before, 'Lady Elinor, it is no uncommon thing, when men and women have been in danger together that. . .' And he gulped; how to say this delicately, without offending, or hurting her?

Nell, cradled in Chad's arms, had never felt so mindlessly happy in her whole life. He was big enough to make her feel small and delicate — no mean feat — and not since she had been a little girl could she remember being held so lovingly, being treated with such careful kindness. She was light-headed enough with shock, excitement, exhaustion, and yes, true love, not to want him to stop caressing her.

At the back of her mind a little voice was telling her where this might end, but in her delirium of mingled love and desire she thought, If Rajah can pleasure White Princess, why should not Chad pleasure me? And she saw no lack of logic in this disgraceful notion; rather it was as though she, Chad, Rajah and the Princess were all partners in a dance of nature, where titles, social conformity and duties to God and King meant nothing.

'Yes?' she said dreamily, aware not only that he had stopped speaking, but he had ceased making love to her, and she did not wish him to do that. 'You were saying, and then you stopped. What was that about men and women?'

'That when they have been in danger together they frequently. . .desire one another afterwards.'

'And that, you think,' said Nell, wishing all this would end and that Chad would get down to the true business of loving again, 'is why we are behaving like this now?'

'Yes,' Chad said briefly, and, as far as he was

concerned, although he was not so sure of Nell, he was lying in his teeth.

By now, Nell was far gone, already on the edge of sleep, a sleep induced by his gentle lovemaking on top of her exhaustion and shock.

'You're wrong, you know,' she said confidentially and sleepily, and how good it was to sleep in one's lover's arms, 'I felt like this about you long before tonight,' and, so saying, she finally drifted into a warm slumber, her changed breathing telling the man who held her not only that he had warmed his Countess into life, but in return she had frankly and freely offered him her love.

And what, he thought, still holding her carefully, and giving her one last, chaste kiss on her forehead, would she think when daylight claimed her, and she was the Lady Malplaquet again, and he was Chad, her groom and stable hand? Would she even remember what she had said and he had done?

The moon, long missing, came from behind a cloud, and threw strange shadows on the moor which lay all about them. Chad could not sleep. First his roused body prevented him, and then when desire faded, and it was enough to hold her in his arms and study her sleeping face, the necessity to stay awake, to guard and protect his woman remained.

Even stranger shadows, quite unlike those on the moor, ran through his head. How did he know that he had never felt like this for a woman before, that the other women he had known had always taken, never given? He did not remember their names or their faces, nor how and why they had loved, and why it had not been satisfactory, as it had been tonight — even though nothing had been consummated.

Chad sighed, and Nell stirred in his arms. In her

dreams she was in a ballroom, full of people wearing court dress, orders and decorations. She was looking for someone, and then she found him. He had his back to her, was wearing an officer's splendid dress uniform, the uniform of an aide; even from the back she could see the bullion on his broad shoulders.

And then he turned and walked towards her and she saw his face plain, and it was Chad! But as she touched him wonder and delight rising her, his arms enfolding her, the dream faded, and she fell into the deep sleep of oblivion, safe in Chad's arms beneath the Throne of God.

CHAPTER SEVEN

TOWARDS midnight, as he later discovered, for he did not sleep, but remained awake to protect his lady from any further danger which might befall, Chad heard the noise of Aisgill's party, heading towards them, across the moor.

Nell lay in his arms, face trustfully turned up towards him; once or twice she stirred, and a small smile crossed her dreaming face, his warmth and hers mingling.

All passion, all desire, had leached from him. All he felt was an enormous protectiveness. He had killed for her once, and knew that he would do so again, if necessary. He was at one with Rajah, or the lion who protected his pride, the falcon who stooped to destroy his enemy. What he felt for Nell had been sealed in blood.

The spilling of blood had not been necessary for him to love her — that had come of itself, born from the gratitude for her saving of him from starvation, nurtured by all that he had seen of her since, come to full-blown maturity when he had taken her in his arms to warm her.

But the bond which had been created by what he had done for her was there, a living thing between them, and the instinctive man he was, who needed no memory to guide him, knew that she, being the woman she was, would acknowledge that bond, as she had already acknowledged her love, before she had fallen asleep in his arms.

The noise below told Chad that the everyday world,

the world where peeress and lowly servant could not meet as equals, was upon them. He heard the sound of horses and men, voices calling, saw the light of lanterns, knew that rescue was near, and he feared that, despite all, once the bright day was on them again what Nell Tallboys had said would be denied or forgotten — but he could neither deny, nor forget.

They must not be found like this, and he slipped out of the coat which they had shared, wrapped it around her lovingly, and, while she protested in her sleep at losing him, he propped her against one of the pillars of the Throne, and left her — to walk, shouting, towards Aisgill and the men with him.

'Praise be to God,' cried Aisgill fervently. 'Lady Nell is safe?' And then, 'I knew it, I knew it, she took you to the Throne — and what,' he demanded fiercely, 'happened to your horses, Newcome, that Rajah should come home without you? Where is Vulcan? Never say you let that mild beast get away from you both!'

'A private word with you, Maister Aisgill,' said Chad, face grim, after he had taken Aisgill's hand, and pointed to the sleeping Nell, half hidden under the Throne's seat, 'before you tell the rest.' For the search party was now upon them.

'As to Vulcan,' he began, leading Aisgill over to the spot where the poor beast lay dead, 'it is as you see,' and he poured the whole story of the attack and its consequences into Aisgill's disbelieving ear as carefully and lucidly as though he were reporting to his senior officer.

Aisgill's early disbelief did not survive the evidence of the bullet which had killed Vulcan, nor the sight of the body and rifle lying among the rocks parallel with the Throne.

'I was sorry to kill him,' said Chad, 'for could I have taken him alive we might have learned something of why he attacked Lady Elinor, but I had no choice.'

'No,' agreed Aisgill. 'You did your duty, Newcome, and protected your mistress as a good servant — and a good soldier — should.'

Nell had been awakened by the noise of the search party and she walked unsteadily towards them, Chad's jacket still around her shoulders, and for the first time Aisgill saw that Chad was shivering in the night air.

'Come,' he said roughly, to one of the lads, 'give Newcome a blanket for his shoulders, and you, Lady Elinor,' he said reprovingly to her, as though she were the child she had once been, whom he had taught and reprimanded, 'may explain to me tomorrow why you should bring Newcome here, so late in the day.'

Nell coloured, and put out a hand in Chad's direction. 'I was wrong,' she said, and then, to Aisgill, 'but he saved me. . .'

Aisgill saw that, despite the sleep she had enjoyed since the ambush, his mistress was exhausted and shocked. He dared to interrrupt her. 'Enough for now, my lady. In the morning you may both tell the whole tale, although Newcome's bravery is plain to see, and fortunate for us all, the day we took him in.'

As they left, beginning the long journey back to Campions, Chad riding one of the horses, Nell's side-saddle transferred from Vulcan to one of the lads' mounts so that she might travel home between Aisgill and himself, he turned once to look at the place of the stones where his Countess had first kissed him in love and gratitude.

* * *

Nell sat up in bed the next morning, being petted by everybody. A great fire roared in the bedroom hearth, and Aunt Conybeare was in a chair by her bed, a magnificent four-poster, its crimson curtains looped into a gilt earl's coronet high above it.

Her aunt was worrying over her, exhorting her not to overdo things, then said, almost reprovingly, 'You look very well, my dear, for one who has had such an unfortunate experience. Half a night in the open, a man and your horse killed in earshot, a long ride back, and you look blooming, positively blooming. Lately you have looked a trifle. . .wan. . .to say the least.'

Nell snuggled into her pillows, drank hot chocolate laced with cream, ate new-made white rolls, with delicious strawberry jam and butter, and tried not to let the dreadful thoughts she was having show on her face. But oh, dear, from her aunt's comments, they obviously did!

Had she really kissed Chad Newcome last night, before he had kissed her, and virtually invited him to make love to her? Worse, had she actually told him, quite wantonly, that she had been wanting him to make love to her from the moment she had first seen him?

No, surely not. She could not have done *that*. Not she, Nell Tallboys, whose reputation had frightened every suitor away, who could by her cold stare reduce strong men to mumbling inanity when they had tried to court her. Icy Nell Tallboys had lain in the arms of her giant stable hand and had invited him to make love to her, in so many words — no, a very few words, and all of them plain.

But if she had not behaved like a lady, let alone a noblewoman, Chad Newcome had behaved like a gentleman. No, revise that Nell, *better* than most gentlemen. He must have distanced himself from her before Aisgill and the other lads had arrived, to stifle any suggestion of improper behaviour, although how Aisgill thought that she had managed to keep warm she could not imagine.

And what should she say when she next saw him — and what would he say to her? What etiquette governed what she had done? Well, he had saved her life, and she had already heard from Aunt Conybeare, so late had she slept, that Henson, Aisgill, Payne and old Challenor the librarian had met in conclave, talked to Newcome, stared at the body which had been brought in, sent for a constable from Keighley, the nearest village, and had discussed putting up bills to try to find out who Nell's would-be murderer was.

All in all, Aunt Conybeare had told her, interest and excitement between Newcome's astonishing resourcefulness and the mystery of who might want to kill her, seeing that no one, rightly, thought that the shot was meant for Newcome.

'And no more riding on the moors with only one groom, my dear,' said Aunt Conybeare tenderly. Nell had only just been able to prevent her spooning bread and milk into her unwilling mouth.

'Oh, no,' she had said determinedly when Aunt Conybeare had processed in with a great china bowl of the wretched stuff, 'you can take that away,' and then, mischievously, quoting from *Macbeth*, which she had been told one ought never to do, ' "Throw physic to the dogs; I'll none of it".'

'What in the world has come over you this last week or so, Nell?' sighed her aunt. 'You have always been so prim and proper. And now, suddenly, you are a positive hoyden — no, that is not the word; I cannot think of one which fits your goings-on. Why in the world, for example, should you drag poor Newcome to the Throne of God, the last thing a stable lad would be interested in, I dare swear?'

'On the contrary, Aunt,' said Nell, looking at her from under her eyelashes, 'he seemed so interested in the Cairn when we rode there that I thought that the Throne of God would entertain him even more, and so it did, until that murdering wretch arrived. And, besides, he said that it was a good thing we did go there.'

Her mouth was now so disgracefully full of buttered roll and strawberry jam that she had difficulty in getting the next bit out. 'He said that we were better off in the shelter of the Throne than on the moor. We were not so good a target for a sniper.'

'Aisgill said that you owe your life to his courage,' remarked her aunt.

'So I do, and I want to see him, as soon as possible, to thank him,' said Nell, mouth free again, 'because I didn't thank him properly last night.'

'But not in your bedroom, my dear,' said her aunt, reprovingly again. Really, what *was* getting into Nell lately?

'Well, the queens of France used to receive their subjects in their bedrooms,' said Nell rebelliously, thinking at the same time, What on earth is making me so frivolous and light-minded? Is this what kissing Newcome has done to me?

'But you are not the Queen of France, my dear,' said Aunt Conybeare, uncontrovertibly.

'A pity, that,' said Nell naughtily, watching her aunt's mouth frame a dismayed circle of surprise. 'No, I will see Newcome in my study, with my face so,' and she pulled her features into a parody of Nell Tallboys at her coldest.

Her aunt looked helplessly at her. 'You will thank him properly or not at all, my girl. But you know he was only doing his duty.'

'His duty, Aunt?' Nell was fascinated. 'Was it his duty to risk his life for me, and then compound that by giving me his coat? No, Newcome went beyond his duty last night, I think.' In more ways than one, Nell, in more ways than one! said the devil which seemed to have taken up residence in her mind.

'Gratitude, no doubt,' offered her aunt. 'For you did save his for him, when you took him in, after all.'

'So I did,' said Nell. 'That makes us quits, you think? I shall tell him so. No, Newcome, I cannot thank you for what you did for me. It was merely tit for tat, although you risked your life for me when you went after my assassin, and I risked nothing when I gave you shelter.'

Except my reputation, said the devil inside her, for I fear that what I so inconveniently feel for him will soon be going to show on my face, or on his!

But there was nothing on either of their faces when she met him in her study after luncheon. She had, for some unknown reason, dressed herself carefully again. Fly-away Nell Tallboys seemed to have disappeared for good!

She was wearing green, a deep green high-waisted wool dress, trimmed with saffron lace, and she had wound round her head a turban which Aunt Conybeare had presented to her, and which she had always refused to wear. It was a flaming thing in vermilions, deep oranges, blues and greens, and she pinned an antique jewel set with rubies to its side, to hold it steady.

Even Henson's opaque stare shivered a little when he saw her unaccustomed magnificence. They were all here, all the Privy Council, old Payne looking frailer than ever — and Newcome, of course.

He looked quite splendid, a figure to match her own. As a reward, no doubt, for faithful service, Aisgill had ordered him dressed to perfection in the Malplaquet royal livery, only worn when Malplaquets entertained kings and courts.

His stock was so white, his boots so shiny, his hands so beautiful in their kid gloves, his body so well set off by the splendid green and gold of his bullion-trimmed coat that he made Nell feel quite weak at the knees — nearly as weak as she had been in her dream.

He held, of all things, a shako in those hands, with the most giant Malplaquet cockade pinned to it that she had ever seen.

And Nell was nervous, as she had never been in her whole life. Her voice nearly came out in a squeak, until she managed to control it, so that his eyes, previously fixed on the floor, or his boots, suddenly lifted, and she saw mirth in them, and yes, an understanding of her predicament — how to speak normally to him after their intimate moment of the previous night?

'I have to thank you, Newcome,' she said primly. 'I was too overset last night through fright, shock and weariness —— ' oh, dear, what lies ' — to make you properly aware of my gratitude for your devotion. . .' What a word, devotion, and what a lie to say that he was not aware of her gratitude, so aware of it had she been that she had virtually offered herself to him.

And by now Nell was in full flow, one part of her saying all the proper things, and the other part having the most improper thoughts at the sight of him, glorious

in full fig — whatever was Aisgill thinking of? Had he no
more sense than to turn Newcome out so completely *à
point* that now it was she who wanted to eat *him*?

'I understand that Aisgill has proposed that you be
offered a bonus on your wages for the gallantry which
you displayed in defending me at the risk of your own
life.' There, she had said it, without falling on her knees
before him, before them all, and saying, 'Take me,
Newcome, I'm yours,' like a mad maidservant in a bad
French farce, by an inferior imitator of Marivaux!

She practised it, in French, in her head, while Aisgill,
speaking before Newcome could, said, 'He has refused
to accept anything, Lady Elinor. He says that he merely
did his duty and wants neither money nor favour.'

'Is this true, Newcome?' asked Nell, willing him to
look at her.

'Yes, Lady Elinor,' he replied, looking her full in the
eyes, so that they met there, if nowhere else.

Nell was suddenly frantic. She felt that she was on
the edge of a cliff, about to slide over, and nothing and
no one there to save her.

Unwittingly, old Payne did. 'An illuminated address,'
he said in his cracked voice, saving her from speaking.
'I think I may still be able to limn one, recording the
thanks of the House of Malplaquet for saving its jewel.'
And he bowed to Nell.

'Perhaps a little premature,' said Newcome, standing
stiff and straight before his superiors. 'With respect, I
hope that you have considered that whoever planned
this might strike again.'

For a moment there was silence, then noise, as all
spoke together, only Nell and Newcome silent, gazing
into one another's eyes.

'Planned this?' said Henson, incredulous. 'A malcontent, a Luddite surely, like the man who shot Cartwright.'

'Do Luddites own or have access to rifles of such precision and quality that a sharpshooter in the Rifle Brigade might be proud to possess it?'

And how do I know all that? thought Chad. Yes, I was in the army, but in the cavalry, and suddenly another series of questions shot into his head, which, in the mental stasis produced by his amnesia, he had never thought to ask himself before. When did I leave the army, and why? I know — how do I know? — that I was happy there.

Aisgill was regarding him steadily. Newcome had told him of his suspicions about the attack the previous evening, but, like the others, he could not bring himself to believe the murder attempt to be by other than a dissident, a Jacobin.

He said so, adding, 'The rifle was doubtless stolen,' only for him to meet Newcome's hard stare. Chad kept his body still, his voice submissive, but he differed from them and was not afraid to say so.

'The man had been a soldier once, had some grasp of how a guerrilla would strike from ambush. Did you inspect his back? I had not time last night. Lady Elinor's safety was my prime concern.'

'His back?' Henson stared at Newcome, puzzled, but Aisgill took the point.

'The marks of the lash, you think, saving your presence, Lady Elinor. The body is still here, awaiting burial. It shall be inspected.'

'Not that their presence would prove anything,' remarked Henson, annoyed that, once again, Newcome appeared to be instructing his betters.

'No,' agreed Aisgill. 'But, if there, they would prove

he was a soldier, and, perhaps, explain the rifle and his stalking skills. And would add weight to the notion that he was hired.'

The room was suddenly so quiet that the ticking of the small French clock over the hearth was loud in it. Nell shivered. She did not like to think herself a target. The face she showed Newcome was now as grave as his.

'My lady should be guarded at all times,' he said, 'if I may say so. We had a saying in the army: better safe than sorry.'

'I shall arrange it,' said Aisgill quickly, before Henson could speak. 'The house shall be protected, too. Best, in future, that Lady Elinor does not leave the park to ride.'

'And I,' said Henson, 'with Lady Elinor's permission, shall write to the Bow Street Runners, asking them to send me some of their best men to investigate this whole murky business.'

He had hardly finished speaking when Payne, whom Nell had given permission to sit, half rose, uttered a strangled cry, and fell forward on to the carpet.

All of them, paralysed a moment, by surprise, stood staring at him, and it was Newcome, flinging down his shako, who fell on to his knees on the carpet, to take the old man in his arms, revealing a livid and distorted face, the eyes rolled up.

'He has had a fit, he may be dying,' he said, and, rising to his feet, the old man in his arms, Chad carried him to the giant oak table in the centre of the room, and swept what was on it to one side to lay Payne down and begin to chafe his wrists and then his poor distorted face.

'The doctor, quickly,' commanded Henson, annoyed at Newcome's speed of reaction and the almost unconscious arrogance with which he had taken charge, and begun to give orders.

Of them all, only Aisgill was not surprised. He had seen Newcome behave like this before, when he was not conscious of himself.

Water was fetched, and the doctor and the footmen came to carry him to his room at the doctor's insistence. One thing was plain to them all — if old Payne had not exactly died in harness his useful life was almost certainly over.

'Poor Payne,' said Nell, tears in her eyes. 'My fault, I should have made him retire.'

'No,' said Henson, 'he would not have been happy to go. He told me so.'

'And now my lady has no secretary,' said Challenor, suddenly conscious of the weight of his own years. 'For Payne has always refused an assistant.'

'May Newcome leave us, Lady Elinor?' said Aisgill. 'He has duties to perform. Rajah needs gentling after yesterday. Leave off your finery, Newcome, and put him through his paces in the riding school. He needs to be reminded who is master.'

'Yes,' said Nell, not wishing to lose Chad but, after all, he had his work to do. She watched the door close behind him.

Aisgill turned towards her, Henson and Challenor.

'Now, Lady Elinor, you may think my wits are wandering. But I sent Newcome away so that he would not hear what I am about to say. You need not look far for a secretary; Newcome would do admirably, I dare swear. I should hesitate to lose him, but perhaps you could release him in the afternoons to school Rajah and some of the better horses.'

Henson began to argue, only to hear Challenor say,

'What an excellent suggestion, if I may say so. The work he has done for you, Aisgill, is exemplary. And he could guard Lady Elinor at the same time. What could be better?'

Nell realised that they were all looking at her, including Henson, who could make no further protests in the light of the other two men's recommendations.

Did she want Newcome as a secretary? Of course she did! Outrageously, proud Nell Tallboys knew that of all things in the world she wanted Chad Newcome to be her secretary, to be by her side. . . She must be careful in what she said.

Slowly and deliberately she lowered her head, looked at the papers on her desk. 'On probation,' she said at last, trying to make her voice sound grudging.

'Oh, of course,' said Henson, eagerly. 'A stop-gap, perhaps.'

'Indeed,' said Nell. 'He might not suit. He seems an outdoors person. Being indoors might be a trial for him.'

'True,' said Aisgill, watching his lady carefully. Still something odd there, where Newcome was concerned. But even Aisgill could not have imagined the truth of the matter. 'But Newcome seems adaptable, and as his memory had recovered, although he has still lost himself, he shows that he has a rare range of skills. Best of all is his application. The army lost a good man when it turned him out.'

'That is that, then,' said Henson briskly. He disliked these eulogies of Newcome, a man rescued from ruin, after all. 'He cannot have been so remarkable, to end up as he did, wandering the moors, memoryless. Best I keep an eye on him, Lady Elinor.'

'A good idea,' said Nell, making her face as serious as she could. The person who most meant to keep an eye on Newcome was herself—and what an eye she would keep!

'Speak to him, then, Aisgill. Send him to Henson for his first instructions.'

'He'll need some clothes,' offered Henson, who disliked the whole idea, but did not care to say so. 'He cannot bring the stables in here with him, begging your pardon, Aisgill.'

'The tailor can make some for him,' said Aisgill, 'and in the meantime, if Lady Elinor does not disapprove, he can wear one of her grandfather's old black suits. He has much the same size as Newcome.'

'So he was,' said Nell, struck. 'You are full of invention today, Aisgill.'

She could almost feel Henson bridle, added gently, 'You can see to that, Henson, I am sure. And my grandfather's old shirts. You could check Newcome's boot and shoe size, as well. Nothing must be wasted at Campions.'

After they had gone, Aisgill with instructions to speak to Newcome when he had finished schooling Rajah, and Henson grudgingly off to check her late grandfather's wardrobe, Nell sat herself down at her desk.

Before he had left the room, Aisgill having gone first, Henson had fixed Nell with a stern eye, and said, 'The world has turned upside-down since that man came here. Aisgill has made such a pet of him as I have never seen. Best watch him carefully, Lady Elinor. After all, we know nothing of him.'

'I know that he saved my life from an assassin, and from the cold after that,' said Nell gently.

'And he is a young man,' said Henson doggedly. 'Not like having Payne in the room with you.'

'Then poor Aunt Conybeare shall sit with me,' said

Nell, exasperated. 'She will not like it, but there it is. Have you any more instructions for me, Henson?'

'I have only your best interests at heart,' replied Henson stiffly.

'Yes, I know that,' said Nell, and thought, and you are right to worry a little, but bonnets over the windmill, Nell, my girl. You may have your giant stable hand by you at all times, and your own Privy Council suggested it!

CHAPTER EIGHT

'BEGGING your pardon, Lady Elinor,' said Chad Newcome respectfully, 'but I should like to re-organise Payne's records for you. He seems to have fallen into a muddle of recent years—his age doubtless.'

Payne was in bed, recovering. He had not died immediately from his fit, but would always be semi-paralysed, and Chad had been her secretary for just under a week.

True to her promise to Henson, Aunt Conybeare sat in a corner of her study, placidly tatting, so that having Newcome with her was not quite the delight Nell had thought it might be.

Besides, he was being most stupidly proper. It was just as though their magic night together, for so Nell thought of it, had never happened.

Perhaps she had imagined it. Except that whenever their fingers touched when he handed letters and papers to her it was almost as though she had been subjected to one of Signor Galvani's shocks. She jumped just like one of his poor frogs was reported to have done. And she was sure that Newcome felt the same. His blue eyes took on a smoky look, exactly as they had done in the Cairn, and that night at the Throne of God.

So it was no use pretending that he was indifferent to her, but what with Henson popping in and out, and Aunt Conybeare sitting there, they might as well be living in a goldfish bowl, and there were times when Nell thought of dragging him off again to see the mere over to Slaitherbeck, and hope that a regiment of Luddites might attack them, so that they could snatch a few more forbidden moments together.

Her study opened into the library — or was it the other way round? — and when he had written the morning's letters he had gone there to do some work for Challenor, that being part of her secretary's duties.

She rose, said loudly, 'I wish to check a quotation from Madame de Sévigné,' to excuse her leaving the room. 'You need not come with me, Aunt. Challenor may play duenna.'

Chad was standing at the big map table, with one of the folios Challenor had found lying on it open before him.

Nell had crept in very quietly, to surprise him, and Challenor was nowhere to be seen. But Chad must have had an extra eye, in the back of his head, perhaps, for he said to her, 'Yes, what is it, Lady Elinor? May I be of assistance, or do you require Mr Challenor?'

'No, Newcome,' she said severely, 'I do not require Challenor, I require you. Pray what are you doing?'

'Mr Challenor has taught me how to collate books, and I am recording the details of this book for him,' he replied, ignoring the challenging note in her voice. 'You know, I have the oddest feeling that I have seen the book before,' and he indicated the map in it.

'Impossible,' said Nell, firmly, taking him literally. 'Challenor only found it by accident, some three weeks ago.'

'Oh, not this book,' said Chad, frowning. 'Another copy. If I am correct in so thinking, there should be a plate showing Terra Australis near the end,' and he turned the pages rapidly, to discover that the last map in the treatise was, indeed, of Terra Australis.

'Yes, you have seen a copy of it before,' said Nell slowly. 'I wonder where?'

'And so do I,' replied Newcome, looking her straight in the eye for the first time since their adventure, and she noticed that his own eyes had gone smoky again. 'But you wanted something of me?'

'Yes,' said Nell, 'I wonder if you would accompany me to the annexe? There is an edition of Madame de Sévigné's *Lettres* there, on a high shelf, and you could hand it down to me, if you would.'

The annexe was a smallish, book-lined store-room, where works not in good repair were kept, and Nell had purposely chosen one on such a high shelf to have the excuse to take Newcome in with her.

'You would wish to remain here while I collect it?' he enquired.

'Indeed, not,' said Nell rapidly; that would not do at all. 'I like the annexe——' another lie; Newcome seemed to provoke them '—and I shall certainly accompany you. I may—check what is there,' she said wildly, trying to think of a convincing excuse to be alone with him.

So there they were in the annexe, and she made sure that the door was closed behind them before she hissed at him, as he lifted the little library steps over to mount them, to reach her book, 'Newcome, pay attention to me and not to Madame de Sévigné. She is not your mistress. Why are you avoiding me?'

Chad put the steps down, and turned to look at her.

'Avoiding you, Lady Elinor? I was not aware that I was avoiding you. We have been constantly together ever since I became your secretary.'

'You know perfectly well what I mean. Do not prevaricate, Newcome,' said Nell, exasperated.

'Prevaricate, Lady Elinor?'

'And do not repeat every word I say, Newcome. Yes, avoiding me, dodging me. Listen to me, Newcome. I am giving you an order; you are not to avoid me in future. You understand me?'

'Perfectly. I am not to avoid you in future. But I have not been doing so in the present, nor in the past.'

'Newcome!' said Nell in an awful voice. 'Were it not that I have no evidence to support what I say I should suppose you to have spent a year in a Jesuit's seminary being instructed in the art of Machiavellian dialogue. You do know what I mean, Newcome. You are the most devious creature I have ever met with. Why are you laughing, Newcome?'

For not only were his eyes smokier than ever, but his expression was so full of honest amusement that she wanted to. . .wanted to. . . 'Quickly, Newcome, speak, or else Aunt Conybeare or Challenor will be upon us.'

'My very dear,' he said tenderly, taking her by the hand, and bowing his splendid head; he looked so handsome in proper clothing. 'You know I must not behave to you as I did that night we spent together. I am your humble secretary——'

'And I am your Countess, Newcome,' she said impatiently. 'Why do you keep telling me things I know, Newcome?'

'Because, if I speak to you as I wish, it would not only be improper, but it would also be unfair.'

'To whom unfair, Newcome? Tell me that, you or me?'

'Both of us. There can be nothing between us, Lady Elinor. You must see that in all conscience. You are a good woman, and to consort with me could only ruin you.'

'Suppose I command you to ruin me, Newcome, what then?'

'I don't think you know what you are saying.'

'Of course I know what I am saying. I want you to make love to me, Newcome. Is that plain enough for you, Newcome? Would you like me to draw you a diagram, Newcome?'

Her expression as she said this, and the low tones in which they were conversing, had him laughing again, but he said, almost roughly, 'Nothing I would like to do better in the whole world, Lady Elinor, than oblige you, but I must not.'

How he was able to restrain himself Chad did not know. Her eager face was alight with passion and impudent mockery, a woman enjoying herself in the lists of love for the first time, jousting with him with her tongue, trying to provoke him into action.

By God, if it were action she wanted, she should have it!

He was upon her, all his restraint gone, conquered by her nearness, his own passion for her, she was in his arms, saying breathlessly, before he stopped her mouth with his, 'Oh, no, Newcome, you do not need diagrams,' and he was kissing her, before common sense ruled, and he released her.

He turned away. 'Sévigné, you said,' and oh, God, it was torment to know that she was there, but duty and honour, newly returned to his memory, must rule him. He could not throw Countess Nell to the ground to love her, however much she wished him to, and however much he wished to make her his.

Nell tried to hold on to him. The passion which ran through her every time they touched one another had her in its grip, stronger than any duty to her name or to

Campions. Ever since her mother and father had died she had lived only for both of them. Her grandfather had seen the steel in her and cultivated it. Careless himself, he knew that Nell was not.

The lonely child she had been had grown into a lonely woman. The education he had given her, intellectually sounder than that of any boy, allied to her natural gifts would have made her senior wrangler had she been a boy. She rode as well as any man, and from seventeen had begun to manage the stud for him, creating it again, making it what it had been in the second Earl's time.

And through it all she had remained proud and cool Nell Tallboys, who at some time in the future would coldly choose a husband, give him a child, but keep her inner self intact. No man should move her, make Countess Nell his toy, his thing, in the end his nothing, as she had seen other women were to their husbands.

Love, what was that? A joke, a myth, something of which poets sang. It had nothing to do with what Nell understood of life. Love was Rajah and the mares he covered, that was all. A name to romanticise lust.

Campions was all she had loved — and all Malplaquet's possessions.

Until she had seen Chad.

Reason had fled, and poetry made sense. The passion previously reserved for Campions was now for him

Conscience, he had said. Now what was that? Conscience withered and died when she was with him. Was it because he was nameless, and she was the queen who stooped, because to stoop was better than to be equal, that she had come to love him?

No, that was not true, because she gloried in him — all of him. Covertly watched him, walking across the room, driving his quill across paper, schooling Rajah.

And what she felt for him was of the mind, as well as of the body, no mere condescension of a great lady, but a woman consorting — his word — with her equal in the sight of God, if not of man.

Joy ran through her. The humour she had never expressed before, hardly knew she possessed, welled up in her, to tease him, to play with words, to watch his face light up — I grow maudlin, she thought, and when he mounted the steps to find her book, and she heard Challenor approaching, she said loudly, in her best Countess Nell voice, 'Oh, dear, Newcome, I could have found that book a dozen times were I tall enough. How long you have taken!'

He looked down at her, the book in his hand, said, 'Madam, you are pleased to be wilful. You're sure you really need the book at all?' and her own laughter rang in the air, as Challenor put his head round the door, said,

'There you both are,' and, being innocent himself, saw innocence in them. 'You have visitors, Lady Elinor. Henson has sent your uncle Beaumont to your study and asked your cousin Ulric to await you in the Turkish room.'

'Visitors!' exclaimed Nell. 'We grow strangely frivolous these days. More new faces in Campions in the last few weeks than are usually seen in a twelvemonth. You may come down now, Newcome, with or without your book. My secretary must meet my uncle, I will not say for him to approve of you; he never approves of anyone.'

And then she added, with such a look on her as Challenor had never seen, so that he gazed after her in puzzlement, 'Do you think that he has come to see me with yet another proposal from some nobleman who would like to take Campions from me to waste it away on the turf or the gaming tables or women?'

Chad would have stayed behind in the library, but she would have none of it.

'No, you must come with me. Old Payne would have done, so why not you?'

Sir Chesney Beaumont, Nell's dead mother's brother, was a fine-looking man, with a strong urbane face, and was busy discussing the day's news with Aunt Conybeare. He had already admired her tatting, and they were well into the affairs of the Princess of Wales, as the Regent's wife was always called.

'My dear,' he said to Nell, as she walked in, Newcome behind her, 'you look positively blooming. So much better than when I last saw you. You looked a trifle peaky then, not at all yourself. Mrs Conybeare has told me the sad news about Payne, and that Henson has rightly sent for the Runners to investigate this strange attack on you. Luddites, I am sure. Luddites.'

'None of my people thinks so, uncle,' said Nell, adding conciliatorily, 'But you may be right.'

'And this is your new secretary.' Sir Chesney's eyes took in Chad, who thought it best to stand submissive. For some reason, Chesney Beaumont made him feel uneasy, and he could not think why. His very name drew odd resonances from the air.

'Yes,' said Nell, walking to kiss him on his florid cheek. 'I hope you have not come to tease me about marriage, my dear uncle, for I am more set against it than ever.'

Sir Chesney was still exercised by Chad. 'I had not thought him to be such a young man,' he said doubtfully, 'and no, I have not come to talk to you about marriage, least of all with Charles Halstead. Particularly not with Charles Halstead.'

He stared at Chad, made waving motions at him, 'We could perhaps talk alone, my dear.'

'Why?' said Nell coolly. 'You would not have sent Payne away. I prefer Newcome to stay. I have no secrets from him,' she added, and threw Newcome a killing look, which had Chad coughing, and looking desperately anywhere but at Nell, or Sir Chesney.

'Well, that must be your choice, my dear,' he remarked, a trifle miffed. 'These matters are delicate.'

'From what I have heard of Charles Halstead, delicate is not the word I would have used,' said Nell, 'but then, fortunately, I have never met him.'

'Nor I, my dear,' said Sir Chesney, 'and now I am glad I never shall, and I am sorry I ever spoke with his father of a match between you. His conduct has been abominable, as you shall hear.'

'Never met him,' said Nell, seating herself, with Chad standing at her elbow, a little behind, as befitted a good secretary, 'and yet you recommended him to me in marriage.'

'Oh, I know his father well — Clermont, a sterling fellow. But Halstead — *there* is a horse of a different colour. He, I regret to say, visited Watier's in a drunken fit, railed against all women, and when your cousin Bobus was foolish enough to exempt you from his strictures, as an example of strict virtue, you understand, made a dreadful bet that he would, he would. . .' Sir Chesney ran down, finding it difficult to say exactly what Charles Halstead had roared in his drunken misogyny.

'Would what?' said Nell impatiently, and then, 'Oh, you do not like to say. Come, Uncle, Aunt Conybeare has been married, I run a great establishment, and I am sure Newcome will not be shocked by what you have to tell us.'

She was wrong. Newcome, if not exactly shocked, was, for some strange reason, distressed at Sir Chesney's news. And as Sir Chesney elaborated a strange red rage seized him.

'Oh, very well, Nell, if you must. He said that no woman was virtuous and bet that, if he cared to try, he might have you, as he pleased, without benefit of marriage, you understand. What's worse, he bet twenty thousand pounds on it.'

Nell rose, paced to the hearth, stared into the fire, face averted, and said in a muffled voice, 'Charles Halstead said that! Before or after you had arranged with his father to offer for me?'

'Oh, before, I assure you. When his father knew what his son had done, he forbade him the house, and withdrew his sponsorship of your marriage to him.'

'Kind of him,' said Nell, satiric. 'I have never wished more that I were a man. Were I so I would have shot Halstead dead for the insult,' and then, a desperate humour in her voice, 'But, of course, if I had been a man, you and his father would not have arranged the match with him. What nonsense I am talking.' She turned towards Chad, whose rage was now so black and strong that he was shaking with it, had bent over the desk, feeling light-headed with a curious mix of—what was it? Shame, surely not—unless it was for all men who lightly spoke of women thus.

'Newcome,' said Nell sharply, 'are you ill, that you look so?' and Aunt Conybeare looked up, equally sharply, struck by the note in her niece's voice.

'Nothing,' gasped Chad, 'a passing malaise. I have had such, once or twice, since I arrived here.'

Which was true. He had thought that it was perhaps his lost memory struggling to revive itself, but why Sir Chesney's story should have such an effect on him was a mystery.

Sir Chesney stared at Nell's concern for her secretary, said indifferently, 'I understand from Henson that your cousin Ulric is here. I hope his presence does not mean that you are thinking of marrying him. Most unwise.'

Since Chad appeared to be recovering, Nell looked over at Sir Chesney, said coldly, 'I don't think you listened to what I was saying, Uncle. I repeat, I have no intention of marrying anyone, least of all Cousin Ulric. And now I must see him. Disliking him, and his proposal, does not absolve me from practising the common courtesies. Newcome, if you are quite well, you may spend the afternoon in the riding school. Aisgill was asking for you this morning.'

She bowed to her uncle, and left him wailing at Aunt Conybeare over Nell's intransigence where marriage was concerned, and glared suspiciously at Newcome when he took his leave. Nell's secretary to work in the riding school — what next?

'Really, Nell,' said Ulric Tallboys petulantly, 'it is too bad that I was consigned here alone, while Chesney Beaumont was admitted immediately to you. You should have a word with that butler of yours, and your man, Henson. After all, I am your heir.'

'Sir Chesney arrived first,' replied Nell briskly. She disliked her cousin, an overweight man, pasty-faced, in his early thirties, and disliked him even more when he continued, still petulant, 'Well, I have come here on business, too. It is high time that you made up your mind to marry me, Nell. That way we keep the Tallboys name in existence, and before you come out with some havey-cavey that you do not love me, let me remind you that you have made it quite plain that you do not wish to marry for love.'

'I don't intend to marry for dislike, either,' retorted Nell, goaded into unwisdom. 'And the Tallboys name will live on without you, for I intend to have anyone I marry assume it. It will be a condition of my marriage — the lawyers can deal with it when they draw up the settlement.'

'But you should marry me,' pursued Ulric blindly. 'Safer so. It is all about the North that you were shot at by Luddites, and that you have nothing better to do than make some stable lad your personal secretary. You would be better advised if I were here to look after you.'

His expression was made the sulkier by the thought that if the first Earl had not insisted on the reversion of his title to the female line, because his only child was a daughter, and a sovereign grateful for his victories in the early eighteenth-century wars had not agreed, he, Ulric Tallboys, and not Nell, would now be the proud possessor of Campions and all the lands and title that went with it — a fact of which he never ceased to remind himself almost daily.

'Oh,' said Nell dangerously. 'And how do you know all that? I never thought that Campion affairs had already become the talk of Staffordshire and Trentham.'

'I heard of your goings-on when I stayed at Habersham Hall with the Gascoynes before I came on here. You are the talk of the Riding, Nell.'

'But then, I always was, wasn't I, Ulric? And I always shall be, because I have no concern in joining Ridings or any other society for that matter.'

'But Nell——'

'Do not "But Nell" me,' said Nell, feeling more like a reincarnation of good Queen Bess than usual, 'or I shall have second thoughts about continuing your allowance.'

'You would not do that?' cried Ulric, aghast. Ever since some eight years ago, after he had squandered his own inheritance, first Nell's grandfather, and then Nell, had made him, as heir presumptive, a generous allowance, on condition that he did not ever go to London where he had once been involved in a scandal so enormous that Nell's grandfather had almost cut him off forever. Nell had continued to support him on the same terms, and he roved round provincial society, tolerated, if not welcomed, because of his Malplaquet connections.

'And what about this secretary of yours, Nell?'

'What about him?' Nell had never sounded so dangerous, but, unobservant, Ulric galloped on.

'I tell you what, Nell, it is not at all the thing for you to make some yokel your private secretary, particularly when he is a young man —— '

'I tell *you* what, Ulric,' said Nell savagely, 'if I cared to make a one-eyed dwarf, with a hunch back, my private secretary, it is no business of yours. And if you feel so strongly about my doings, why, to save yourself pain, you may leave within the hour. Out of my kind consideration for your own feelings, I would not stop you.'

She had never spoken to him so before, had always been courteous and patient, and he stood there with his mouth open. 'I say, Nell,' he began, only for her to reply, as she strode to the door,

'And I say, Ulric, that if you do not care to remain for luncheon I shall quite understand, and now I must

leave you. I have work to do. My days are not spent in
fiddle-faddle and gossip.'

'Have a heart, Nell,' he protested as she swept
through the door, 'I've only just got here, and dammit,
I'm your heir.'

'So you keep saying,' were Nell's last words, 'and a
great pity for Campions that it should be so,' and she
was gone, leaving him gasping, but determined to stay.

After all, he had his own fish to fry at Campions.

Luncheon was a somewhat constrained meal. Ulric sat
there with an aggrieved expression on his face, and Sir
Chesney felt a strange annoyance with Nell, stronger,
perhaps, than her mere refusal to marry deserved.
Something odd going on at Campions, but what he
could not decide.

As was usual since Nell had taken over, the place ran
like clockwork. The food was good, the service perfect,
the whole estate was in splendid order, and he looked
forward to a visit to the stables and riding school in the
afternoon, although he could have done without Ulric's
company.

To prevent Nell's sending him away, Ulric stuck like
glue to Sir Chesney, whom he disliked as much as Sir
Chesney disliked him. He thought that Nell would not
be so deuced rude to him before her uncle, and he was
right about that, if little else.

The stable and the stud were in splendid fig, too,
thought Sir Chesney crossly. It would be nice to have
something to complain about, so as to put Nell down a
little, but, dammit, with Aisgill there to give his usual
friendly meeting, there was little he could say, and like
Ulric he was surprised to see the supposedly unmanageable Rajah being given a dressage work-out.

'Who's on Rajah, hey?' he said, to nobody in particular, to hear Ulric grind out,

'I thought Nell said that she never had suitors here, so who the devil's he?'

Chad was up on Rajah, dressed in one of the late Earl's country suits, charcoal-coloured jacket, modest cravat, grey breeches, beautiful boots—his feet, Nell had been pleased to discover, were the same size as her grandfather's—and he was wearing a dated bicorne hat, which made him look particularly dashing.

Swinging Rajah around the circle, keeping him under tight control, for he had been wild ever since the attempt on Nell's life, he was suddenly aware that he had an audience, and that Nell, dressed more smartly than he had ever seen her, had added herself to the group.

Some mischievous devil made him sweep off his bicorne to her as he passed them, and when Rajah, annoyed, reared, he treated the group to the spectacle of a superb piece of horsemanship, which culminated in Rajah performing a splendid caracole—an extravagant sideways leap, which had him apparently standing in the air—much against his lordly will.

'Oh, bravo,' cried Nell.

Ulric asked again, 'Who the devil's *that*, Nell?' to hear Sir Chesney say, in a hollow voice,

'Good God, it's the secretary! Damme if it ain't.'

'You mean that's the yokel?' gasped Ulric, looking from Rajah's rider to Nell, and back again.

Nell's pride in Chad was almost visible, she suddenly realised, and quelled it.

'Yes,' she said, in her most bored Countess Nell voice. 'I understand he was a trooper once, which I suppose was where he learned to do that.'

Sir Chesney looked down his nose. 'A trooper who

has visited Vienna,' he muttered. 'Damned difficult
trick, that. You've a jewel there, Nell. Wasted as a pen-
pusher, if I may say so.'

'Well, I need a pen-pusher more than I need a circus
turn at Astley's, so a pen-pusher he'll have to stay,' said
Nell, not wishing to have Sir Chesney begin to make all
kind of suggestions about Chad Newcome's future, and
pleased to appear to put him down a little. It would not
do for her uncle to begin. . .suspecting things. . . And
surely, she thought, amused at herself, females must
possess a natural talent for intrigue, for no one has
taught me to be so devious.

She was thinking this later that afternoon, when she
met Chad on the stairs, about to return to his quarters
on the top floor, to change out of his riding clothes into
his secretary's drab uniform.

'Lady Elinor,' he said, staring at her a little. She had
already changed for dinner, and was magnificent,
simply magnificent. He had heard Aisgill say that the
gentry thought Nell plain, but to him she was the most
stunning thing he had ever seen.

She was dressed in white and silver satin, high-
waisted, with an over-dress of gauze and net floating
about her tall person. Around her throat, her wrists and
on her fingers, and finally as a crown in her gleaming
chestnut hair, were the famous Malplaquet diamonds
which she rarely wore. And tonight she wore them like
the glorious Diana she was.

They shimmered and sparkled in the light of the
chandeliers, fully lit because Sir Chesney and Ulric
Tallboys were dining with her.

'You will attend me tonight, Newcome,' she said, all
arrogance, like her stance, the tilt of her neck, which the
diamonds adorned, a monarch to her humble subject.

But Chad, standing straight and tall, was equal to her. If desire roared through him at the sight of her, he quelled it as well as he could. 'I think not, Lady Elinor. Unwise perhaps.'

'A command, Newcome, you hear me? A command.'

'Sir Chesney will not like it, nor, forgive me, will your cousin.'

'Servants'-hall talk, Newcome. Henson will be there, and Challenor, too. Old Payne would have sat with us.'

'I am not old Payne.'

'Very true, and to both our advantages. You will attend me. I will brook no denial.'

'You are as wilful as Rajah, my lady, and far less manageable.'

'A compliment, Newcome, a compliment. You grow more courtier-like by the instant.'

Face to face they stood, and any watcher could not have failed to see the tension which crackled between them.

'Not meant as such, but if you choose ——' and she interrupted him, like lightning.

'Oh, I choose, Newcome, to take it as one, and I choose to have you sit at my table, which I would never ask Rajah to do.'

As so often, Chad could have taken her, there on the spot, as she was almost defying him to do, for whenever they met the battle of words between them was merely a symbol of the sexual heat which passed between them.

Nell saw his face change, his eyes begin to smoke, and whispered, face wicked, 'Confess, Newcome, confess. You wish to call me your lady in every way, Newcome, in every way, and this very moment, too. And if I am your lady you will wear my favour, do my bidding,' and she took the scrap of lace which was her pocket hand-

kerchief from where it hung from the fortune in diamonds on her wrist, and leaned forwards to wipe his
sweating brow, sweating as much from frustrated desire
as from his exertions in the riding school.

He could not deny her further. He took the lace scrap
from her, and put it to his lips, but before he could
speak a door on the landing opened, and Sir Chesney
emerged.

Chad stood back, bowed, said submissively, 'As you
will, Lady Elinor,' and made his way up the stairs,
bowing, equally submissively, to Sir Chesney, who
looked after him, a worried look on his honest old face.

But Nell, sweeping an arm into his, as he exclaimed,
'My dear, you look radiant, radiant! Why you will not
come to London and conquer society I shall never
understand,' laughed and replied,

'But Uncle, dear, I have everything I could want, or
desire, here in Yorkshire; what could London offer me
better than that?'

And if she was speaking of Chad Newcome, neither
Sir Chesney nor her cousin Ulric could yet have an
inkling of that.

CHAPTER NINE

FOR Chad and Nell it was heaven, and it was hell. To be so near, and yet to be now so hedged about by others that they could only enjoy snatched moments, two-edged conversations and the touching of hands, was to suffer the torments of Tantalus in the old Greek legend.

Not that any yet suspected them. Only as Countess Nell, and still unmarried, she was rarely ever alone. When Chad had only been her stable hand they could go on the moors, mistress and man, but now that he was her secretary they could not even do that. He could school Rajah and her other prime horses occasionally, but that was in public, too, and then she could only yearn at him, in the riding school, on the excuse of seeing her horses being properly trained.

Yes, there was an atmosphere, something in the air, for Nell was now so volatile, after so many years of being sober. Her laugh rang out, her happiness was plain for all to see, but her people were glad merely to see her happy.

The Runner and his assistant arrived. Cully Jackson was a big, raw-boned, red-headed man who questioned them all, made something of Chad's newness, until he heard the full story. Of them all, as he first sniffed about Campions before disappearing into the Riding, he saw what existed between the Countess and her secretary — but said nothing. *That* was not his business.

The year ran towards Christmas, and Newcome was no longer new. The women servants still followed him with their eyes, but he made nothing of them. He burned for Nell; his body, not his memory told him that he had been long continent, and that made the burning worse, but he would not betray the mistress to whom he had never made love.

Sir Chesney left the day after he had arrived; Ulric stayed a little longer, leaving shortly before the Runner was due. The Runner was told of him, the dissolute heir, nodded at the news, but said nothing about that. The dead murderer had borne the marks of the lash on his back as Chad had suspected, but the rifle he carried remained a mystery. 'A gentleman's piece,' Jackson said to Chad, holding it in his big hands. 'You must have seen such in the army, perhaps?' and he watched his man as Chad shook his head ruefully.

Jackson knew of Chad's lost memory, and tried, Chad was sure, to trip him up, to test him, but left Campions on his journey of enquiry certain that Newcome was not lying about himself.

'And now, Newcome,' Nell said teasingly to Chad one morning, shortly after Sir Chesney had left, and Ulric was packing to go, 'you know exactly what my worth is, do you not?'

Chad looked up at her. He was writing at his desk, placed near to hers, Aunt Conybeare dozing gently in her corner by the fire. 'How so?' he said, abstracted. He was checking accounts for Henson, for though he claimed no special talent for figuring Henson had found him useful with figures, too.

'Why, Charles Halstead set my price,' she said gaily, 'at twenty thousand pounds, no less. A high price for him, perhaps, but small, is it not, for Campions's owner, and Malplaquet's lady? Would you kill him for his insolence to me, Newcome? He wished to murder my reputation, not my body. I wonder which crime God considered the worse of the two?'

For some reason to hear of Charles Halstead's bet always disturbed Chad. He looked up at his lady, as usual turned out *à point* these days, her cheeks flushed, and the look in her eyes which was for no one but Chad Newcome.

'I would gladly kill such a cur for you, my lady,' he offered, 'should you wish it, and should he arrive here to try to win his bet.'

'No, I do not wish it, Newcome,' she said. 'He may stay in exile for me. My uncle said that he has gone to live in Scotland, and that his father talks of transferring the estate to his younger brother, leaving him only his title.'

Chad cursed beneath his breath. His hand had shaken unaccountably as she spoke and ink splattered over the virgin page.

Greatly daring, there being no one to see her, Aunt Conybeare's snores growing louder, Nell placed her small hand over Chad's large one.

'Does it trouble you so much to hear me traduced, Newcome?'

'Yes,' growled Chad. 'I'd like to break his damned neck, begging your pardon, my dearest. The sound of his name is enough to distress me.'

He stroked the hand which had been so lovingly offered, and then, as Nell bent her head, Aunt Conybeare growing noisier, and kissed him on the cheek, he lifted the hand to kiss her palm.

Nell felt him shiver, said gently, 'Oh, you burn as fierce as I. Is there nothing we can do, nothing?'

He looked squarely at her. 'Nothing. And there is

nothing we should do. I have told you that, my love, my own, and you must believe it.'

Aunt Conybeare's noise stopped, and she gave a great sigh, said 'Where are you, Nell? And where am I?'

The lovers pulled away. 'In the study, dear Aunt,' replied Nell gently. 'Playing chaperon.'

'Oh, yes,' said her aunt vaguely. 'So I am. Not that you need one,' and she went back to sleep.

'You heard that?' said Nell softly to Chad, her face so amused that he leaned forward and kissed her absently on the corner of the mouth, and, pulling away, muttered thickly,

'You almost destroy my resolution with your humour, but mere passion would not answer for us.'

'My passion is not mere,' she riposted, 'nor, I think, is yours. Tell me, Newcome, if my aunt, wise monkey that she is, the one who places his hands over his eyes, and says, "I see nothing", has no suspicion of us, why, then, are we not innocent? And being innocent, may we not do as we please? What the world does not know cannot exist.'

Chad put a hand to his forehead, said hoarsely, 'And you accuse *me* of logic-chopping.'

'Oh, I learned it from you,' said Nell sweetly. 'My servant, who will not obey me in the only thing which matters to me in the whole wide world,' and she held him with her eyes.

'Lady Elinor —— ' he began.

'Why, who is that?' she interrupted him.

'The lady whom Mrs Conybeare chaperons,' was his eager answer to her. 'My mistress — who can never be my mistress.'

'Never, Newcome, never?' She saw his hands rise, to twist together, agonised. The hands which could not hold her. 'Is the man who is not afraid of Rajah afraid of me?'

'Shall I be no better than Charles Halstead?' he muttered. 'For he betrayed you with his talk, where I shall betray you with my body. Your reputation, your honour, what of them?'

'My spotless reputation did not prevent Charles Halstead from staining it. You see, Newcome, you cannot defeat me in the combat of words; defeat me in the combat of love instead. I wish to die in your arms. You may kill me in that contest; I shall not allow you to win in any other.'

Their eyes met, and oh, his smoked, were smouldering into flames. She was winning! She knew it!

There was a knock on the door, and the spell was broken. She called, 'Come in,' and Chad turned away, was at his desk in a trice, head down, quill driving, and she was at her own, as Henson entered. Nothing there to see, although Nell felt that her recent passion was written in letters of fire in the air.

Henson could only read words on paper. Fire was beyond him. 'Ah, Lady Elinor,' he intoned. 'A dispatch from Jackson. He has traced your murderer,' he said, placing a budget of letters on her desk. 'I have read what he has to say — do you wish to read yourself, or shall I save you the trouble?'

Nell thought that reading was beyond her. 'Tell me,' she said.

'Newcome was correct in his suppositions. The man was an ex-soldier, turned off in the peace. He lived at Bradford for a time, turned footpad, had a small gang of men. The rifle was stolen, they say, and some weeks before he shot at you he left his gang and his usual haunts, none knows why. It was supposed by his associates that he was hired.'

'Hired!' said Nell. She saw that Chad had stopped writing, was alert. 'By whom?'

'Jackson does not know. He will endeavour to find out. Meantime he asks what others beside your cousin stand to gain by your death.'

Nell shivered, rose impulsively, walked by Chad, placed a hand on his shoulder as she passed him.

'Ulric! He surely cannot think that Ulric would stoop to that.'

She remembered his anger when she had last refused him. 'I know he envies me — all this.' And she waved a hand at the splendour around her. 'But murder, that is quite another thing.'

'Desperate men seek desperate remedies,' said Henson slowly. 'Jackson accuses no one. In the meantime, he says, you should go carefully.' He turned to Chad. 'You will guard my lady with your life, will you not?'

'Willingly,' said Chad, 'with my life, seeing that she gave me mine.'

He spoke quite levelly, but perhaps Henson could read letters of fire, after all. Something in the quiet intensity of Newcome's speech reached him.

'See that you do,' he said roughly. 'You will not go out, ever, madam, without Newcome, and a footman, or a groom with you until this snake is scotched.'

Nell could not protest. With a sinking heart she faced a future in which few opportunities would be given her to. . .deal with Chad as she wished.

'I hear you,' she said in a hollow voice, staring out of the window at the magnificent view. 'But you cannot really believe that it is Ulric who wishes to kill me.'

Chad spoke. 'With respect, Lady Elinor, you would be foolish to ignore Jackson, and Mr Henson's advice.'

'You hear him,' said Henson, face impassive. 'We are of a like mind, and I'm sure that Aisgill and Challenor would tell you the same. Your advisers are agreed — you must take no risks, whether it be your cousin, or another, who threatens you.'

The bright day had grown dark, even though the November sun shone across the moor. Nell shivered, wrapped her arms round herself, turned to face the two men, Chad standing now.

'I must obey you,' she said, 'in all things,' and that message was for Chad, a two-edged one. 'Until —— ' and she hesitated ' — my judgement tells me otherwise. You all advise me; you do not rule. I will not be wilful, but I will be mistress.'

Henson bowed his head. 'You are my Countess, madam, and you have never been unreasonable, have always consented to listen, and to understand.' He looked hard at her. 'For that reason your people serve you with love as well as loyalty. I know you will take heed for yourself, and of yourself.'

Nell looked at the two men. Henson, after his fashion, loved her, too. He did not merely serve her for his pay. And, for the first time, she understood Chad's reluctance to take her without thought.

But I love him, ran through her mind, truly love him, and I know, because he holds off, that he truly loves me, and they say love finds a way, and I must clutch that thought to me — for it is all I have.

Thus, thought Nell, exasperated, was how it always went. Snatched moments when, at the crucial point, they were always interrupted. And now it was worse than ever, with men guarding her all the time from any possible threat.

Her mind went round and round, a whirligig, she thought, pondering possibilities. If Rajah wanted Princess, the whole of Campions arranged for his pleasure, but if Campions's owner wanted her lover, all of Campions — were they to know — would conspire to keep her from him.

Why could she not have fallen in love with one of the sleek young men whom Uncle Beaumont had paraded before her? They would have handed her over to Charles Halstead without a thought, wretched though he was, but Chad, whom she loved, would be almost whipped from the grounds were it known what she and he felt for one another.

For everyone would assume that it was he who was seducing her, when, ever since the night of the attack, it was *she* who had been pursuing *him*. He thought only of her honour; she thought only of him.

If I were a man, hissed Nell furiously to herself, making angry faces in her mirror, I could have as many lovers as I pleased, and no one would think anything; they would admire me, rather, for my virility. Even well-bred young women would snigger knowingly when I walked in a room, 'Look, there is Malplaquet, a devil with the women — won't marry unless he meets one of whom *he* approves and not his advisers. And when he does marry, why, he will *still* go on his merry way.'

And I, I can have no merry way. Why was I not a boy, or the Empress Catherine of Russia, who had all the men she pleased in her bed? I only want Chad, none other, and, damn them all, I *will* have him.

She rose, walked downstairs, busy brain scheming. The last time that they had been able to meet privately

was when she had pursued him into the annexe. Well,
she could take him there again, could she not?

But when she reached the library they were all
present, the whole Privy Council, Newcome with them,
wearing the new suit which the tailor had made for him,
which fitted him perfectly, showing off the length of his
legs, and the strength of his thighs. His cravat was so
white that it looked like a fall of snow. His whole
appearance did nothing for her equanimity.

Nell stared at them. 'What's to do? I had not thought
we were to meet today.'

They must have agreed that Chad should speak for
them all, for he bowed, and said, 'The Runner, Jackson,
is here, Lady Elinor, and wishes to speak to you. He
will not trust what he has to say to the post.'

'He is here?' Nell looked around.

'In the ante-room,' Henson spoke. 'I thought, we all
thought, that he ought to speak to you with your council
present. It is our duty to guard you, and we must know
everything, if we are to do that.'

Nell could not argue with them, so inclined her head,
said briefly, 'Admit him, then.'

It was Chad who went to do her bidding, and Jackson
followed him in, a rough figure in the splendid room,
only Aisgill, sturdy in his country clothes, having any
common ground with him.

'My lady. . .' Jackson made an awkward reverence.
'There has been a strange development, of which I must
tell you, and your people here. It is about the rifle which
Mr Newcome here thought must have been an army
man's. I have traced it, and an odd turn-up indeed.' He
paused.

Strangely, of them all, it was Henson who was
impatient. 'Spit it out, man. Why stand havering?'

'I took it with me, as you know. Returned to London, and showed it to a gunsmith who has his shop in the Strand. I asked him if he had ever seen it before; the piece bore signs of a cunning repair. He recognised it at once, although it was nigh three years since he had last seen it. He would not say who had brought it in until he found its details in his books.

'And there it was, repaired shortly after Waterloo; he identified it by the roses engraved on its steel, and by the coronet he placed upon it for its owner——'

'A coronet?' interrupted Nell. 'Not Ulric Tallboys, then?'

'No, indeed,' said Jackson, 'and here is the puzzle, for Viscount Halstead, old Clermont's heir, bought it off a friend of his, and took it in to be overhauled and repaired, and there is no doubt that it is he who owns the rifle which was used to fire at you, my lady.'

There was a babble of voices. 'Charles Halstead?' said Nell, incredulously. 'You are telling me that *Charles Halstead* owned the rifle? Are you saying that it was he who organised the attempt on me?' She hardly paused before adding, 'To prevent the need to pay out twenty thousand pounds when he lost his disgraceful bet? What did he say when you spoke to him of this?'

'He is not to be found, my lady. I went to his father's home. His father refused to see me. I saw only his secretary who said that Lord Halstead was in Scotland. He knows nothing of him, said that Lord Clermont wished to know nothing. I showed him the rifle—although I did not tell him why I needed to know whether it was Halstead's—but the secretary knew nothing of it, merely that it bore Halstead's initials and arms—which I already knew. He added that Lord

break through, and just then, in there, while Jackson was speaking, I had the strangest sensation. I felt on the brink of I know not what, I had a sensation of dizziness, a feeling of disaster.'

'Disaster,' said Nell thoughtfully, 'that's an odd word, Newcome.'

For the moment her personal feelings were in abeyance. He looked so ill that rather than make love to him she wanted to mother him, feed him gruel, hold his head — these were, of course, different ways of making love to him.

'You wish to be relieved of your duties, to rest a little?' offered Nell tenderly.

Chad looked at her ruefully. 'No, indeed. The malaise is merely a passing thing.'

'Like Aunt Conybeare struggling to stay awake in here,' said Nell, trying to lighten the situation a little. She seemed to have gone from a state of mad desire for Newcome to be in her bed to an equally mad desire for him to be in his own bed — with her as his nurse.

She fantasised him needing to be returned to his room, where she would put on her brown holland apron, feed him soothing drinks, sit on his bed, stroke his brow, stroke his. . . She blinked.

'I trust you to tell me if you are not well. Campions needs you to be in the finest fettle, Newcome, and so do I.' She could hear the note of love in her voice and looked across at Aunt Conybeare, in case that lady had heard it too.

But Aunt Conybeare was sitting there lax, her canvas work forgotten on her knees, dreaming of summer, perhaps, or her coming good dinner.

Impulsively she put her hand on Chad's brow, found it cool; he took the hand, kissed the palm, returned it to her. 'You are too kind, my love.' For he also had seen that Aunt Conybeare had effectively left them alone again.

'Well or ill, Newcome, I need to see you alone, and soon. You understand me?'

'Too well,' said Chad.

'Then we must arrange it,' said Nell firmly, ignoring his answer. 'Tomorrow, I shall require you to be in the annexe, to solve a matter of grave intellectual import. I am concerned about what Kant actually meant when he spoke of the Moral Imperative. Judging by the answers you have been giving me when I have been trying to seduce you, it would seem that you know a great deal about it.

'Instruct me, I command you, on that topic, Newcome. You are so very moral that perhaps you do not need Kant, whereas I, I need not only Kant, but a whole library of philosophers to make me behave properly. On second thoughts, perhaps I ought to instruct you on Immoral Imperatives! At two-thirty tomorrow, then, on the stroke. Aisgill and Rajah require you this afternoon, and I would not wish to disappoint them.'

Chad's expression as he looked at his wilful mistress told its own tale.

'Why are you not making a note of my appointment with you, Newcome? Do so immediately; I want no excuses for your absence. None at all. I need succouring after this afternoon's revelations, and you are large enough to succour anyone. Now, I must go to Henson's office to sign papers, and give silver coins to deserving servants.'

She turned at the door, blew him a kiss as Aunt Conybeare slept on. 'Tell me, Newcome, what present shall I give to my most deserving servant of all?'

CHAPTER TEN

THE annexe hardly seemed the most romantic of places: no windows, narrow, lined with bookshelves, a glass window in its ceiling the only light, but to Nell and Chad it was a haven, the one place where they might catch a few moments together — if their luck held, that was.

Luck was with them. Challenor was unwell; he had retired to his room, leaving Chad alone there, collating at the map table, for Nell to find him, and Aunt Conybeare was gone to her sitting-room, after her morning's stint in the study overlooking Nell with her secretary.

Nell, aware of Challenor's absence, burning with impatient desire, controlled herself, and as Aunt Conybeare made off said, 'A moment; I must consult with Henson, Aunt. I will join you later.'

Amorous conspiracy had made such a liar of her that now her voice carried no false overtones, and without the slightest trace of guilt she pushed the library door open to see him standing there, broad back to her.

She did not even need to speak, put up her hand, and he followed her into the annexe where she closed and locked the door behind them and they stood face to face.

But oh, dear, *his* face! He had yet another noble fit of conscience on him, that was plain.

Nell drew a ragged breath, said wearily, 'Yes, Newcome, what is it this time? A sudden religious conversion, or another inconvenient attack of honour?'

'Neither,' said Chad, face grim. 'My wits recover slowly, but they do recover. Two things struck me this morning: first of all, if I accede to your wishes, and my own love and yes, desire for you, the chances of you falling with child are great,' and before he could continue she was there before him.

'Oh, Newcome, what of that? Are you fearful that I shall not make an honest man of you, somehow?'

Despite himself his face lightened, even if, as Nell was pleased to see, his eyes began to smoulder. 'No, it won't do,' he said, blunt with her for once. 'Consider — and I must truly have lost my wits as well as my memory not to think of this before — I may have a family, children, somewhere, and, if so, what of them?'

'What indeed?' said Nell, who wondered what her own wits had been doing — struck down by mad desire, she supposed. 'You do not seem a married man to me,' she offered, 'a derelict wandering the moors. Had you deserted them, Newcome? Or have you remembered your family, and this is a kind way of telling me of them?'

Chad closed his eyes, and as so often tried to conjure up his past. Nothing — vague clouds passing over the sun, blackness with lights in it, a dying horse squealing, soldiers shouting, an old man's angry face, despising him, a sensation of falling, sorrow, regret and pain felt — for what?

'Nothing,' he said at last, 'nothing. The harder I try to remember, the less I can recall. Flashes come when I am not attending to my condition. I do not feel that I was married; on the contrary, my deepest self tells me I was not, but——'

'Oh, what a but that is,' said Nell sorrowfully. 'Let us think of what you are, and what it tells us. You had an education, a good one. You speak like a gentleman, but you were not in the condition of one when you were found. Aisgill says you were undoubtedly a cavalryman. "He knows the brand", he says. A gentleman fallen on hard times, penniless perhaps, enlisted in the army as a private, one supposes, turned off in the peace with nowhere to go — does all this seen reasonable to you, Newcome?'

Chad nodded. Reasonable but wrong, something beyond reason told him, but he followed Nell's line of logic. 'Such hard times that I could find no occupation, began a-wandering, somehow ended up attacked and my memory gone. I do not sound married, and such instincts as I possess tell me I was not, but oh, my dearest lady, that may be my wishes, my love speaking, not the truth.'

'What is the truth?' said Nell softly. 'The present truth is that you are here at Campions, my secretary who saved my life, and whom, God forgive me, for reasons which are no reasons, I love beyond reason. I do not care if you are married, and have twenty children, Newcome, do you understand me? I do not care. I am Nell Tallboys who has lost her wits, and about whom Charles Halstead was right — when we love, all women are the same. Light-skirts, everyone of us! He has won his bet — and will never know it. Forget your conscience, Newcome, as I am forgetting mine. What price my being a Countess and owning half Yorkshire, and a quarter of England, if I cannot have the man I love?'

'You love the wrong man,' said Chad hoarsely. Proximity was fuelling desire; the sight of her, the scent of her, was working in him. Oh, yes, he might have twenty children, but what of that?

In the here and now there was only Nell, and she was

offering herself to him, and if what they snatched together
would be brief, at least he would have that to set against
the dark, which was all that he possessed of himself.

Conscience, honour, reason worked against them
both, but 'Amor vincit omnia' flashed though his mind;
love conquers all, and against love nothing could stand,
nothing.

He moved forward. So did she. Nell saw on his face
the message that she had won. What she offered him he
could not refuse. They were so close together now, in
the narrow room, that no man or woman could be
closer, outside of the act of love itself.

Nell trembled as Chad's hands rose to cup her face,
and then he brought down his face to kiss her. And the
kiss was not like any of his previous ones. It was fierce.
It almost bruised her mouth, which opened beneath his
to take him in, his tongue and hers meeting and
touching, as though all the words which had passed
between them had been made flesh, killing the need for
speech.

His tongue was the first of him to enter her. She
exulted in the sensation, wound her arms around his
neck to draw him even closer, to feel the long length of
him against her, his arms around her, equally demanding, as though they could sink into one another, become
an entity which, being both, was neither, but something
new.

How long they stood like that Nell did not know.
Only, suddenly, his busy hands were at work about her.
He was pulling her dress down from her shoulders so
that her breasts sprang free, and he was caressing them,
first with his hands and then with his mouth, so that
her head fell back, and she gave long shuddering gasps,

gasps which were in rhythm with the shuddering ecstasy which ran through her body.

The sensations which Nell was experiencing made her knees weak, her head swim, and she gave an inarticulate cry, steadied herself against him, and then her wanton hands did something quite disgraceful, something she had never dreamed of doing.

For she undid his breeches flap and it was his turn to spring, hard, into her hand, which grasped and stroked him, so that he groaned beneath her loving hands, and now his hands peeled her dress up, up.

Nell was on fire, lost to everything but the fact that they were at last on the verge of doing what she had hardly dared to dream was possible, and when his hands transferred themselves to her buttocks, to clasp her to him, ready for the final act, she said thickly, 'Oh, yes, Chad, yes.'

Her voice broke the spell which bound him. He shuddered, put a hand down to take her hand from him, said hoarsely, pulling away a little, 'No, Nell, no.'

'No?' babbled Nell, who by now had only one idea in her head — to impale herself on him. . .on what her hand held. 'What do you mean by no, Newcome? I say yes. Your Countess orders you, Newcome. Yes, immediately. Now.'

'No, not like this,' was all that he could say, trying to detach himself from her and Nell resisting.

'What do mean, not like this, Newcome? I thought that this was how one did it. Is there another way? If so, pray show me, at once, Newcome, at once!'

She felt him, rather than heard him, give a half-laugh, half-sob. 'Oh, by God, Nell, you tempt me sorely with tongue and body. This way, any way you please, but not here, not now, hugger-mugger. I don't want to take you like a drab in an alley, I want to love you, slowly, properly.'

'Oh,' she wailed, 'I want you now, properly or improperly, my love, or I shall die. Here on the spot I shall die, and how will you explain that, my darling, when Challenor finds me stark and cold, slain by your Moral Imperative, an unwilling sacrifice to virtue?'

'No, never cold,' he said, free of her, facing her, trembling with unfulfilled desire, his body reproaching him as much as she. 'In life, in death, Nell, never cold. But not now. . .not here. . . It should be a sacrament. . .'

'But where, Newcome, Chad, my own love, where?' Nell was frantic. 'No private place for me or you. Oh, here and now is heaven and hell,' and she put out her hand to stroke him again, so that he rose on tiptoe, said roughly, chokingly,

'For God's sake, Nell, would you have me pleasured without my knowing you? I can only stand so much. . .'

Nell was on the brink of she knew not what. The excitement she felt was so powerful that it sought release. If he would not pleasure himself within her, then she would give him release without her, for she had brought him to this with her wilfulness, and at least she could give him that.

'I would give you fulfilment,' she said, 'this way, if not the other.'

His grip was suddenly on her wrist, stilling her hand. 'No,' he said. 'No. Without you, nothing.'

'For you,' she whispered, 'for you. For I have done this to you.'

'My love, my life, my dearest lady. . .' he was articulate *in extremis* '. . .it is *you* I want. Our pleasure together. Oh, Nell, you must take, as well as give. Take my unfulfilled flame of love, it is all I have to give you, against what you wish to give me. I will contrive, somehow, that we meet in a place more fitting, that we may make a ceremony of it. Please, Nell, please.'

Nell stopped, her head drooping on his chest. They panted together, self-denial more exhausting than fulfillment.

'If that is what you want, then I want it too. Oh, I am greedy, I know, but I want all of you, not just your hands and mouth.' She hardly knew what she was saying, and for a moment they stayed there thus, unmoving, content to hold one another. Except that at the end Chad turned to face the wall, leaned against it, his whole body shaking, and Nell dropped to her knees, shuddering, her forehead on a low cupboard's top, passion contained, not destroyed.

And then they turned towards one another. He straightened her dress for her, and gently, gently, she restored him, refastened the cravat she had pulled undone in her passion to get at him, rebuttoned him, still without speech between them. They had gone beyond words.

But once outside, in the library, the clock ticked above the fire in the hearth, the busts of the Roman Emperors looked down on them, blind, and the books stood in their rows behind their lattices as though nothing had happened, as though in their precincts two lovers had not suffered and inwardly bled, torn by their forbidden passion.

Nell walked to the door, turned there before she left, to say but one word. 'Soon!'

The word was easily said, the doing difficult. The guard kept on Nell, the duties which bound him, the presence of her aunt, servants, Aisgill, Henson,

Challenor, her duties, all contrived to keep them apart.
The annexe they avoided.

Christmas, its pleasures and further duties, was upon
them. Nell entertained the Riding. Men and women
arrived for a great feast. They stared at her. Despite
sexual denial, she was radiant, for was *he* not always by
her side, to sustain her, if he could not physically love
her?

'I never thought Nell Tallboys beautiful before,' said
one bluff squire to his wife, as Nell moved among them,
magnificent in toffee-coloured silk, wearing her rarely
seen diamonds, the knowledge of being cherished plain
upon her face for the perceptive to see, 'but, by God,
she's a marvel tonight.'

Chad was there, sporting a new silk suit, especially
made for him, black, with knee breeches and stockings
also of silk, standing in the background with the rest of
Nell's council, one or two staring at the size of him.

Memory still lost, he had bad dreams. The night after
the scene in the annexe he had shouted so loud in his
sleep that he had woken up Sandby, Henson's assistant,
who had a room next to Chad's small suite on the top
floor, and Sandby had gone in to find him tangled in
the bedclothes, sweating and shaken.

He could remember little of what had disturbed him
so. Only a feeling of desolation, and of falling, of clawing
himself up a steep slope, and then losing himself. Nell
had been there, but the sight of her had distressed him
so badly that he was suddenly beside himself with pain
and shock, after the first joyful sight of her.

He had had such dreams when he had first arrived at
Campions, but of late they had disappeared. Perhaps
the encounter in the annexe had brought them back.
One thing did surprise him, and that was that just

before Sandby shook him awake he had seen in his hands, quite plain, the rifle he had taken from the would-be assassin. But the hands that were holding it were wearing white gloves, and he was talking to an officer in full regimentals in terms of cheerful equality, almost of authority, and then the scene vanished into the dark.

Like all dreams, it ran away from him in the day, and little was left of it. He had learned to accept his condition, to accept that perhaps he would never find himself again, and to live with that knowledge. The dogged dedication with which he worked owed a little to his determination to forget himself in his duties, and a great deal to his love for Nell, which he tried, for her sake, not to betray to those around him.

But the big event of the Yuletide season for those at Campions was the party that Nell always gave for her staff, the day when the state dining hall was given over to those who created and maintained the estate, and not to those who simply lived off it.

Chad, with the rest of Nell's council, dressed again in his black silk suit, walked in that evening. The hall was decked with boughs of holly, every chandelier was aflame with light, fires blazed in the two hearths, and Nell was even more stately than she had been on the night she had entertained the Riding.

She had dressed herself like a bride in white and cream; she wore not the diamonds but the emeralds which Catherine the Great of Russia had given to the third Earl, when he had been ambassador in St Petersburg, after she had taken him to bed as her lover.

It was a suite of even more splendour than her diamonds, consisting of a tiara, earrings, necklace, bracelets, rings, and a belt of gold, set with pearls as

well as emeralds, cinched under her breasts. Her fan
matched the suite, huge, decorated with parrots of green
and scarlet. Annie had dressed her hair high beneath
the tiara, and if she took Chad's breath away she had
the same effect on everyone else. Even mild Aunt
Conybeare was a little stunned.

The boar's head had been carried in, the plum
pudding served, drink of all kinds handed around, and
at a signal Nell rose, and the company adjourned to the
long gallery, where there was a small collection of
musicians, brought especially from York to play for
Nell's people, and a group of waits who broke into 'God
rest you merry, gentlemen' at the sight of Nell.

Chad knew one thing. He had never before been
present on such an occasion—he needed no memory to
tell him that. Old Challenor, her senior council member,
led his mistress out for the first minuet, for court dancing
alternated with the country dances put on for her staff.

'And you,' Nell murmured to Chad, after Challenor
had returned her to her place on the small dais set up
before the great window which ran for a third of the
length of the wall, 'will take me out for my fourth dance
after Henson and Aisgill. We follow strict precedence
here, you see. After you, the butler!' and her eyes shone
with mirth.

Strangely, they had been easy together since their last
powerful encounter in the annexe. It was as though they
knew who they were and how they stood with one
another; that they could be patient, hold off, and work
together in a comfortable amity, even though a cauldron
of passion might lie below the smooth surface of their
lives.

'Biding our time,' murmured Nell, when he stood up
to lead her out. 'What good creatures we are, to be

sure.' The Yule log roared in the hearth, Nell's people clapped their hands each time she took the floor, and many clapped louder when it was Newcome who took her hand. He was liked — and not only by the women, who yearned over his size and his rugged charm; the men respected him, too, a pen-pusher who could match them at many of their outdoor pursuits, and beat them in some.

He was Rajah's master, and recently had been discovered to have a punishing blow in the ring. He had stopped one day to watch young Seth training — he was a useful fighter at little bouts in the Riding — had offered him some advice, and then been challenged to put his fists where his mouth was, a challenge he had taken up with some success.

He had arrived in Nell's study with a black eye, but he had managed to put Seth down twice before Seth put him down, and Aunt Conybeare had clucked and fussed over him, to Nell's amusement. She thought that all Campions was falling in love with Chad, not merely its mistress!

They moved through the pattern of the dance, meeting, parting, symbolic of life itself, Nell thought, and thinking so she arrived back at him again, and unselfconsciously, naturally as she met him, there in the centre of the floor, for a fleeting moment all that she felt for him, and he for her, was written plain on their faces.

In the hurly-burly of the dance it might have gone completely unnoticed, the spark which betrayed them both. One man, and one man only, saw it.

Aisgill, whom all such occasion as this bored, found his entertainment not in taking part but watching others. He was leaning against one of the pillars of the fireplace, half-cut, but even so the shrewdness and knowledge of man and beast which made him so successful as Nell's lieutenant were still with him. His lazy eye was on the dancers; he saw Nell turn, saw her and Chad meet, and it was as though lightning flashed in front of him to illuminate a landscape he had never seen before.

He had no doubt of what he had seen; his only doubt was how far the lovers had gone. He knew his Countess, and the lightning illuminated something else — the change in her, and what had provoked it.

Nell watched Chad move away from her, turn, to greet her again, and joyfully, she curtsied before him as the dance ended, and he bowed, to lift her, to take her hand, to escort her to the dais, passing Aisgill on the way, his shrewd, sad old eyes on them both, his mistress and the man he and she had rescued, half-naked, from the moor.

CHAPTER ELEVEN

IT WAS six weeks since they had broken off their lovemaking in the annexe. Snow covered the moors; Nell thought that her heart was frozen too, and wondered at Chad's. She had not thought it possible that they could be so cool with each other.

They met, worked together, spoke as in a dream. Had she dreamed it, their passion? Had he dreamed it? No, of course they had not, for if they were foolish enough to let their hands touch, ever so slightly, the fever sprang up between them again. Nell felt her body grow lax, saw his eyes begin to smoulder with desire, and then for the rest of the day she needed to control herself.

And how, and when, had he learned to exercise such iron control? For Nell had come to recognise that he did. How fortunate, she thought bitterly, they they were so strong, for none watching them could see what they meant to each other, she was sure of that.

She walked towards the stables in the dim light of early morning. White Princess, her mare, always known as Princess, was in foal, due to bear Rajah's progeny any day. She fantasised herself as Princess, and Chad as Rajah. How simple it was for the members of her stud, and how difficult for her, Nell Tallboys, who had everything, but who had nothing.

Aisgill met her in the yard. 'Lady Elinor?'

'I have come to learn of Princess, Aisgill,' she said, pulling her coat tighter about her, against the cold. 'You said that she was about to foal at any time now.' She paused, went on, 'You will think me stupid, but I awoke, worrying about her.'

'Not stupid, my lady,' he answered. 'Sometimes I think that where your horses are concerned you have an extra sense. I am worried, too. She has begun to have her foal, but things are going ill. I had hoped that they would go better before I needed to tell you of her.'

'I may see her?' asked Nell. She had assisted at births before, insisting that she needed to know all of the work of the stud, not just the pleasant, easy bits.

'Yes,' he replied curtly. Nell thought that for some reason Aisgill was short with her, and she wondered why.

He led her to where Princess lay, and there, kneeling by her beautiful mare, now *in extremis*, was Chad, wearing not his fine black suit but the rough clothing he had been given when he first arrived at Campions.

Aisgill saw her eyes on Newcome, sighed. He had thought, after the Christmas dance, when the tenants and the servants had gone, that perhaps he had been wrong, deceived by the drink he had taken; and the impassive masks his mistress and her lover had worn in the days after Christmas reinforced his belief that he had been mistaken. But here, in the gloom, the look which Nell gave to Chad, assisting at the primal moment of birth, told him that after all he had been right.

Nell moved over to Chad, fell on her knees beside him. He had looked up on seeing her enter, and looked away again, fearful that he might betray himself.

Aisgill, behind them, spoke. 'I thought that Newcome,' he spoke the name roughly, as though Chad were still only one of his hands, not the almost-gentleman he was in the house, 'would be of most use here.

He helped me when Lady Luck had her foal and things went ill. You owed that foal to him, Lady Elinor. He has good hands for birth, as well as for controlling Rajah.'

'Yes,' said Nell, almost absently. 'What is wrong, Newcome?'

'Her foal is wrongly positioned,' said Chad. 'Not like Lady Luck's was. Worse, I fear. Her chances are not good.'

There were several other stable hands present, all with grave faces. To lose Princess and her foal would be a blow to them all. For no good reason that Nell could think of, it suddenly seemed desperately important that Princess lived. It was almost as though the beautiful beast, lying there helpless, was Nell herself, about to die — or, rather, that Princess symbolised the love she felt for Chad, and could not express.

She rose to her feet, said, 'No!' and walked over to the wall, to stand there facing it, leaving them all surprised that she, usually so cool, who had seen all this before and had not flinched, could show such emotion.

Chad could not stop himself. Something of what she was experiencing passed from her to him. He rose, regardless of etiquette, and what Aisgill might think, and he walked over to her, and touched her arm. 'Lady Elinor,' he said, and the sound of his voice eased Nell's torment a little, 'Lady Elinor, we shall do our best to save her, and the foal as well.'

Nell turned towards him, showing him a face of such grief that he retreated a little.

'Poor Princess,' she said. 'There are times when I feel ——' and her voice thickened ' — that running the stud is more than I can endure.'

'It is the way of life, Lady Elinor,' he said gravely,

fighting the wish to take her in his arms and comfort her. 'With or without the stud, mares would be in foal, and occasionally their lives would be at risk because of it.'

It was as though they were alone, and the frustration which Nell felt that she could not be Princess, lying there, having *his* foal, even at the risk of her life, was in her voice and manner.

'Where did you learn such wisdom, Newcome? Or have you forgotten that, along with everything else?'

Oh, she was being unfair to him, she knew, and saw that he understood why she spoke as she did, that the rapport between them was now so strong that it went beyond words.

Aisgill spoke sharply. 'The mare needs you, Newcome, more than Lady Elinor does.'

Both lovers were so engrossed that the full import of what he was saying did not strike them. Chad heard only the command to action, Nell hardly heard him at all.

Until Aisgill added, 'This is going to be difficult, Lady Elinor. I think that you should leave us to it. Not a fit place for you.'

'My mare,' said Nell, proud, 'my stud. You would not say that to me if I were the sixth Earl, instead of your Countess. I shall stay.'

Aisgill bowed his head. He could not deny her. He knew that she had been present at births before, but in some fashion, and why he did not know, he felt that she should not be present now. But he could not gainsay her, and for the next hour of blood and pain and noise Nell stayed, carrying buckets of water for them, until Princess's foal was pulled into the world, and Princess, though sorely hurt, and beside herself with pain, still lived.

Nell had willed the mare's survival, that Chad and Aisgill should succeed, wanting an omen for herself that she thought to be good, and once all was over her legs turned to water, not with desire, as they had done in the annexe, but for sheer blessed relief.

'And now will you go, madam?' said Aisgill, surlily mutinous for once, Chad washing Princess's blood from his hands and arms in the pail which Nell had carried to him, the foal—which Aisgill had announced was to be called Lightning, in a voice which brooked of no argument—staggering about, and Princess trying to rise.

'I will escort Lady Elinor back to the house,' announced Chad; he was towelling his face now.

'No,' said Aisgill sharply. 'Go and eat with the lads; you need to rest. I shall see Lady Elinor back.'

'I need no escort in Campions's grounds in sight of both house and stables,' said Nell, equally sharply, wondering what had got into Aisgill that he should be so surly. 'You need your own breakfast. No, I will brook no denial,' and she walked off, head high, Countess Nell at her most icy cold, almost as she had been before Chad's arrival at Campions.

Chad ate his breakfast hungrily, although sorry that he was denied Nell's companionship on the way back to the house. The hands' fare was simple, but good, and he was grateful for the plain food after all the kickshaws at Nell's table. What did that tell him of his old life? he wondered.

Aisgill came late to breakfast, and when Chad rose to return to the house, to dress himself to be Nell's secretary again, said to Chad, still harsh, 'A word with you, Newcome, before you leave.'

Like Nell, Chad was a little puzzled by Aisgill's manner, the more so when Aisgill led him to the stable yard, away from any overhearing of what he was about to say.

'Do not misunderstand me, Newcome,' began Aisgill, his colour high, even for him. 'You are a good worker, the best, and I understand from Henson that you have made a good clerk. But remember, the Lady Elinor is your Countess as she is mine, and I do not want to see any hurt come to her, especially from those to whom she has shown kindness. You understand me, Newcome. I should find means to turn you away tomorrow, if I thought that your presence here was a threat to Campions.'

The thunderbolt had hit Chad. Aisgill knew! But how? He was certain that he, and she, had done nothing to betray themselves. But Aisgill knew men and animals. Could he scent them, then? And if he could, could not others?

'I would do nothing to bring harm to Lady Elinor, or Campions,' he said, 'seeing that they have given me life. Without her, I should be cold on the moor.'

'Then see that you remember that, man,' said Aisgill, showing his teeth. 'You are her secretary, who was her stable lad, and before that you were nothing, scum, starving, naked, plucked from the ditch. Keep that well in mind, and you cannot go far wrong.'

What could he say? God help me, I love her, and she loves me, and that stands before everything, even my honour, and hers.

Instead, he bowed his head stiffly before her faithful servant who wished only to protect her, while he, what did he wish to do but dishonour her? And Aisgill's words were one more barrier between himself and his love.

Nell, newly dressed for the day, elegant in tan, was expecting to find Chad in her study, at his desk. But only Aunt Conybeare was there, placid, her sewing on her knee.

'Where's Newcome?' she said, abrupt.

'He came in, went out again.' Aunt Conybeare was unruffled. The weeks of sitting in on Nell and Chad and nothing happening had left her used to his presence. The undercurrents between the two escaped her. Gifted at reading novels, Aunt Conybeare could not read life.

Nell sat down at her own desk. There was an envelope on it, her name written there, in Chad's hand.

She opened it, read the short sentence inside.

'Lady Elinor. I must leave Campions. With, or without, your permission,' and then his signature, bold, firm, like himself. Chad Newcome, plain, no flourishes.

Nell's heart clenched inside her. She could have screamed, thrown herself about. Of all the things which she could have imagined—never this, never this! To lose him. No, no, it was not to be borne. To be alone again, and this time to know what she was missing. She could never be uninvolved Nell Tallboys again.

Where was he? He must be in the library, if he was not with her, or in Henson's office. She must see him, speak to him. What had brought this on?

He was in the library. He was sitting on the booksteps, a book in his hand. Challenor was nowhere in sight.

Chad saw Nell advancing on him, the letter in her hand, an avenging fury.

She walked to where he sat, waved the letter at him, and, careless of whether Challenor was about or not, said, 'What is the meaning of this, Newcome? Tell me at once.'

Chad made no effort to leap to his feet, to pay her his due respects, but said, from his sitting position, 'I thought the meaning of what I have written quite plain, Lady Elinor.'

'Did you, indeed, Newcome? Get down, at once, pay me the respect due to my rank from yours. I am your Countess, Newcome! Remember that!'

Chad rose, stood before her, head bowed, deferential, said, 'I am remembering that, Lady Elinor. And *that* is why I have written you my letter.'

'Oh!' Nell's desire to scream was almost not to be denied. 'Stop it at once, Newcome. You are back in the Jesuit seminary again. Answer a plain question plainly.'

He could temporise no longer. The anguish which tore at Nell tore at him.

'It is not right that I should stay. For your honour, I must go. We are. . .remarked upon.'

At last something to give Nell pause. To have her staring at him, face white.

'We are. . .' and then the intuitive leap. 'Aisgill! I knew it, somehow, this morning. He was odd, strange. But how in the world could he guess at such a thing? For guess it must be.'

'Does it matter?' said Chad wearily. 'He knows. That is enough.'

'He knows nothing, Newcome, for there is nothing to know.'

'Now you are enrolled with the Jesuits, Lady Elinor,' said Chad. 'For there is everything to know. I must go, and soon. To save us. . .' And then since Challenor seemed absent, and for a moment they were safe, 'Nell, I would not have written the letter else. I *must* go.'

'Go! Where will you go, Newcome, my love, my own? To starve again? To die on the moor this time? You have no home, no haven, not even a name. I will not let you go to. . .nothing.'

She but echoed what Aisgill had said earlier.

'What am I,' he said, and, since Aisgill had spoken to him that morning he had dredged his mind for memories, something to tell him who he was, but nothing, nothing, 'but a piece of scum, found and cared for, betraying those who cared for him, by seeking to dishonour their lady?'

'No dishonour, Newcome, when your lady commands. Was Princess dishonoured by Rajah?'

Chad closed his eyes, that he might not see her face. He would carry the memory of her to his death. His gallant lady.

She took his silence for consent, pressed home her advantage, as she thought. 'Besides,' she said feverishly, 'you are now my secretary. I shall demand three months' notice, you hear me, Newcome? Three months' notice, before you leave. And you are not to try to run away; I shall set the dogs on you, to haul you back.'

The tears were rolling down her face; she was frantic. No thought for those who might find them, her only thought was not to lose him.

'Hush,' he said, pulling out his handkerchief, and leaning forward to mop her face with it. 'You are brave, my Countess. Remember your ancestor on the field of battle. "The day is lost, surrender", his enemies told him, and his answer, "I scorn to surrender my living body; you may take it only in death". And saying so he

fought on, but not to lose his battle, to win it against all
odds, in the end.'

'Fine words,' she said, through her tears, 'from one
who is running away.'

'Oh, it is you who carry the banner, not I,' he said,
his mouth twisted. 'I am only your slave, whose duty is
to die for you, or sacrifice himself to save your honour.'

'But you sacrifice me, too,' she wailed, 'for what is
left for me but a loveless marriage, and an empty life? I
have no battle to win, unlike the man whose name I
bear. I would be a cottager's daughter and have the
man I love rather than be what I am. You must not
leave me.'

Chad saw that she was distraught, which moved him,
and he knew also that what she said and did came from
her heart. But he saw Aisgill again, and the contempt in
his face for a man who would do what he thought he
saw Chad doing.

Again, it was as though she had picked up his very
thoughts.

'Am I, are we, to do what Aisgill tells us? Is Aisgill
master here ——?'

But Chad came back at her, 'He thinks of Campions,
as well as you.'

'Campions!' Nell almost choked on the word. 'Do
you, does he, love Campions more than you love me? If
every great lady who loved where she should not were
to be punished as I am, the nobility would be
decimated.'

'But you are not every great lady. You are Nell
Tallboys, brave and true.'

'Words, Newcome, words. I cannot compel you, I
know. Whatever you were, you are a strong man; I
could not love a weak one. No,' she said, eyes blazing.

'If I give you leave to go, it will not be yet. Give me but a little longer, before my life closes in on me for good. Only that! I ask only that.'

What could he say or do? What was his honour, or hers, before such suffering?

He hesitated. Nell knew that she had won. 'You will stay a little longer, and we shall be careful. Just to have you near me will be enough.'

But even as he assented, saying, 'The usual notice, three months, and it must be known that I am going,' Chad knew that it would not be enough, for what lay between them was too strong for that.

CHAPTER TWELVE

FRUSTRATION and desire were one word for Nell—and that word was Chad.

The self-control which had ruled her life for twenty-seven years, which had created the icy Countess Elinor, noted for her stoic uprightness, her austere virtue, the woman who had turned away suitors until suitors had ceased to come, had disappeared when she had met Chad.

The woman who had proclaimed so confidently that love was not for her, that she would marry someone, anyone, when she chose, merely to secure the succession, and, that done, her partner could go hang—she treating him as a man might treat a woman he had married for her money and lands—that woman no longer existed.

She had discovered in herself a well of passion. . .no, not well, that word was too placid for what she felt for Chad. It was a cataract, or a fire, a raging fire, the flame of which the poets sang, which consumed her.

When she read Lord Byron now, it was not with superior amusement; she knew only too well of what he wrote, and she forgave him for what he was, and what he did, because, knowing what love had done to her, she knew what it had done to him.

How could Chad be so strong? She could almost feel the iron control which he maintained over his emotions, and in the face of the temptation which she knew that she presented to him. For the first time, she truly asked herself what he had been in his lost past. Where and how had he learned to deny himself? And what toll had it taken of him, was taking of him? She knew, because nothing that happened at Campions was unknown to her, that he never touched the women servants who yearned after him, being quite unlike most of the men servants in that respect.

Nell had said to him, and to herself, that she could only love a strong man, and had told true. Otherwise she would have taken Ulric as a husband, and, she now knew, contrary to her earlier beliefs, that she could never have married the weak man whom she thought she could have used to serve Campions.

She had fallen in love with a man whose will and control matched her own — so how had he managed to arrive on the moor and at Campions, abandoned and derelict? And now she must know, somehow, what she thought had never mattered — Chad himself having been all that she had previously wanted — what the man she loved had been before his memory had gone.

Sitting at her desk that afternoon, his resignation formally written out now, lying before her, she made her resolutions. She had three months in which to keep him, to change his mind, to try to bend him to her will.

Chad was at the riding school when Henson came in to her, carrying the account books relating to the estate, and a further budget of letters. Before she opened them in Chad's absence, she showed him the letter of resignation.

Surprisingly, Henson was annoyed and offended. 'What maggot's in his brain?' he almost grunted. 'Where will he find work to equal what he has achieved here?'

'I thought you disapproved of him,' commented Nell mildly.

'I did.' Henson was brief. 'But the man has compelled me to admit both his competence and his honesty — to say nothing of his courage in saving you. Besides, his devotion to his duty is exemplary. I had not thought him ungrateful to wish to leave what has saved him.'

Nell began to close her eyes in pain, said, 'I don't think it's ingratitude, Henson.'

'Then what the devil is it? Has he recovered his memory?'

'No, it's not that. I. . .taxed him with that. He says —— ' and Nell invented wildly, and reminded herself to tell Chad of the excuse which she had found for him, for *something* must be said to Henson ' — that he wishes to leave to try to discover who he is.'

'I suppose that makes some sort of sense — so long as he does not end up as a vagabond again,' replied Henson grudgingly. 'In the meantime, we must try to persuade him to stay. Campions must not lose good servants. To lose first Payne and then Newcome would be too bad.'

Payne still lay in his bedroom in the attic, and would never rise from it again, another old servant dying in harness and cared for by the family.

Nell opened the first letter, read it, handed it to Henson, who had taken a seat at Chad's desk. The letter was from Scotland, and its message was simple. The writer, factor to Charles, Viscount Halstead, had received the letter from Campions asking for information about my lord's rifle, but no answer could be given: the Viscount Halstead was not at Glen Ruadh, and no word had been received of his arriving there. Campions was advised to write to Clermont House in London.

Henson handed the letter back to Nell. 'Another dead

end,' he commented bitterly, 'and where the devil is the man? Saving your presence, Lady Elinor. And isn't it time that Jackson reported back to us?'

'Yes.' Nell had opened, and was reading, another letter. 'He hopes to be back with us tomorrow. He say he has little to report, but would like to confer with us.'

Henson shrugged his shoulders at that. 'Nothing satisfactory for us today,' he snorted. 'First Newcome off, then Halstead missing, and now Jackson at *point non plus* by the sound of it.'

'I know,' said Nell, and then naughtily — cheerfulness would break in, even in her misery, 'I know, Henson, the world is going to the dogs. But it always has done, and it always will.' And if that doesn't comfort Henson, she thought sadly, why should it comfort me?

'So there it is,' said Cully Jackson to Nell and her council, all in Nell's study the next afternoon. He had arrived, as he had said he would, and his news was that apart from the rifle, which he had asked to keep, he had nothing tangible with which to work.

'I am certain, beyond a doubt, from all I have learned since I last saw you, that Mr Ulric Tallboys was behind the attempt on you. But I have no proof, no proof at all. One of the dead man's associates awaits hanging in Bradford gaol, and I am to see him there soon. He might, facing his end, tell me a little more of his dead leader; throw light on where Halstead's rifle came from. A slim chance, I fear. And I shall make more enquiries there. I have set up a nice little ring of informers in these parts, who may be of use to me in the future, if not now. . .'

'And that's all,' Henson almost snarled. Of them all he hated the attack on Nell most. A civilised, orderly

man, he saw it as a giant crack in his world, as well as
an attack on his mistress.

'After that,' said Jackson, mildly, ignoring Henson's
bile, for he had met such before, 'I shall hie me to
London again, to try to find a clue to Halstead's
whereabouts. He has certainly been in these parts once,
but must have left. None here knows of him. Clermont
House might have some information on his whereabouts
now. And after that, if I fail there, you must save your
money; the trail is dead.'

'You will stay here tonight,' said Nell. 'I insist. The
housekeeper will find you a room, and the butler will
see that you are properly fed.'

Jackson bowed. 'Before that I should like to speak to
Mr Newcome again, if I may.'

They all, Newcome as well, stared at him.

'Oh, I do not suspect Mr Newcome of any wrongdo-
ing,' said Jackson, 'but he may know more than he
thinks he does. Witnesses often do, and he is our only
witness.'

Nell rose. 'Pray accept my thanks for your efforts so
far, and Jackson, I would wish to speak to you alone
before you leave. Tomorrow morning, after breakfast,
here.'

If Nell's council was surprised by this, none indicated
that he thought so. Jackson looked across at Chad, said,
'I should like to see you in the riding school, Mr
Newcome. I understand that this is the afternoon you
work out there. My interest in horses has previously
been with the money I have put on their backs, but I
have a mind to see a stable in action.'

'So you shall.' Aisgill was jovial. 'You shall see
Newcome on Rajah—that is a sight.' He felt that he
could be generous towards Newcome, seeing that he

was doing the decent thing by taking himself and his temptations from Campions.

So, that afternoon, a good lunch inside him, Jackson stood in the riding school watching Chad on Rajah, as Aisgill had promised. Both horse and rider had come on since their early days together. Rajah still hated all men, including Chad, except that with Chad he did strange and wonderful things, and, which, although he did not want to do them, there was an odd magnificence in the doing.

First Jackson watched horse and rider go through a series of tricks which Jackson had seen previously, in simpler forms, at Astley's Circus in London. The caracoles and airs above the ground entranced him, as did the obvious control which Newcome was exercising over the unwilling stallion.

And then the lads put out fences around the arena, and Chad took Rajah over them, snorting, blowing and foaming, hating his rider and the admiring spectators, but compelled to do as he was bid.

And when the show was over two lads warily led Rajah away, and Chad walked to where Jackson was standing. 'You wanted to speak to me?'

Jackson was fascinated by Newcome. There was something so ineffably haughty and commanding about him when he was unselfconscious. He had his own theories about what Newcome might have been, and they were not those which obtained at Campions.

'Yes,' he said. 'As I said earlier, I wanted to ask you some questions about your finding of the rifle.'

For some reason Chad did not believe him. His intuition, which he knew — how? — had been powerful in dangerous situations, but not in emotional ones, was working in him. He answered Jackson's innocuous

questions calmly; he had no desire to make an enemy of
the man. They were now quite alone. It was cold, and
the lads had drifted indoors, and Aisgill had gone to his
little office.

'And that is all?' asked Jackson. 'You have no conscious memory of having seen the man before?'

Chad's expression grew dangerous, his whole body
quite still; he said softly, 'Are you suggesting that I was
in some way connected with the attack on Lady Elinor,
that I was a Trojan horse planted here to lead her into
danger?'

'No,' said Jackson, recognising that the man who had
tamed Rajah so easily might not hesitate to tame him.
'I have no doubts about your honesty. It was Lady
Elinor's decision that you rode to the Throne; she was
adamant that you tried to dissuade her to the point of
mutiny. But I have the strangest feeling about the rifle
every time I hold it, and I have not learned not to ignore
such feelings——'

'And that is?' prompted Chad, his voice still dangerous.

'That you, Chad Newcome, and the rifle are somehow
connected. It is what makes me a good thief taker.
Feeling, not reasoning connections.'

'I would not argue with you,' said Chad, easing a
little, the aura of danger about him dispersing. 'Because,
not from memory but from my own instincts, I know
such things may be true.'

'And you are leaving Campions, when your notice is
up?'

'Yes,' said Chad.

'And you will let me know where you are going, when
you go. You may do so through Lady Elinor,' and then,
daring danger, 'You are leaving because of Lady Elinor,
are you not, Mr Chad Newcome?'

Jackson was on his knees gasping, Chad Newcome's hands were about his throat. Old campaigner that he was, he had not seen Chad move, only knew that he had done so when he was overwhelmed.

'Say that again, to anyone but myself, and I shall not hesitate to kill you, Mr Jackson,' said Chad, almost conversationally. 'It is no business of yours, nor your investigation, why I am leaving. Mention her name to me again and I shall step on you and crush you as I would a beetle.'

He released Jackson, who began to laugh, although his throat pained him. 'Oh, my fine gentleman,' he choked, 'I have properly smoked you out. A trooper, were you? Someone's servant? I think not.'

He had the satisfaction of seeing Newcome's face change, lose its colour.

'And what the devil do you mean by that?' Chad grated.

'You may work it out for yourself, sir. In the night watches. It might help you to recover your memory, tell you why you chose to lose it. No, do not attack me again, I know you are not faking. But you might try asking yourself why you do not wish to know yourself, a man of honour, such as you most plainly are.'

The Runner strolled off, laughing to himself. He had not needed to bait Newcome to find out that he and Lady Elinor were involved, he had seen that for himself, but he had discovered to his own satisfaction that Newcome was rather more than the poor ex-trooper that Campions thought him to be. What exactly he had been was quite another matter. He took that knowledge with him to his meeting with Lady Elinor.

Nell had spent her time wondering what to say to Jackson. When he came in with his ill-made, dangerous body and face, the thief taker *par excellence*, she decided that the simple truth might be the safest.

'I have another task for you, Jackson,' she said, without preamble, 'and it is this. You know that Mr Newcome has lost his memory, that he is shortly to leave Campions. I am disturbed that he may leave us without being able to sustain himself properly. Consequently, I'm asking you, without his knowledge, to try to discover where he came from, how he arrived, injured and starving, on the moor. It seems to me that you could make your enquiries at the same time that you pursue the mission for which Campions has employed you.'

Jackson kept his face straight. He did not fear that Lady Elinor might attack him, as Newcome had done, but it would not be safe to be on the wrong side of such a powerful woman.

'Yes, my lady,' he said. 'I can do what you wish, and, of course, I shall say nothing to him.'

'And I will tell you all I know of his arrival here,' began Nell, and proceeded to do so, so lucidly that at the end Jackson said respectfully,

'If I may say so, Lady Elinor, I could do with you as my assistant. Few of the ones I possess are as clear as you in the reports they make to me.'

Nell laughed at that. 'When I am no longer Countess Nell,' she said gaily, 'I shall come to Bow Street and ask you for work.'

It was not difficult for Jackson to understand why Chad Newcome, and all her people, for that matter, loved her. He determined that if it were possible he would try to find out who was plotting to kill her, and would nail him.

Nell watched him leave the room, dour and honest.

She felt as though she was betraying Chad by setting Jackson on his trail, for who knew what he might find?

Jackson turned at the door before he left, and said, 'Whatever I discover, of both good and ill about him, you will hear of it from me, will you not?' and his tone was almost a challenge.

'Yes,' she said, 'yes,' and then thought, as he left the room, All's fair in love and war, and only myself and my God know how much I love you, Chad.

CHAPTER THIRTEEN

'NEWCOME!'

Chad was in the library; his time when he was not acting as Nell's secretary was divided between the stables and the library, which Campions did not find strange since their Countess's time was similarly shared.

He was standing at the lectern, working, when Nell came in, his back to the door from her study by which she had entered. The few occasions on which they had been alone together were either in the library proper, or in the annexe. A little earlier Nell had seen Challenor walk by her window, away from the house, knew that Chad would likely be working there, and had immediately seized her opportunity to speak with him unchaperoned.

Chad turned, gave her his smile, the smile which wrenched her heart. Dressed as he was, he was virtually indistinguishable in appearance from the aristocrats and gentry who had once besieged her, except that he was Chad, and none of them had stolen her heart from her bosom.

Nell treasured the smile for it was all that he gave her these days — they had reached the stage where they dared not touch.

'Lady Elinor?'

He was suddenly so grave, so proper, so all that he should be that the devil whispered in Nell's ear. Oh, to destroy his hard-won composure. She spoke, eyes glinting, dark brows lifting, her whole aspect one of such innocent wickedness that the man before her clutched at the shreds of his reason.

'I have not given up, you know, Newcome. I shall never give up!'

'I know,' said Chad, his eyes smoking, Nell noted happily; Not so composed after all, my love, she thought. Let us see if I can shake that nobly intransigent front of yours. 'I know, Lady Elinor. You take after your ancestor in that.'

'Oh, no,' said Nell, still naughty. 'It was his body he refused to surrender, whereas the body I refuse to surrender. . .' and she paused, her eyes hard on his face '. . .is yours.'

Chad could not prevent his smile from broadening at her impudent wit.

'Do not smile, Newcome,' commanded Nell severely. 'You are not to smile when my heart is breaking.'

'If I do not smile, Nell,' replied Chad softly, 'I shall shriek to the heavens for what they deny me.'

'Oh, you feel as I do, then,' she said. 'How can you be so strong, to deny yourself and me so calmly?'

'As strong as you, Nell,' he said, still standing aloof from her. 'As strong as you.'

'No, I am weak,' she returned. 'Touch me, Newcome; you will see how weak I am.'

Chad put his hands behind his back. They now stood face to face, but apart, neither moving towards the other.

'Infinity,' said Nell, pointing at the eighteen inches of parquet floor which separated them.

'An eternity,' said Chad. 'Two names for the same thing.'

'And what name is there for love denied?' asked Nell.

'Honour,' Chad returned, as quick as she.

'Honour?' Nell repeated sadly. 'I think it a word for men to use.'

'Ah, but you play a man's part, Lady Elinor,' said Chad. 'For you are Countess as a man is an earl. No husband gives you that title. It is yours by birth and by right. So, men's words are your words.'

It was as though an arrow pierced Nell's heart, as though a bell had tolled, or a sentence had burned itself in letters of fire before her in the air. She almost staggered and fell. For he had unlocked the door, found the heart of the maze in which they stood, liberated them both from the bonds which bound them.

'Why, so I am,' she said. 'And their deeds are my deeds, their rights mine. I am blessed among women, for whatever a man can do, so may I do. Oh, Chad,' and she laughed joyously. 'You have played with words as other men play with dice, and this time your throw is so true that I, your Countess, salute you,' and she dipped into a great curtsy before him, as though he were her monarch, chestnut head bent. 'And now I must leave you, to think on what you have said—and to act!'

Why, what have I said to affect her so? thought Chad, puzzled, watching her face, glowing as it had not done since they parted, love refused, in the annexe all those miserable weeks ago.

Nell turned at the door, to find that he had not moved, had followed her going with his eyes alone.

'You do not ask me where I am bound, Newcome,' she said, her eyes sparkling, her whole mien changed from the stoic one of the recent past.

'To your room, I suppose.' For once he was at a loss for words.

'You suppose wrongly, Newcome. I am bound for the long gallery, to where my painted forebears hang, for I think that they have a message for me. You have reminded me of what I am, and what they are, and love may yet conquer all. It is *au revoir* I bid you, Newcome, not goodbye.'

Eyes still shining, Nell paced the long gallery, staring up at the family portraits, at the first Earl, godlike in his early eighteenth-century battle dress, banners and plumes, cannon smoking behind him. At the second Earl, Hanoverian George's minister, sardonic in dark blue court dress, the man who had founded the Campions stud, at the third Earl, who had combed Europe for the treasures which filled the house, and had refused office because he disliked his monarch, at the fourth Earl, who had died young, but not before he had created the library which was Challenor's treasure, and at her grandfather, his brother, painted in his old age by Sir Thomas Lawrence.

Their word had been law, they had defied kings, princes, done as they pleased, as the male Tallboyses had always done. She looked at the first Earl again; she had thought him the founder of the House of Tallboys until her grandfather had told her otherwise.

'Oh, no,' he had said, one rainy evening, as she sat at his feet, looking at the first Earl. 'He simply acquired for us the Malplaquet title. We go further back than that. Not him, my dear; he was already noble. Never forget that we are sprung from nothing, or so the legend says.'

Strange that she had forgotten this, and that it should come back to her now.

'What does the legend say?' she had asked him, as he fell silent.

'Why, that one day in the mists of time, long ago, in

King John's reign, the unmarried lady of Barthwaite rode from her manor, and, being tired, stopped at a cottage where a tall woodcutter rested on his axe. Ivo of the Woods was all the name he had.

'"You may give me a drink," she said to him, "for I have a great thirst."

'"I would give you more than that, lady," he said, bold eyes on her, leaving no doubt as to what he meant.

'"Why, so you may," she said, looking at the size and strength of him, "and in exchange I will give you myself and Barthwaite, too," for she knew that here was the only man who could match and master her, and she would have him, for was not she the lady and he the serf?

'"I have no name to give you, lady," he said.

'"Then I will give you one, woodcutter, and a good French one it shall be, and then you may give it to me when the priest weds us. You shall be Taillebois, the man who cuts wood, and so shall all be to whom we give life."

'And so it was, and Taillebois — Tallboys — we are to this day, for we are all their descendants, and you, barring Ulric, are the last of the line, my dear.'

'And is the story true, Grandfather?' she had asked him.

'I would like it to be so,' he said, 'if only to show that, noble or simple, we are all the same beneath our clothes. I am at one with the Radicals in that, if in nothing else.'

Remembering this, Nell struck her hands together fiercely. She was the last lady of the line, and, through the first Earl's doing, she also stood as the last man, with all of a man's rights and privileges. She knew what she had to do, and, being practical Nell Tallboys, who

organised her life so well, she decided to organise it
further — and at once.

'I shall go to York tomorrow,' she said aloud, and she
almost ran from the gallery, calling on Annie, her aunt
Conybeare, and the butler, all of whom she would take
with her to her house in York, which stood in the lee of
the great cathedral.

'I have a mind to play, to shop, for a week,' she lied
to a puzzled Aunt Conybeare, 'and my council shall
rule Campions for me in my absence, for I shall take
none of them with me. They may work while I dally, for
the house there needs to shelter its owner a little.'

Exactly when Guy Shadwell first began to worry that
he had heard nothing from his brother since he had left
for Scotland he could not say.

All Guy's life his elder brother had loved and protected him. His relationship with his other brother
Frederick had always been a cold one. But Shad had
taught him to swim, to shoot and to ride — not as Shad
rode, for Shad was a marvel with horses — and he had
always encouraged him to study hard as well, the eleven
years between them making Shad more of an uncle than
a brother.

And when Shad was away at the wars he had written
constantly to Guy. A little reserved in speech, on paper
he was a witty and informative correspondent, and Guy
had always looked eagerly for the post to bring him
Shad's latest letter. He had tried to show them to his
father, for Shad's letters to the Earl were stiff, dutiful
things, the constraint between them operating on him,
but his father had always pushed them away pleading,
'No time.'

Shad's last words to Guy as he had left for Glen

Ruadh had been quite clear. 'I shall write to you, Guy —
but not immediately.'

Time passed, and no letters came. At first, Guy
thought nothing of it. He knew that Shad had been
mortally hurt by the final breach with his father, but
surely, he thought, he must have recovered sufficiently
to write to the brother who he knew had always loved
him? Unless, of course, he had cut himself off from
everything that was related to Clermont, and that
included Guy, too, which Guy found difficult to believe.

Shortly before Christmas, growing troubled, Guy
wrote to Glen Ruadh, but nothing came back. He wrote
again, still nothing, until one day, after his third despair-
ing letter begging Shad to remember that he, Guy, still
loved him, on a blustery day in early March, a letter
came from Shad's factor at Glen Ruadh.

He wrote that correspondence had arrived so constantly for Lord Halstead that the factor, in my lord's
continued absence, had opened it, and was further
writing to say that if my lord had set out for Scotland
he had certainly never reached there. What was worse
was that this first letter had been two months on the
way; a second from the factor, written within the last
fortnight, was delivered only a few days later and said
that my lord had still not arrived and asked for
guidance.

Guy stared at the paper before him, face going slowly
white. It was now nearly six months since Shad had
flung out of Clermont House, announcing that he was
off to Glen Ruadh, and no one had seen or heard
from him since. Guy had thought him in his Highland
fastness, refusing to acknowledge the rest of the world,
which was bad enough, but to learn that he had dropped
off the edge of the world. . . Guy had spoken to several

of Shad's friends in London, none of whom had heard from him, and were themselves troubled by his disappearance from his old haunts, and lack of any news from him.

Carrying the letters, Guy went to his father's study, put them on the desk before him, and poured out the tale of Shad's disappearance.

'I would have a search made for him, Father,' he finished. 'But better that such an initiative came from you. Your name is a powerful one.'

The Earl, who had stared, face hard, at Guy while he spoke, looked down at his work again, said coldly, 'Most convenient if he has disappeared. You may, after due formalities, be Halstead and my heir. A more satisfactory eventuality than I could have hoped for.'

The obedience which Guy had always shown to his father broke on that.

'No!' he said violently. 'You shall not speak so. No! You wrong him, Father. You have always wronged him. Shad is good, brave and true, as the whole world knows, aside from yourself. What maggot works in your brain, sir, that you have never given him his due? The Duke himself——'

His father interrupted him. 'Do not bore me, Guy,' he began.

'Bore you, sir! Bore you! It is time that you knew the truth about Shad—and about Frederick, too. Shad forbade me to tell that truth, but if by bad chance he is dead his death absolves me from my promise to him. It is time you knew what Frederick really was, and what Shad did to save the family honour and to spare you pain.'

He had his father's attention now. The Earl rose, face stern.

'Explain yourself, sir — or I will deal with you as I did with Halstead.'

'Oh, you may cut me off, too,' said Guy furiously, quite unlike his usual mild and charming self. 'But you *shall* know the truth. Frederick's death was no accident as you and the world thought. Frederick shot himself, committed suicide. He. . .' Guy choked on the words, could hardly say them. He ignored his father's suddenly ashen face, began again.

'Frederick loved boys; he always did. He could not live without his. . .vice. He frequented special houses. . . Shad knew, he always knew; I didn't know until just before his death when I heard Shad and him talking.

'He was being blackmailed, had been blackmailed for years, was threatened with exposure if he didn't pay large sums of money over. He was bleeding the estate dry to pay the swine off. And when ruin and exposure finally stared him in the face, because their demands became impossible, he. . .shot himself, leaving a letter for you, to tell you what had happened, and why he did it.

'Shad found the letter, and Frederick, dead in the gunroom at Pinfold — it was when he was recovering from that dreadful wound he got in Spain. He knew what it would do to you, and to the Clermont name, but particularly to you, who loved him so, if you knew the truth. He fetched me, I was there that weekend — you were over at Broadlands at the time — and together we secretly arranged it to look like an accident. No one ever guessed the truth.'

The Earl's face was livid, ghastly. 'And how do I know that this remarkable story is the truth?'

'Oh, the agent knew that Frederick was robbing the estate; he may even have guessed why — but there's more than that. Shad thought that he had destroyed the letter, but I—and I don't know why I did it, I was only fourteen at the time—but perhaps I felt that the truth should not be completely destroyed. I substituted blank paper for it, and Shad burned that. I have the letter still, and you shall see it. He never knew what I had done.'

The Earl sat down, all his beliefs in ruins about him. He could not speak. Guy, uncharacteristically voluble, continued. 'And that, sir, should tell you how Shad loved you and protected you and the family name both, for he dealt with the blackmailers as well—how I never knew—and put straight the estate which Frederick had nearly ruined. That should tell you how unworthy you have been to prefer Frederick to him, and now he is likely dead, taking your unfounded dislike to the grave with him.'

Guy saw that he had broken his father, and, even though it was for Shad that he had done it, it gave him no pleasure.

'I believe you, sir,' said the Earl, at last. 'But I would like to see the letter,' and he sank his face into his hands, a man suddenly grown old before his time. Which son he was grieving for he could not have said, the one whom he had wrongly valued, or the one he had never valued—and both lost.

Finally, he raised his head, said, 'You are saying that Halstead set out for Scotland, but never reached there, and has not been heard from since he left here?'

'That is so, sir.' Guy's throat had closed, his revelations over; he could hardly speak. He had always thought that one day he might tell his father the truth about his two older brothers, but had never thought to do so in such tragic circumstances.

'Then I shall institute enquiries, and also I must. . . order my thoughts. Come to terms with what you have told me. You say that he did what he did to save me pain?'

'Yes,' said Guy sturdily, 'and to save Clermont's honour. Think of the scandal if anyone other than Shad had found him.' He did not add that Frederick had been careless of that as well as of everything else — he did not need to. 'Shad is what I said he was, good and true, but you were always fixed on Frederick. He understood that, although it grieved him.'

The Earl looked sadly at his youngest son, said, 'It seems that I have never known any of you. I think that I have never properly valued you either, sir. You showed a shrewdness beyond your years when you saved the letter. When you have given it to me, you will leave me alone with it, and we must both pray that somehow, somewhere, Halstead still lives. My greatest punishment would be never to see him again, to rectify the lost years.'

CHAPTER FOURTEEN

NELL had arrived back from York late in the evening. She retired to her room without ceremony, without seeing her council; she pleaded tiredness, but sent a message to Henson that they should all meet in her study on the following morning, no exceptions.

She sat in her bed that evening eating buttered rolls and drinking hot chocolate, feeling one moment like the cat that had stolen the cream, and the next moment like the cat turned out into the rain at midnight. What would they say when she threw her bombshell on the carpet before them all in the morning? What would Chad say? Would he kiss her, or kill her? She had no idea how he would react.

She thought she knew how the others would, and she was inwardly bracing herself to face them. She could not sleep for excitement. The lawyer whom she had brought back with her from York was given a room on his own — and told to talk to no one. His cynical old face was even more cynical than usual as he ate his excellent food, and drank his good wine.

Morning broke, the sun was up, and the scents of an early spring were everywhere. Nell dressed with uncommon care in a deep green wool, cut on classic lines, belted high under her waist, and which emphasised the depth of her magnificent bosom, and although the neck was high with a tiny man's cravat the whole effect was voluptuous. She looked a far cry from the icy Nell Tallboys of the past.

She could not eat her breakfast, the food stuck in her throat, and she could hardly wait to reach her study, Aunt Conybeare consigned to the drawing-room; this was not an occasion at which she ought to be present. The lawyer Nell had banished to an ante-room, to be sent for, if required, and Nell had a stack of legal documents on the desk before her. I am armed at all points, she thought. A military metaphor seemed suitable, seeing that she was about to deal with an ex-trooper.

Promptly at ten, the appointed hour, her Privy Council arrived. Almost as though they knew that this was a solemn occasion they were all dressed *à point*. Henson and Challenor were grave in charcoal-grey, Henson was wearing cream riding breeches tucked into shining riding boots; later in the day he was to tour the tenant farms in the Riding around Campions.

Even Aisgill was smart in his country clothing, and Chad was wearing his best black silk suit, and he had, in Nell's honour, although she did not know this, tied his cravat in a waterfall favoured by the late leader of London society, George Brummell.

Standing before his mirror that morning, Chad had had a flash of memory. He had seen himself standing before another mirror with a splendid frame of eagles soaring high above its top. And he was tying his cravat, and talking to someone behind him, whom he could not see, 'And this is a waterfall,' he had said, and tied the cravat *so*, and then everything disappeared again.

The flashes were disturbing because they were inconsequential, had no beginning, and no end, came from nowhere, and disappeared into nowhere. This one was particularly disturbing because he had felt that his surroundings were luxurious, and how could that be?

All in all, he looked severely magnificent, but then he always did. Severe was a good word to describe him. Well, thought Nell, mischievously, we shall see if severe is a good word for him in another hour. She begged leave to doubt it.

'Lady Elinor,' said Henson, almost reproachfully, 'this is not our usual day to meet you.'

Nell smiled at him. 'I agree, but this is not going to be a usual day for anyone.'

Henson, she saw, frowned. He did not like surprises; he wanted life to be orderly. Chad, Nell was amused to see, looked wary, as though a sniper were hidden behind the boulle cabinet in the corner. What intuitive message was passing between them that of the four of them he seemed to be the only one to have some inkling that she was about to commit a most outrageous act?

'I have called you in. . .' she said, quite cool; she was, indeed, astonished at how level her voice was. She could see herself in the Venetian glass over the hearth, and she looked quite calm, the portrait of a lady totally in command of herself, not one about to breach every canon of etiquette which controlled the actions of ladies.

She began again, almost absently, 'I have called you all in to tell you that I am about to follow the advice which you have so frequently given me.' She paused dramatically; some devil inside her was drawing this out, so that what she was about to say would be all the more devastating to them all when they heard it.

It was Henson who broke when she did not continue. 'And that is, Lady Elinor?'

'Oh,' said Nell, 'there is only one piece of advice on which you have all agreed, ever since I inherited, and I am about to take it. I have decided to marry.'

Nell saw Chad's face change. He undoubtedly

thought that he had lost her, that she had done the honourable thing, gone to York to arrange a loveless marriage which would remove them both from temptation. She smiled inwardly.

As usual, Henson constituted himself spokesman, forestalling Aisgill. 'I think that I speak for us all,' he said, 'in offering you my felicitations, Lady Elinor. Your decision is welcome, if a little overdue. I take it that we may expect suitors to be arriving here at Campions.'

'No, you may not,' said Nell, smiling sweetly; she was beginning to enjoy herself, even if Chad wasn't. 'I have already decided whom I will marry.'

There was uproar. All but Chad began to speak as one, her Countess-ship quite forgotten, she was amused to note. Chad was silent, his face more severe than ever. Oh, how he was suffering, her darling, her poor love; her heart bled for him.

'Not Ulric Tallboys, after all, Lady Elinor,' began Aisgill, red in the face. 'Not after what Jackson has told us of him. You could not be so unwise.'

'No, not Cousin Ulric——' said Nell, to be interrupted, almost rudely, by Henson.

'And not, I hope, to someone whom you met only last week in York, and hardly know, I trust.'

'Oh, no,' said Nell, 'I would not inflict Cousin Ulric on you and Campions. Nor is it someone I met last week in York; that is not my way, either. But it is perfectly true that I went to York to arrange this marriage.'

She paused, held them all in turn with her eyes, finally arriving at Chad, almost compelled him to look at her, which he did, so that for a moment it seemed to Nell that there was no one in the room but the pair of them.

'I am,' she said, 'entitled to arrange my own marriage, for am I not Countess of Malplaquet with exactly the same rights and powers as though I were the Earl? I am, in short, in the same case as a man, and as a man I need no one to arrange a marriage for me and I may propose to my future partner as a man would. I therefore propose a marriage which will please me and benefit Campions.

'I have decided that in view of my. . .inclination for him, and the talents and devotion to duty which he has shown since he arrived here, I can do no better than to ask Mr Chad Newcome to marry me, and for you all to support me as I do so. Accordingly, I formally ask you, Mr Newcome, to take my hand, and Malplaquet, and all that goes with Malplaquet's name with it.'

Chad, who had gone quite white, so that Nell's stunned Privy Council could see at once that this was as great a surprise to him as to them, said something inarticulate, strode to the window, and stood with his back to the room and to Nell, staring out at the wild and beautiful view over the moors. It was plain to them all that he was the prey to strong emotion, was struggling to control himself.

The stunned silence gave way to uproar, Henson, Aisgill, Challenor all talking at once. Nell ignored them, and in the moment of silence which followed as the three of them endeavoured to collect themselves and their scattered wits she said steadily, face white, coming from behind her desk, to pass her Privy Council, addressing Chad's straight back, 'You reminded me, Mr Newcome, sir, that I stand in the place of the Earl. I ask you to recognise that fact, turn to face your Countess, and give her your considered answer.'

Behind her, her Privy Council muttered as Chad

slowly restored his self-control. He now knew why she had reacted as she did that day in the library, when he had so idly said that she stood in the Earl's place, and he could guess why she had gone to York. He refused to turn, for Nell had placed him at a disadvantage by the manner of her proposal, and he was seeking to restore the balance between them.

Henson spoke. 'May I advise, madam?'

'No, you may not,' said Nell again. 'I am Earl and Countess here. I await Mr Newcome's answer.'

Chad stood, unmoving. And Nell, suddenly nervous, for oh, he was strong, stronger even than she might have thought, would give her neither yea nor nay easily, would make her bleed her heart dry, to test how true this proposal was, said, 'I may advise *you*, Mr Newcome, as you have no lawyer, no family to help you. The special licence for our marriage, given at York, should you wish to accept my offer, stands on the desk here. The marriage settlement between us, which is the same as I would offer any man, gentle or simple, is also there for you to sign. My grandfather's ring is ready for your finger; as the Earl would give his pledge to the partner he chose, I will give you mine. So do I honour you, Mr Newcome,' and as she had done that last day in the library she sank down before his turned back in her most elaborate curtsy.

At last, Chad turned, and the man they saw, although neither he, nor they, knew it, was the man he had been before memory deserted him.

His soldiers in Spain would have known his manner, as his fellow officers and the Duke had done. As Jackson had shrewdly noted, when unselfconscious, as he now was, he reverted to the haughty aristocrat birth and military training had made him. Cold, hard and imperious, it was the face of a man who gave orders, and expected them to be obeyed.

'Madam,' he said, 'though the manner is not one I would have chosen, you do me the greatest honour a woman could do a man. You offer me, a landless nobody, taken naked from the moors, the noblest prize in England. You are sure that you wish to do this thing? That you understand what you are offering me?'

'None better,' answered Nell, quaking internally, for all her brave front, for here was a Chad she had never seen, nor her Privy Council either. 'I offer you myself, and the guardianship of Malplaquet, for guardians are what we shall be. We shall jointly hold it in trust. It owns us. We do not own it. Those are the terms of the settlement.'

Aisgill spoke, breaking the paralysis which had seized the three of them at Nell's monstrous proposal. 'Madam, I cannot remain silent in the face of this.'

'But you will, Aisgill, you will,' said Nell, not turning her head. 'For I am Earl here, and you would not so have spoken to my grandfather, without he asked you to. I do not ask you.'

Aisgill would not be quiet. 'The man may have wife and children, he has no name, he is nobody. . .'

'As to the first,' said Nell, 'I think not. As for a name, I shall give him that. As with the first of the line, so with the last. Should he so wish, he shall be Tallboys.'

Chad had remained silent. If anything, his hauteur had grown.

'No,' he said. 'If I accept, madam, you will take *my* name. I will not take yours. You may be Countess, and Earl, I grant you that, but you will still be my wife, and I shall not be your servant. I shall be your partner — or nothing. And, should I accept, they —— ' and he waved a hand with the utmost arrogance at the Privy Council '—they must accept me, and accept, too, that I had no part in your decision to do this thing, that you made it freely and without my knowledge, that I shall be master here, as you will be mistress, but they will still advise.'

Henson had said nothing so far, only now, before Chad made his final decision, spoke.

'You have still not given a straight answer, man, and what the world will say if your answer is yes will be a scandal and a year's wonder, and I will advise you now. If Campions needs a master, and Malplaquet an heir, and you are her choice, and I would not have chosen you, yet your answer must be yes.'

Of them all he was the one whom Nell and Chad would have thought the most adamant against such a marriage.

'You may offer me your advice, as I said——' and Chad's face was closed and cold '—I did not say that I would take it.'

'So you refuse me,' said Nell, white to the lips, head high, bleeding internally; her gamble had failed, after all.

'Oh, no,' said Chad, and smiled at her for the first time, his brilliant white smile. 'In honour, I could not accept you in less than marriage, in honour, I accept your offer of marriage, and now, in honour, I must offer for you. Lady Elinor, will you marry me? I can give you nothing but my signature on a piece of paper, and my love and reverence for you, ever and always.'

And he bowed his proud head in answer to her earlier curtsy, while Aisgill hissed, and old Challenor looked bemused, and Henson's face was a sardonic mask.

Nell murmured a whispered, 'Yes,' suddenly shy, 'yes, with all my heart,' and curtsied again. He put out his hand to lift her, kissed her hand, and then she pulled from her thumb, where she had placed it before she came into the meeting, her grandfather's ring, the ring which the first Earl had been given by Prince Eugene of Savoy after the battle of Malplaquet.

'I seal our betrothal with this,' she said, handing it to him, for him to slip on his finger, and then he pulled from his pocket the lace handkerchief which she had given him at the time of Sir Chesney's visit.

'My lady, I have little to give you, so you would honour me by receiving back the favour which you gave me. I have carried it ever since.'

Nell took the handkerchief, after he had kissed it, and she too kissed it, before tying it to her belt.

The ice which had enfolded them both throughout the whole passage broke as Chad finished speaking. The face which he had shown them lost its sternness, Nell's lost her air of cool command, and for a moment the look which passed between them was unguarded, and of the fiercest passion. The Privy Council could have no doubt but that this was a marriage for love.

'And now we must fetch the lawyer who has been patiently waiting in the ante-room, settlement papers shall be signed, the parson brought from Keighley, and the marriage shall be solemnised in Campions chapel tomorrow, with Campions people around us.'

'So soon,' said Henson.

'No delay.' Nell was firm. 'Neither he nor I wish to wait, I am sure. And I have no wish for outsiders here.'

'Sir Chesney. . .' began Henson, to fall silent at Nell's raised eyebrows. 'No,' he said resignedly. 'This is enough of a turn-up, without having Sir Chesney's bellowings about it, begging your pardon for my disrespect, Lady Elinor, Mr Newcome,' and his sardonic eye

took in Chad. Like the others, he had noticed his
changed demeanour during the proposal ceremony, and
that Chad had now reverted to the pleasant man he had
been since he had first recovered from the confusion
which had gripped him on his arrival at Campions.

He was not to know that Chad's own soldiers had
always noticed the difference between Chad in a tight
corner, the commander on the battlefield, and the
courteous man he was in daily life.

Aisgill had the last word when all the legal business
was over, and Chad and Nell had retired to the long
gallery, where Nell had said that he must be properly
introduced to those who had preceded him.

'It might be worse,' he said to Henson and Challenor.
'He is young, personable, has many talents, has
obviously been a soldier, and a gentleman, but who and
what he is God knows; we probably never shall.' He
hesitated. 'The thief taker Jackson said a thing I thought
was strange at the time when he last left us. He said—
and God knows how he knew what even I was not sure
of—that passion lay between them—that I was not to
worry about the turn events might take, that Lady
Elinor and Campions would be safe with Newcome.
God grant it may be so. She has leapt into the dark
today, and taken Campions with her.'

Challenor spoke for the first time. 'There was never
any stopping Lady Nell. She is a true Tallboys, and the
first Earl would have been proud of her. As for the man,
I think him honest, but as you say, Aisgill, only time
will tell.' He paused. 'He is a good bookman, and that
says much for him.'

CHAPTER FIFTEEN

NEITHER of them spoke until they reached the long gallery. Once inside, now alone, permitted — nay, encouraged for the first time to be alone, Chad turned to her.

'It is not too late to change your mind——' he began.

Nell interrupted him, her expression dangerous. 'You regret your proposal to me, then?'

'No, not that,' he said. 'Never that. But you, are you sure that you know what awaits you? You rule Campions, but what of the rest of the world? It can be harsh, unfeeling, to those who break the code which binds us.'

Chad said 'us' without thinking, making himself one of the great ones of the world, part of the cousinry, the network of nobility which owned and ruled England.

Nell was so troubled by his questions that she did not notice this unconscious assumption, and nor did he.

'Oh,' she said, lip curling, 'they have always disapproved of me. I have simply given them a real reason for their dislike. And you, are you afraid to marry me? Or is your honour troubling you again? It need not; we are to be married, and honourably. I have no fear that you will do other than deal well with me and Campions — which is more than I could have said had I chosen to marry Ulric, or another of his kind.'

He took her hand, and kissed it. He could wait now, to love her as he wished to, for when they finally met together in her great bed their union would be blessed,

not something illicit, love celebrated hugger-mugger in
a corner, but nobly, in the open, Nell's people about her
at the wedding ceremony.

'I hope,' he said simply, 'that I shall prove worthy of
what you have given me.'

'No fears for me on that score,' said Nell, 'and now I
must show you your inheritance, the painted images of
those who have gone before you,' and she waved a hand
at the Tallboyses who lined the walls, their wives beside
them. 'Bravery and beauty combined,' she said with a
smile, 'until they reach me. For bravery,' and her smile
at him was a mischievous one, 'I showed today, but as
to beauty — I have no illusions about that.'

Chad knew that she was not saying this simply for
him to deny it indignantly. He took her by the shoulders
and turned her towards him, gently held her chin in his
big hands, and tipped her head back slightly. 'I do not
think,' he said softly, 'that you do yourself justice.
Beauty without character is not worth having, and
character is beauty, and so you are the most rare of
Tallboys ladies, since you possess both.'

'Oh, my love,' and Nell's smile was dazzling, 'you
play with words again. Were you a lawyer, after all, and
not a soldier? Challenor says that you are a man who
should have been a scholar, but I have seldom seen a
scholar who looked as though he could go into the ring
with the Game Chicken and acquit himself respectably!'

Chad laughed at that, and released her so that they
paced the gallery together, and before she introduced
her recent ancestors to him she told him the story of the
lady of Barthwaite and Ivo of the Woods.

He listened to her in silence, and thought of the gulf
which she had leapt in order to offer him herself, and
thought that in the shock which had followed that offer,

against all common sense and urgings of the head, he had followed his heart and now on the morrow, like the lady and her serf, she was to be his.

His bright blue eyes hard on her, the eyes with which he had done such execution, he said, 'And you are the lady and I am Ivo?'

'If you like,' she answered him. 'As the beginning, so the end. I wonder what my grandfather would have said, were he to have known of this day. But he told me once that all men and women are the same under their clothes, so we are not Countess and secretary, but simply Chad and Nell, man and woman.'

'Chad and Nell.' His voice was grave. 'So be it, then. And you have no regrets?'

'None, and that is an end of that. I know that you and I will serve Campions well, and love one another in the doing, and that is all I need to know. The omens are good, Chad.'

Chad nodded his head, and let her tell him of the pictured men and women, long dead, who had sprung from that meeting in the woods. He thought of the dark behind him, and the brightness before him, and paradoxically, now that his future was secure, was settled, he suddenly needed to know his past. He had thought himself reconciled to his loss of memory; indeed, in the days when he had first come to full consciousness of himself and his surroundings, it had been enough for him to know that he existed.

He knew that Henson and the others had made enquiries about him, but everything had led nowhere. He had appeared on the moor as though he had been dropped from heaven, and none had known nor seen him before he had been found lost and wandering.

Short of his memory returning to him, his past was

gone, not to be recovered, it seemed, with no clue to lead him to his origins. And then, as Campions claimed him and he became part of it, first in the stables and later as Nell's secretary, that had come to seem enough. The brief flashes of memory annoyed him, and his attempts to remember distressed him so much by their uselessness that he abandoned them altogether.

Except that now he was to marry Nell he had a sudden passionate wish to know himself.

'Perhaps,' he said, when her tale was done, and they were to return to the others, 'when we have been married for a little, we might try to find where I came from, how I arrived on the moor.'

'We must have no secrets between us,' said Nell. 'When Jackson left us last month I asked him to try to trace your past. He wrote privately to me, two days ago, that all his efforts so far had ended in failure. He had scoured the Riding, and you had not been seen before you were discovered begging by the farmer. He also said something I thought strange; that he connected the rifle with you, and that when his search in the North was ended he would visit London to try again to speak to Charles Halstead, to discover whether he had sold, lost, or even had the rifle stolen from him. His answer might give us some lead to the assassin, or even, unlikely as it sounds, to the mystery of your origins.'

'He told me that, too,' Chad said, and frowned. Somehow Charles Halstead's name always had the power to disturb him. 'But I cannot think what the rifle has to do with me, except that I found it by the man who tried to kill you.'

'Chad, my love,' said Nell quietly, taking his hand, distressed by the unhappiness on his face. 'Let us not talk of this now. I am marrying you, not your past, and what I know of you, as all Campions knows, and Henson and Aisgill admit, is good and true.

'The future is all that matters to me. I cannot think your past disgraceful. Unfortunate, perhaps. . .and now I fear we must return to the others. Tonight we dine with the Privy Council, and after we must retire separately; the conventions must be honoured. We shall not meet again until we meet in the chapel. I must go to Aunt Conybeare tomorrow morning, and you will be attended before the wedding by Challenor. Henson shall give the bride away, and Aisgill, as is fitting since he first rescued you, shall stand at your side as your best man.'

Her face was full of mischief. 'I am only sorry that Rajah cannot be present. He shall have a new set of plumes, and we shall both visit him after the ceremony so that he may know that we have not forgotten him!'

Chad bowed solemnly. 'It is, as you said to me when we last parted, *au revoir*, and not goodbye. I trust and pray that you may never regret today's work, my gracious lady.'

'Not I,' said Nell, 'and now Aunt Conybeare and Campions must be told that their mistress has found her master.'

After dinner, a formal occasion, all the participants splendidly dressed and the best dinner service — the china from the present given to the third Earl by Catherine the Great of Russia after he had taken her to bed, the silver given him by a Bavarian princess for similar favours, and the great epergne in the centre of the table showing Hercules killing the Hydra, brought home in triumph after a conquest so noble that he never

even named the lady—fetched out in honour of Nell
Tallboys's marriage to her servant.

Afterwards Nell and Chad, equally formal, bowed
and parted to their own quarters, Nell to her splendid
suite of rooms, Chad to his small and humble pair in
the attic under the roof.

Before he went there, he returned to the study, to pick
up his copy of the settlement, to study what he had let
himself in for by marrying Nell.

The door to his rooms was ajar, and someone had lit
the candles there. He raised his eyebrows, walked in, to
discover Henson waiting for him, leaning against a chest
of drawers, the book from Chad's nightstand open in his
hand. It was a copy of *Les Liaisons Dangereuses* in the
original French.

He raised his eyes from it as Chad entered, made no
apology for his presence, merely said coolly, 'So you
read French, too. When did you discover that?'

'Early on,' said Chad. 'It hardly seemed worth
mentioning.'

'Difficult to plumb all your talents,' drawled Henson,
and Chad did not know whether it was praise or
criticism which he was being offered. 'But the one talent
which might benefit you, your personal memory, is still
missing.'

'Yes,' said Chad briefly, 'I am not fooling you, though
the expression on your face suggests you do not necess-
arily believe me.'

'Oh, I believe you,' returned Henson, his face
expressionless. 'Your choice of reading is interesting—
in the circumstances.'

Chad chose to ignore any inference which he might
draw from Henson's suggestion that a novel which dwelt
so constantly on human wickedness and sexual intrigue

might have some point, some connection with Chad's own astonishing rise to fortune. He said instead, 'To what do I owe your visit?'

Henson closed the book, put it carefully down. He was particularly finely dressed, at all points one with the mighty whom he so faithfully served.

'I came to warn you,' he drawled.

'Ah,' said Chad, face watchful. 'I thought your acquiescence in Lady Elinor's wishes odd, in view of your care for her and her interests. Of you all, I would have expected opposition to such a marriage to come from you.'

Henson shrugged his beautifully tailored shoulders. 'And what, my fine young man, would the lady have cared for my opposition? Nothing. She was determined to have you. No, I could only lose by gainsaying her. I have watched you since you came into the house as her secretary, and ——' He paused.

'And?' said Chad, giving him nothing.

'And — and nothing. From the moment you began to recover yourself you revealed a man of education, a man who has undoubtedly been a soldier. There is also no doubt that at great risk to yourself you saved my Countess's life, and for that I am grateful. Nell Tallboys is a remarkable woman; it is a pleasure to serve her. But, on the other hand, who the devil are you? And have *you*, despite what my Countess believes, angled for this match, used the attraction you undoubtedly possess for her to make yourself master of Campions?'

'Guardian, guardian only,' was Chad's answer to that.

'Words,' said Henson. 'You may or may not be as honest as you seem, but if you are not, beware. My duty is to her, and only to you through her. She is Countess, you but her consort, and, if you prove false, why, God help you, for Campions will deal with you, sir, and hardly.'

Rage stirred in Chad. The temper which he usually kept in firm control, the temper which he knew must have played its part in his old life—perhaps, unwisely used, he had sometimes thought, might have brought him to destitution and beggary—rose and filled his throat. His hands clenched.

He mastered himself. His true inclination would have been to seize Henson by the throat, force him to his knees, make him retract the unspoken accusation. Reason told him that the man was a good servant, the best, who sought to protect his mistress from harm.

The calmness of his voice did not deceive Henson; the man who could control Rajah, charm Nell, and charm also the men and women about him, was no tame tiger. The hint of wildness behind the self-control was always there. He shivered a little despite himself as Chad spoke, 'Rest easy, Mr Henson, sir. I shall guard Campions, as I would Lady Elinor, with my life. Do you be careful that you are as honest with both as I intend to be.'

'Bravely spoken,' replied Henson, giving not an inch himself. 'Enough; we know where we stand.' He walked to the door. 'I bid you goodnight, Mr Newcome. From now on I serve you, not you me. I must tell you that the staff of Campions, indoor and out, have been informed of tomorrow's ceremony. Representatives of all parts of the house and estate will be at the chapel; the rest will attend you later, and you will be expected to show yourself and your lady to them, in due form.

'Tomorrow morning Challenor will escort you to the guest suite, and will help you to dress, with the assistance of old Wilson, the late Earl's valet, brought from his retirement to be of service to the late Earl's successor. From what I have seen of you, you will play your part properly. I bid you goodnight, and I hope that your dreams are more pleasant than I hear they usually are.'

He bowed. Chad returned the compliment, saying coolly, 'I know, Mr Henson, that anything you arrange will be both correct and apropos. You need have no fears that I will let my lady and Campions down.'

He was gone, and Chad sat down on the bed, his hands sweating, his whole body racked from the necessity to hold himself in. But, in all honesty, he thought wryly, what could he expect? He had told Nell earlier of the commotion which this strange marriage would cause, and he could not fault Henson for seeking to protect his mistress's interests.

He slept at last, for sleep, not surprisingly, was long in coming, but he did not dream until daybreak, and then his dreams were confused, but not painful, until the last one. He was in a hot and crowded room. He thought that he was drunk. The men around him were laughing and staring; one pulled at his arm, saying, 'Quiet, Chad, quiet,' but he would not be quiet, he would have his say, and improbably, as he started from sleep, it was Nell's name that he was crying out, and where and to whom he said it he did not know.

Nell also could not sleep. First there had been Aunt Conybeare to tell, to ask her to be Nell's matron of honour, to hold her bouquet when the ring was placed on her finger. As she had expected, even Aunt Conybeare's usual placidity was shaken by such momentous news. 'But Newcome,' she had said, bewildered. 'I knew that you liked him, of course, and he saved you. But to marry him!'

'I love him, Aunt,' she had said simply. 'And I had never thought to love anyone.' She did not say that she loved him beyond reason; she did not need to, for even innocent old Aunt Conybeare knew that she would not have married her servant, of unknown origin, unless her passion for him was so strong that it transcended common sense, and the conventions that governed the class to which Nell belonged.

The servant's hall thought the same. 'Wants a man in her bed, a real man, don't she?' being the most common comment, and said admiringly, not sniggeringly. 'Better than Maister Ulric and them pretty boys what have come up here from London. One of us now, you might say.' For Chad, although not a seeker after popularity, was popular. From the moment he had tamed Rajah, he had been accepted, and there were many who connected that event and the marriage. 'Our Nell's a grand lass, and needs a real man to hold her,' being another remark. 'Besides, he's almost a gentleman himself, for all he was taken starving off the moor. You might say that Campions is all he's ever known, seeing that he remembers nothing before he came here.'

The last was the butler's comment, and served as Campions's opinion of the match. The only thing lacking in him being, as young Seth said, 'Pity he's not really a Yorkshireman, but he's a tyke by adoption.'

And so, as a fine March day dawned, Campions prepared for the event which many had feared might never happen—the marriage of its Countess, and the settlement of Malplaquet's lands.

CHAPTER SIXTEEN

NELL had awoken that morning with such a feeling of well-being as she had never experienced before. She stretched herself, lifting her arms above her head, so that her toes almost touched the bottom of the great bed.

She did not wait for Annie to come, but leaped from it, ran to the window, pulled back the curtains, and looked out across the lawns, beyond the giant fountain, where sea-nymphs and dolphins, the latter spouting water to the heavens, frolicked in the kind of joy she was feeling, beyond the grove of trees planted by the third Earl, the giant obelisk commemorating the first Earl's glory, to the moors above them, rising grand and glorious, until they reached the Throne of God itself, far, far beyond her sight — but not her memory.

Oh, she had defeated them all, Chad included! She thought of his dear face when she had finally cornered him, how it had changed from the stern severity it normally wore to the joy and delight he had shown her as they parted in the long gallery, secure in the knowledge that their love was outrageous, but that they were about to fulfil it in honourable marriage.

Yes, Nell Tallboys was about to defy them all. Charles Halstead, when he heard of this, could make further disgraceful bets, tongues would buzz wherever she went — but what of that? She was the lady of Barthwaite, who had married whom she pleased, or the first Earl, who had made his own rules on the battlefield and in life. Tallboyses all, living up to the house's motto, emblazoned on the ribbon which ran below the arms: 'As the beginning, so the end'.

And the arms themselves, the shield which bore three tree stumps, in honour of Ivo. She hugged herself. I shall petition the College of Heralds; I shall have the shield divided, the trees on one side, Rajah rearing on the other, for Rajah is Chad, the strong man who tamed the strong horse — and his Countess. Unknowingly, she echoed the comments of her staff.

Yes, she was the lady of Campions, and today would marry her choice, the first time both parties to a marriage had proposed to one another, she dared swear.

Annie came in, Aunt Conybeare behind her. Annie was carrying a breakfast tray. Aunt Conybeare carried nothing but a grave face. She said what Chad had. 'It is not too late to change your mind, Nell.'

'Change my mind!' Nell had jumped into bed again, was stuffing hot rolls into her mouth, drinking coffee this morning. 'Why should I do that, when I am marrying my heart's desire?'

Aunt Conybeare sighed. Nell had never looked before as she now did. It was almost, outrageously, as though her lover had already pleasured her, and, had not Aunt Conybeare known for sure that both partners to this mismatch had spent the night chastely apart, she would have thought the opposite. There would be no shy bride in Campions chapel today, that was for sure!

Nell's joy continued, through the bath, its water full of scents, and through the dressing for the ceremony. The parson had arrived shortly after dawn, sent for by Henson, and after she was dressed she went into her drawing-room, so that the bed could be stripped, new linen put on it, herbs strewn between the sheets, a new fire lit in the grate, all to celebrate Campions's proudest day for many years.

Annie had put a little bag under the pillow. 'And what is *that* for?' Nell had said.

Annie blushed. 'It is to bless the bed,' she said shyly. 'Granny Goodman says that the Mother will give you a son, after this night's work, if a virgin places it there, and the bride goes virgin to her man.'

'A son!' Nell was enraptured. She, who had scorned men and marriage, could hardly bear to wait for her true love's child. She knew that when Annie and old Granny Goodman spoke of the Mother they meant the Earth Mother of the old religion which had never really died out in these parts. A century earlier and Granny Goodman might have been in danger of being burned as a witch. Now, she prescribed her herbs and simples to the suffering, and blessed marriages, high and low.

The thought of a child changed Nell's mood. She became girlish and trembling, not the madcap who had risen with the dawn. Aunt Conybeare, who had left to eat her own breakfast, returned to find her niece as modest as a bride might be, except that every now and then a fit of such delight passed over her that her face took on the shining aspect of her early morning ecstasy.

Finally, carrying a spray of early spring flowers, brought from the hothouse, Aunt Conybeare, resplendent in deep blue satin, with Nell herself in cream, a pearl circlet in her hair, a small string of pearls around her neck, Chad's handkerchief tucked into the lemon silk sash at her waist, walked downstairs to the great salon where Henson, Challenor, the butler and the senior servants of the house, including her housekeeper, magnificent in black satin, awaited her.

They bowed as low when she walked in as they would

have done had she been marrying Britain's premier
Duke, instead of her former stable hand.

Henson, who seemed to have constituted himself as a
kind of benevolent grand vizier, despite his private
thoughts, said, 'Madam, I am to tell you that, if you are
prepared, everything is in train. The groom awaits you
in the chapel, the priest is at the altar. The ring and the
book are ready. If you will take my arm, I shall escort
you there.'

He bowed low, low, and when he straightened up his
eyes were hard on her, and the message was Aunt
Conybeare's, 'It is not too late,' but Nell knew what she
wanted, and, shy and trembling although she now was,
all her bold hardihood quite gone, she was a girl again,
the girl Henson remembered from his first day at
Campions when he had walked into the Earl's study to
see her standing by old Malplaquet's side.

'You know the way, Henson,' she said. 'And today it
is your privilege to give away your Countess and. . .
revive Malplaquet's line, which otherwise would die
with me.' For she had no faith that Ulric would do
anything but waste himself and the estate.

Together, they walked through the great house, past
everything which Nell had known all her life, her staff
behind her, past lines of her other servants, the
occasional, 'God bless you, my lady,' offered by the
bolder spirit.

And there, before her, was the paved forecourt to the
chapel, where another group of servants was set, waiting
for those behind her to take their places, and there at
the altar *he* stood, Aisgill beside him, magnificent in his
livery as master of the horse, a livery worn only on great
occasions such as this. Nothing, nothing, was to be
omitted from this wedding, all was to be done in proper

form, until finally, on Henson's arm, Aunt Conybeare behind her, she walked towards Chad, and they were there together, the wondering parson before them, Challenor now at the pianoforte to play for them.

Joy contained, her face as white as his, bride and groom suddenly nervous, bold spirits though they normally were, faced one another, for life, as it were, he tall, his black curls clustering about his head, wearing a fine suit once worn by Nell's grandfather, possessing neither name nor fortune, only the manifold talents of which Henson had spoken.

Nell, for her part, had been granted a strange beauty, which came from knowing that she was loved, that she had found a mate for whom she could feel respect, as well as passion, who had held off when he could have taken her on the library floor as though she had been a poor girl from the village, but who had preferred to leave her, so that she and he might keep their honour intact.

The service began, and when the priest issued his challenge to any who might gainsay the match there was silence, and then they were man and wife, neither voice faltering, and when Chad pushed on Nell's finger the marriage ring of the Tallboyses the expression on his face and his smouldering blue eyes told Nell all that she wanted to know.

And then they processed out of the chapel. Tables had been spread with food and drink in the long gallery, and the only guests were Nell's people — the marriage was a marriage for Campions and no one else. Bride and groom and the Privy Council ate nothing, but drank a toast proposed by the butler, and enthusiastically seconded by every voice.

Nell thought that the long day would never end; her

face ached from smiling. Later, as she had promised, they visited the stables, and Nell's small bouquet was hung over Rajah's stable door.

The day was fine, and hand in hand they walked the length of the gardens to stare together at the moor where Chad had been found, a barely conscious derelict, and now it and Campions were his, as much as they could be anybody's.

But still they were not private. Tenant farmers came in, to see their lady and her chosen husband, until at last evening arrived, and now they were to dine alone for the first time, in the great state dining hall, in the same splendour as the night before, but now as the Countess and her husband.

For a moment, they were alone, and Chad embraced her, kissed her cheek, saying softly, 'A pledge for tonight, Mrs Newcome,' and then the door opened, and the servants entered with the food, and facing one another, absurdly, at each end of the table, they ate the fine fare set before them, more to honour the staff who had prepared it than to satisfy their non-existent hunger. The true hunger they felt was for one another.

At the meal's end, the double doors were thrown open by the butler, and Henson entered, the Privy Council at his heels, carrying bottles of wine, for yet another toast.

'It has long been the custom in this part of the world,' he announced, his eyes for once merry, 'for bride and groom to be publicly put to bed before their servants and dependants. But these, I think, are more civilised times. We shall not demand that of you, my lady Countess. Instead, you shall have Campions to light your way to bed.'

He put down his glass, beckoned to them both, said, 'Come,' and Nell, wondering what she was about to see, walked from the dining-room into the great hall from which the stairs rose for full two storeys of the house.

Before her, to the stairs, was an alleyway of servants, each carrying a candle. On every step two servants stood, also holding candles, and along the landing, and all the way to the state bedroom where Nell and Chad were to sleep, Nell's lonely days being over, servants lined the way, candles in their hands, smiling and lighting them, as Henson had said, to their bed.

Nell felt tears pricking her eyes, and each man or woman said as she passed, 'God bless you both, and Campions, too,' until finally they stood at the great oak doors, which Henson threw open, bowing — and, at last, they were alone.

Nell sank on to the bed, eyes alight, as though the flames through which she had passed had found their home there.

'You see, my love, you are accepted; Campions welcomes you. Let the rest of the world think what it will — here we are at home.'

Chad stood for a moment, looking down at her. The day seemed unreal. Any moment he expected to open his eyes to find himself — where? At this point of fulfilled love and triumph his lack of a name and past seemed the doubly cruel; he felt that he had nothing to offer his mistress, and he said so.

'No,' said Nell, passionately, opening her arms to him. 'You offer me yourself, and what is better than that? Oh, I am unmaidenly, I should be shrinking. Perhaps,' and she coloured, 'that will come later.'

Nell knew that she was not being strictly truthful. Whether it was the effect of the long day, or the many eyes upon them which knew exactly what they were going to do on the great bed, once she and Chad were

alone together—just as though the pair of them were
Princess and Rajah, performing for Campions—she did
not know. She only knew that the maidenly reserve
which she had felt for so long and which had flown
away from the moment in which she had first met Chad
had returned some time during the wedding ceremony
and was with her again.

She looked up at him almost fearfully. She felt her
legs weak beneath her, sank on to the bed, and everything about her alerted the man before her to what had
happened.

His viking, his valkyrie had gone; the passionate
woman passionately demanding fulfilment from her
mate had disappeared. Nell Newcome was what Nell
Tallboys had never been with him, the shy virgin, who
loved her new husband, but was suddenly aware of
what that love meant.

Chad went down on one knee, reined in his own pent-
up passion, the desire to take her immediately into his
arms and begin to make love to her at last, took her
hand, said gently, 'Do not be afraid, Nell,' and for once
she did not spark back at him as she would have done
in the past, but looked at him, her great eyes full of a
loving demand for his consideration.

'I love you, and I would do nothing to distress you.'
He hesitated, then added, 'Suppose I go to the dressing-
room and change there, while you ready yourself for me
here?' He saw, in retrospect, that it might have been
better if Annie had stayed, to help her to prepare for
him, and he had come to her later, but the ceremony
which had preceded their entry into the room had pre-
empted that.

Nell looked up at him, grateful for his consideration,

his understanding that what had happened today had temporarily quenched the fire within her.

'Yes,' she answered him, and then almost with a sob, 'Oh, you will think me a fool, after all I have said and done, to behave to you like this, but. . .' and she shook her head.

'No,' he said, 'no,' and, as he reached the door to the dressing-room, 'Oh, Nell, you are as precious to me in your modesty as you were in your pride, and I hope to prove that to you, if not tonight, then another.'

He was gone, and Nell was alone with what she had done. Oh, she had no regrets, and the way in which he had reacted to her untoward fit of the vapours, once they were alone together, told her that her choice of him had been no mistake, so considerate was he of her.

She rose, slowly began to take off her beautiful dress, until she stood naked before the roaring fire, which cast its rosy glow on her, so that she was not a marble woman, but a glowing nymph whose image she saw briefly in the long mirror before she took her night-rail from the bed, to hide away what she would so soon share with him.

Nell debated anxiously whether to enter the bed, or sit on its side, and laughed at herself a little — what matter, either way? But to enter the bed might look as though she were trying to hide from him, and Nell Newcome must not be more fearful than Nell Tallboys had been.

He knocked on the door, another concession to her new-found shyness, and she called, 'Come in,' to see him enter, dressed in an overgown which had belonged to her grandfather, a magnificent brocaded thing, and the familiar sight of it reassured her, and when, after extinguishing several of the candles which stood about

the room, so that they were bathed in a dim red-gold
glow from candle and firelight combined, he came and
sat by her, she said, with something of her old fire, 'Oh,
I sometimes think that I fell in love with you because
you so resemble Grandfather, not in looks and manner,
but in body and carriage, the man he must have been in
youth.'

Chad took her face in his hands, but gently, 'I see
that my fiery lady is back with me again.'

Nell blushed beneath his gaze, the touch of his hands
having its usual effect on her. 'Not entirely,' she said,
shyness still with her. 'I am stupid with love for you,
cannot really believe in what I, we, have done.'

'Believe it,' he said, 'believe it,' and then, 'Nell, my
darling, I may have no memory, but I do know this. I
am a man who has not made love to a woman for a long
time, and I will try to be kind to you, but I desire you
so passionately that the body may subdue the mind. I
will try not to hurt you too much, or frighten you by the
fierceness of my passion for you, but. . .' And at the look
she gave him, passion and innocence combined, he said
thickly, before bending to kiss her, 'Oh, you do understand me, I am sure, and will forgive me if. . .'

'Hush,' said Nell, beginning to drown in sensation as
his kisses awoke her sleeping senses. 'There will be
nothing to forgive, nothing.'

'At last,' he said, and she echoed the words, but he
was so gentle and so slow with her that his very holding
back excited her, as first his kisses were light, innocent
things, ranging around her face, her neck, before he
found her mouth, and even then the first of them were
like a child's, so gentle, until suddenly, giving a harsh
sob, he forced her mouth open below his, and they
kissed as they had done in the annexe, his tongue

meeting hers, and hers welcoming it, so that, as then, fire ran through Nell, and she grasped him by his thick black curls, pulling his head closer to her, to force him even further into her mouth, as though they might consummate themselves there.

By now, his hands were busy about her, unbuttoning her nightgown, to find the treasures of her bosom, his hands on her breasts, stroking, his mouth following, and her hands were a reflection of his, loosening and untying the bedgown, and even in her passion her wit returned to her, and she muttered as she found his bare chest, the black curls thick on it there, too, 'So far, so good, my darling,' to hear his choking laugh, as her hands grasped and stroked him there, finding his nipples, like hers, already erect.

'Oh, Nell, you witch, my witch.' His voice was hoarse and shaking, his hands now ranging around her naked body, his mouth on her breasts, her own hands wildly stroking him, finding his sex, holding it hot and throbbing in her hand, so that as his hands found her buttocks he stopped, body shaking, to say, 'Oh, God, Nell, no, not there; it's difficult enough for me not to take you before you're ready as it is.'

Nell hardly knew herself; the need for him, contained over the weeks since they had denied themselves in the annexe, the daily necessity to renounce such thoughts of him, had taken their toll. She was more than ready to receive him, on fire all over, her body an aching void to be filled.

'Oh, no, Chad, I cannot wait, either, no need to deny yourself,' and, her mouth now on his, he having turned her above him for a moment, he swung her beneath him, stroking her inward thighs, until he pulled his mouth away to gasp,

'Be a soldier, my dearest girl, bite the bullet, for a quick hurt is kinder than a slow one,' and with one hard thrust he was in her, and they were one.

And being one was so satisfactory that the pain was worth it, even though she cried out at the shock, so that he began to draw back, until she clutched at him, crying, 'No, you are mine now, Chad, we are one, not two, and that is all I want.'

After that, for both of them, sensation took over; thought and coherent speech flew away. Countess and secretary disappeared, and the great bed consecrated their love as they reached fulfilment together, Chad Newcome pleasuring his Countess so thoroughly that, climax achieved in a great wave of pleasure, Nell was near to fainting from it.

Chad's own pleasure was so strong that his memory, long dormant, almost revived, so that in the aftermath of calling Nell's name he knew that, although he had made love to other women, never before had he felt the satisfaction he had just achieved with this one.

Beneath him, Nell, who had been laughing for sheer joy, now, in the final transports of all, long and slow, was suddenly weeping, her tears — born not of sorrow but of joy run beyond its bounds — slowly falling.

Her sobbings alarmed Chad, who tightened his grip on her, raining tender kisses on her tear-stained cheeks, pausing only to say, 'Oh, my love, my darling, what a brute I am, I have hurt you. Forgive me.'

'No, no,' said Nell, stroking the anguished face he bent over her. 'A little pain at first, but, later, what I felt, what you made me feel, was beyond anything.'

She kissed him back, and, reassured, he cradled her in his arms as though she were a child, kissing and stroking her gently, until she put a finger on his mouth to stop him, saying mischievously, 'I liked it so much, pray tell me, is it possible that we can do it again soon, and often?'

Chad's shout of laughter was spontaneous. 'If you look at me like that, and say such things, you will rouse me to such efforts as Hercules might envy! Give me but leave to hold you like this a little, and your pleasure shall be mine. You are as generous in love as you are in life, my own.' For she had given herself to him, and to helping him to secure his pleasure, as she had given herself to Campions and its people.

They had both given and taken, they had shared their love in mind and body both, and their mutual pleasure had been so strong because, although Nell and Chad had disappeared when they became one, they still gave and shared, and when they were separate again the knowledge of the one thing remained with them.

Spirit had been involved as well, and, because of that, although their first pleasure was over, he had the impulse to stroke and soothe his partner as he had never done before, so that gradually their sweating, panting selves, for two athletic bodies had celebrated their strength, were slowly brought back to peace and harmony.

'The calm before a new storm,' he whispered in her ear. 'That was merely the first of many such delights.'

'Oh,' said Nell, laying her head on his shoulder. 'That was even better than I might have hoped. Such joy, such bliss, I wonder anyone is ever out of bed.'

'If every man had the pleasure of loving such a beautiful body as yours,' was his answer to that, 'then I would agree with you.'

Shyly, her old fears about her lack of looks reviving

again, she said, 'Unlike my face, then,' only for him to cover her mouth with his big hand.

'You are the most beautiful woman in the world to me, Nell, and, have no fear, few look more strong and true. I have had enough of empty prettiness.' And where did *that* come from? he wondered, for the thought to disappear in the glory which his words had evoked on her face.

And later, when they had made love again, this time slowly, so that she had screamed her pleasure at the end, clutching him so fiercely that her nails scored his back, and she lay, half-asleep, a satisfied houri in his arms, she whispered to him, 'No regrets, then?' to hear him say,

'For me, Nell, none, but for you? Even in my pleasure I know that gossip will follow you everywhere, the Countess who married her stable hand. Only the thought of what we have shared tonight, and what I hope we share in the future, life and love both, comforts me.'

Nell was suddenly all proud fury. She sat up, magnificent in her nakedness, rosy in the fire's ebbing glow. 'Gossip!' she said fiercely. 'How can you be so foolish? It is not like you. I have done nothing, nothing until I fell in love with you, and yet gossip has always followed me everywhere. You know as well as I do that Charles Halstead made his shameless bet about me when I was still virgin, unawakened and untouched. What could be worse than that?'

For no good reason that he could think of, Chad's breathing became short and painful when Nell repeated this tale, first heard several months ago. It had affected him badly then, and did so again.

'Oh, Nell,' he said hoarsely, 'how can you trouble

yourself about what such a brute as he must be says about you —?' only to be interrupted by Nell's kiss on his mouth, and her drawing away to say,

'Oh, come, my love, only a moment ago you were worried about people blowing on my reputation, and now you tell me not to worry about Halstead's bet. Where is the logic which you so often show? Of which Henson so often complains?'

'He does?' asked Chad, suddenly sidetracked.

Nell rolled on top of him, kissing him whenever she reached a comma or full stop in what she was saying, her whole face and body amused, provocative again. 'Oh, yes. He once said that you must have been a divinity student gone to the bad, you were so able to rout him with such pitiless and carefully reasoned arguments based on such undeniable premises.'

'Now, now,' said Chad, imitating her, but giving her two kisses at each stop, 'not only are you funning, my darling, but of one thing I am sure. I was never a divinity student, even one gone to the bad.'

'Well, all I can say is that if,' remarked Nell, 'a divinity student gone to the bad is as good at pleasing a woman as you are we shall have to arrange special examinations in which the prize will be failing, not succeeding!'

'For that suggestion, Mrs Newcome, you shall be properly punished,' said her husband, 'and the victim shall choose its manner.'

'When, and if, you fully recover,' said Nell thoughtfully, stroking his broad chest, running her fingers again through the black curls there, 'such a *satisfactory* body you have, my darling, a regular work of art —'

'As you saw in the stable yard,' interrupted her spouse, equally naughtily.

'Oh, yes,' said Nell, not at all ashamed, 'I'm sure that from that moment on I was determined to have you in bed with me so that I could do — this,' and she tweaked a vital portion of his anatomy. 'Why, I do believe, Mr Newcome, you are almost ready to begin to administer punishment! Which of us deserves the praise? You for your virility or me for my powers of temptation — ? Oh! Chad!' For he had rolled her beneath him, and the whole delightful business had started again.

'And I was wicked in the stable yard,' he said hoarsely, before all speech stopped once more, 'for I was so entranced by you and your delighted face — yes, it was delighted, do not deny it — that all my decent modesty flew away, and I was slow to cover myself!'

Later, much later in the night, when, after that final bout, sleep had claimed them both, Chad slowly surfaced for a moment, to find his body lax after loving, Nell in his arms, sleeping quiet against him, body and tongue still at last. He had been dreaming, and dreams of happiness and fulfilment, not the fear and horror which sometimes came to him of a night. How satisfactory it was to make love to a woman who matched him physically, And why, he thought drowsily, did I always believe I liked little, clinging women? Isabella and Julia were both little, and they were similar in their ways, quite unlike Nell, both flutteringly modest and submissive on the outside, but whores inside, whereas Nell — Nell is the opposite, frank and fearless in manner, but at heart a truly modest, good woman.

He sat up suddenly, wide awake, his heart thudding, but instinctively careful, even so, to try not to disturb his sleeping wife. Isabella and Julia! Who were they? He had for a moment remembered them, and then they were gone, into the dark, and, strive as he might, he could not bring them back.

Chad lay down again. Nell turned in his arms, said, half-awake herself, 'Chad?' questioningly.

'Nothing, my love. Nothing. Rest easy,' for whatever else he had forgotten he knew that he had never felt like this before for any woman, and not simply in the business of sex and bed, but for the whole of living, and that his lost memory had surfaced to tell him so.

Nell's warmth against him, her love freely and frankly expressed, his own sense of having met, at last, his other half, was so strong that the memory could not disturb him, and he slept with Nell in his arms, and both their dreaming was of love crowned, love fulfilled.

CHAPTER SEVENTEEN

EVERYTHING had changed — and nothing had changed. Chad's desk still stood by Nell's, and he worked there daily, but not as her secretary, as her partner. The Privy Council met each week, and Chad, as Nell, was one of them — but the one to whom Nell listened the most. His judgement, as Henson grudgingly admitted, was sound. He proposed some changes, and all were useful, and needed. They involved not only the running of the stud, but the manner in which the estates were administered. He did not put them forward all at once, but was tactful, so that Henson, who had been fearful that, once married, Nell's upstart husband might show himself in colours far removed from those he had worn as stable hand and secretary, was reassured: Campions looked to be in safe hands.

More, Chad suggested to Nell that she lived at Campions too much; that Malplaquet's other lands and homes needed to see more of their mistress, but although she argued with him a little she at last agreed.

'For,' he said, after examining the accounts which had come in from Wroxton and Sheveborough, and the Welsh estates, 'I think that not all may be well there. Agents left to their own devices may grow careless — and greedy.'

Henson was compelled to echo this advice, and was ruefully pleased to see that Nell intended to take it — because Chad had put it forward.

'Grandfather spent most of his time at Campions,'

she said, a trifle defiantly, one evening, as they sat alone
before the fire, the Privy Council, who now dined with
them twice-weekly, having left. Aunt Conybeare had
taken her leave shortly after the wedding to visit her
sister, she said, adding,

'You no longer need me now, as chaperon or companion. You have your husband to guard you.'

She had never criticised the marriage, was unfailingly
polite and kind to Chad, but Nell was not sure what she
truly thought.

'You will come back, dear Aunt Honey-bear,' she had
said.

'Perhaps,' said Aunt Conybeare. 'When the children
arrive, you may need an old woman then.'

Chad, who was setting out the backgammon board,
looked up at her and smiled. 'You have said yourself
that your grandfather was not always wise in his rule.'

'Sophistry,' Nell flung at him playfully, 'to turn what
one says against the sayer.'

He laughed at that, and put out a hand to her. 'Come,
your turn to win.'

'And that,' said Nell, 'will be a day to run up the
union flag, unless you are chivalrous enough to let me
win — which I do not want.'

'Brave girl,' replied her husband affectionately. 'For
that sentiment you will be suitably rewarded.'

Their marriage was, of course, a scandal. The Riding
visited, to stare at him, his size and strength, his good
manners, and his equally good speech. 'A gentleman,
down on his luck,' was the usual verdict. 'But to marry
him!'

Chad, and Nell too, bore it patiently. It was inevi-
table. Sir Chesney did not come immediately; he was
away, and the news was late in reaching both him and

Ulric. Ulric had left the Riding to visit his mother's family in Ireland, he had said in an ill-scrawled letter, and did not know how long he would be gone.

He would return soon enough, was Nell's wry reaction — when he heard the bad news. Sir Chesney's visit came when they had been married for a fortnight, and were still the wonder of the North, as Nell frequently joked.

Chad was at the stables, working out Rajah, a Rajah who was pleased because they so often took him out on the moors, Nell and Chad riding together, unsupervised these days, doing everything together, and, if the world disapproved of them, Campions did not.

Nell, working in her room, heard the noise of his arrival, and sighed when the butler told her that Sir Chesney was in the Turkish room.

She put off her brown holland apron, to reveal beneath it the modish dress which she now always wore, her hair carefully coiffed, feet perfectly shod, face soft, the very picture of a satisfied woman, and went to join him; she hardly dared think that he would welcome her, any more than she welcomed him.

He turned as she entered. 'Nell! I ask you to tell me that this story is not true. You cannot have married your stable hand!'

She kissed his warm cheek as though this were a normal visit. 'Not my stable hand, my secretary,' she said calmly.

He dismissed her chopped logic. 'Piff-paff, Nell. It's all one, and you know it. How could you do such a thing? What would your grandfather have said? Do you know what the world is saying? Such a marriage cannot stand.'

'Come, Uncle,' replied Nell, still calm. 'The deed is

done and I am happy with it. He is a good man, and even Henson approves of him, and you know what Henson is.'

'Oh, by God, damn Henson; who's he to decide who Malplaquet marries? You are wanton, my girl, seduced by a strong body and ——'

'Do not say handsome face,' responded Nell incorrigibly. 'My husband has many attributes, but he is not handsome.'

'You have taken leave of your senses and your modesty both,' shouted her uncle, now thoroughly roused to anger. 'A pity that we are no longer allowed to thrash our womenfolk. A good beating twice a week would soon restore you to your senses.'

Before Nell, eyes furious, could respond, a cold voice spoke from the door. Chad had returned, to be told of Sir Chesney's arrival, to hear him shouting even before he opened the door, to be in time to register his displeasure by threatening Nell.

He walked over to his embattled Countess, slipped an arm around her. True, he could never be called conventionally handsome, but even Sir Chesney had to recognise his physical power and the air of effortless authority which had returned to him permanently on the day he married Nell.

'I allow no man to speak to my wife in such a fashion,' he said, his voice ice and fire, the voice his men had heard in the Spanish mountains, and on the night before battle. 'Unless you are civil to her both in and out of her presence, you are not welcome in this house, sir.'

'Why, you. . .' Words failed Sir Chesney, faced with the man himself, standing there so cold and sure. 'Who are you to tell me whether I may or may not visit Campions, see my niece?'

'My husband, Uncle.' Nell was as cool as Chad, and, to Sir Chesney, equally infuriating. 'I do not wish to lose you, Uncle. I have few relatives, God knows, but if you wish to see me you must respect the fact that I freely chose the man by my side to be my partner, to run my lands with me, to father my children, and nothing you can say or do will alter that. Your choice, Uncle. Go or stay, as you please, but I will not allow *my* choice or my husband to be traduced.'

'You are shameless, madam, shameless,' almost gobbled her uncle. 'I shall have this piece of trash you have chosen to elevate from the gutter investigated. Better for you to have married Ulric than for you to do this.'

'I give you leave to go, Uncle.' Nell was still calm, but shaking a little. 'You will not, I am sure, wish to remain here longer, and, much though it pains me to see you go, I cannot have my husband miscalled. As he protects me, I will protect him.'

'Protects you!' was Sir Chesney's answer to that. 'Pillage you more like. Mark my words, my girl. You will rue the day you married him.'

'I am not your girl, Uncle, I never was, and my judgement tells me I have done aright. But right or wrong, done is done, as we say here, and I joy in the doing. I am sorry that you have had an unnecessary journey. Should you wish to eat before you travel home, I will arrange for you to dine alone, so that we do not disturb you by our presence.'

He saw that there was no shaming her, no shaking her.

'God damn it, madam, the food would choke me. What a work you have made of this. What can have possessed you, I ask myself?'

Nell could not resist the opportunity offered. 'Why,

Uncle,' she whispered sweetly, 'I did but follow the Tallboys motto: "As the beginning, so the end". What was good enough for the lady of Barthwaite is good enough for me.'

'You were like to have given him a fit,' said Chad, a little ruefully, when he had stamped out, 'but I could not allow him to speak to you so in your own home.'

'Nor I hear you miscalled,' sighed Nell. 'You were right, of course, when you foresaw trouble. But I cannot allow it to affect me. I am sorry to have made an enemy of him, yet Ulric troubles me even more. I cannot think what he will say or do when he finally hears that I am married—and to whom.'

'Nothing useful,' said Guy Shadwell dispiritedly to his father, 'and really, after all this time, not surprising. Only an innkeeper in South Nottinghamshire who thought that Shad "might" have passed through last autumn. He seemed to remember Vinnie—made them all laugh, trust Vinnie—and if Shad's missing, where's Vinnie? He was always watching Shad, guarding him—that was quite a joke, only it ain't one now.'

'What I expected,' sighed his father. 'So it seems that he disappeared somewhere between South Nottinghamshire and Glen Ruadh, which leaves a lot of country to cover after nearly seven months. And the carriage and horses—what happened to them?'

'Attacked by footpads somewhere lonely,' hazarded Guy bitterly. 'After all he went through in the war, surviving that dreadful wound, to disappear somewhere in England—or Scotland—and be lost without a trace.'

'I'll not give up.' The Earl rose, his face distraught. 'I cannot believe that I shall never be able to see him again, ask his forgiveness for thirty lost years. I cannot refrain from thinking of him. I ask myself why it was I disliked him so much for so long. Perhaps it was because he was always so much his own man, whereas I now think Frederick always consciously sought to please me. The Duke asked after him yesterday, said he was sorry that he was lost to the army. I nearly told him that Shad——' the first time that Guy had heard his father use the affectionate nickname '—was lost to life, but I will not give up hope. The search must go on. See to it, Guy.'

It was Guy who was despondent now; he thought his father's hope was based on a desperate desire to make up to Shad for the cruel indifference he had shown to him all his life. He left, to prepare to visit again the old ex-Runner whom he had employed in the attempt to trace his lost brother.

The Earl sat at his desk after Guy had gone, his head in his hands. Despite his brave words to Guy, who he knew mourned his brother sincerely, he had no real hope that Shad might be found after all this time.

His secretary put his head around the door. 'My lord?'

'Yes.' The Earl lifted his head—life must go on. 'Yes, what is it?'

'The Runner is back, my lord; says he needs to speak to you urgently.'

'The Runner? What Runner? Guy is dealing with him.'

'Not that one, my lord. The one who came before Christmas about Lord Halstead's rifle. The man you refused to see then—I spoke to him. He insists that he needs to speak to you personally, no one else will do.'

How wrong he had been to refuse to see the Runner. Halstead's rifle might offer some clue to his disappear-

ance. Anything to do with Halstead must be investigated, my lord thought. 'Send him in,' he said curtly.

Cully Jackson, who had been waiting in the ante-
room, carrying the mysterious rifle in its leather case,
was not abashed at the prospect of meeting such a great
man as Lord Clermont. On the contrary, he stared
about him, taking in the splendid room with the trained
eye of a man used to summing up his surroundings for
his professional purposes.

The study was superb, bookshelves in the bays on
each side of a hearth elaborate in white marble, nymphs
holding up its mantelshelf. Above the hearth was a giant
painting, which he offered only a cursory inspection —
neither the books nor the painting were of real interest
to him; the man standing behind the desk was. He drew
in a long breath, let it out again. He knew that he had
seen this man before, or someone younger, very like
him. One mystery, he was sure, would have been solved
by the time that he left the room. But he was wary, was
Cully; he had to make sure.

'My lord,' he began, 'I am sorry to trouble you and
your office about this matter again.'

The Earl put up his hand. 'You are right to do so. I
should have made it my business to see you before. Is
that my son's rifle you carry?'

Jackson lifted the rifle from its leather case, handed it
to my lord. 'With respect, you may tell me, sir.'

The man opposite took the rifle, inspected it carefully,
said slowly, 'This rifle belonged to my son. His initials
are there, engraved beneath his Viscount's coronet. I
remember it.' He looked up, his face ravaged. 'He
showed it to me once when. . .when we were on good
terms. It almost certainly went with him on his journey
north last autumn. He bought it from his best friend

who was later killed at Waterloo, and treasured it because of that. He would not lightly have parted with it. And now he is lost, almost certainly dead, I fear, and how the rifle came into your possession is something which you must explain to me.'

My lord's face disturbed Jackson. He thought that he knew why. He had not been on the best of his terms with his heir, but now that he thought that his son was likely dead. . . He looked away from naked grief to stare more closely at the painting over the fireplace.

His stare held. He knew at once that his search was over, and that my lord's grief was misplaced. But why, and how, the rifle had come into the possession of the dead thief and would-be murderer, and my lord's son was — what he was, Jackson did not know, but was sure that he could find out.

'Forgive me,' he said. 'The question may seem strange to you. But is that painting there,' and he indicated the portrait over the hearth, 'your son, who is missing?'

The Earl was surprised; it was his turn to stare a little at Jackson. 'Indeed,' he said, 'that is my son Charles, Viscount Halstead, done after he came home from the wars, when he had recovered from his wounds. Yes, that is my worthy son,' he said painfully, 'whom I spent years neglecting for my unworthy son. I am rightly served that I lost him before I found him.'

'A cavalryman?' asked Jackson, still staring at the painting.

'Indeed,' said the Earl, turning to look at the portrait, which hurt him every time he passed it. 'A good one, they tell me. A wonder with horses and at commanding men. Not so fortunate with women.'

'Oh, I wouldn't say that, my lord,' offered Jackson with a sly grin, referring to the last part of my lord's judgement on his son, 'but, I agree, a wonder with horses.' He thought of Chad Newcome, the man without a memory, last seen controlling the uncontrollable Rajah in the riding school at Campions.

For the sumptuous painting by Sir Thomas Lawrence, flaming in its glory above the hearth, was of Chad Newcome, but a Chad Newcome whom Campions had never known.

He was standing, straight-backed and tall, face stern, magnificent in full regimentals, black curls blowing in the breeze, his left hand on his sabre, his right hand holding a superb white horse. His breast blazed with decorations, including a giant star. The bright blue eyes gazing down at Jackson he had last seen some weeks ago, and like Chad Newcome's were those of a man of pride, will and astonishing self-control.

The Earl's voice broke into his reverie. 'You admire the painting, I see.'

Jackson turned, said coolly, London in his speech, 'Yes, but I admire the man more.'

'You have met my son?' The Earl's voice carried incredulity.

'Yes,' returned Jackson, suddenly man to man; Earls and thief takers had no place here. This man was grieving for what he thought was lost — but how would he take the truth? 'I beg pardon, my lord, for my effrontery, as you will see it, if I ask you to sit down before I speak to you of your son and where he may be found, although the finding may be painful to you, and what it will be to him I cannot even guess.'

He held the Earl with the eyes which had frightened thieves into confession, and consigned murderers to the gallows, so that the Earl slowly sank into his chair, and

began to listen, in mounting shock, to what Jackson had
to tell him.

Guy had been sent for, caught as he was about to leave
to initiate further search for Shad.

'And Shad — Halstead — is alone, you say,' said Guy,
'and does not know who he is, only that he was Shad,
which, of course, they translated into Chad, and he did
not know enough to correct them? And where, then, is
Vinnie, his faithful shadow and protector?'

'Shad?' said Jackson, for up to now the Earl and his
son had spoken only of Halstead.

'Yes,' said Guy, 'he was so nicknamed from a boy,
Charles Shadwell, you see — Shad.'

'And Vinnie, you said. Who and what was he?'

'Shad's factotum, old sergeant, valet, groom, man of
all work. They'd saved one another's lives in the war.
He would never, living, desert Shad.'

'You're sure that he was with him?' asked Jackson —
everything must be double-checked in his line of work.

'Quite sure,' replied Guy. 'I saw them drive off, and
it was Vinnie who was remembered in the last trace we
have of them.'

'All I know,' said Jackson, 'is that Chad, Lord
Halstead, as I believe him, was found alone, starving,
half-naked, mind and memory gone, wandering on the
moors. It's my guess that they were set on, robbed,
Vinnie killed, Lord Halstead not quite finished off,
horses and possessions, including the rifle, stolen by a
gang led by the thief who later tried to kill Lady
Malplaquet.'

Even in his relief that Shad still lived, Guy could not
help laughing. 'And what a turn-up that is,' he

exclaimed, 'to be saved and employed by Nell Tallboys, of all people!'

'Oh,' said Jackson with a grin, 'there's more to it than that. He became her secretary, and, begging your pardon, sir——' he turned to the Earl, who had sat silent, listening '—he and the lady are sweet on one another. So sweet that he gave his notice, and is due to leave any day—doing the honourable thing, you see. We'd best hurry north, the young gentleman and I, to catch him before he disappears again.'

Jackson had no knowledge of what had happened at Campions since he left—the proposal and the marriage.

'Sweet on Nell Tallboys!' Guy was incredulous. 'Even more of a turn-up. And you're sure he has no knowledge of who he is?'

'Quite sure,' said Jackson.

'Poor Shad,' said Guy obscurely, thinking of the scene at Watier's the night before Shad left, and his oft-repeated statements that the last person he would ever marry would be Nell Tallboys!

The Earl rose. 'We owe you our thanks, Mr Jackson. You have given us hope. And this Chad, you say, who you think is my son, saved Lady Malplaquet from an assassin, worked as a stable hand, and then as her secretary—and that they. . .favoured one another?'

'Indeed, my lord,' said Jackson with a grin. 'I taxed him with it, and got half killed for my pains. A man of honour, your son, for so I believe Mr Chad Newcome to be.'

'Well, Guy shall go north with you,' said the Earl, ringing the bell for his secretary, 'to check whether your belief is correct, but what he will do if Charles's memory is still gone he will have to decide when he meets him.' He paused and for the first time his stern old face cracked into a smile, albeit a grim one. 'I can tell you one thing, Mr Jackson; if my son does recover his memory to discover that he is. . .sweet on Nell Tallboys, that shock will be a profound one, too!'

CHAPTER EIGHTEEN

NELL found that each day as a new wife brought its own pleasures. She and Chad, who had now been married for a month, an anniversary which they had happily celebrated during the previous night, were due to visit one of Nell's properties situated in north Nottinghamshire, an old hunting lodge-cum-country house known as Penny's Hall. Word had been sent ahead that my lady and her new husband would be expected to arrive on the Friday afternoon, that their baggage would come by coach and cart, and they would ride there, suitably attended by grooms and outriders.

Nell had protested at the state in which she was to travel, but Chad had agreed with Henson and Aisgill that she should not only be protected — the outriders would be armed — but also that the people at Penny's Hall would be flattered by their Countess honouring them so, after all these years without a visit from the family.

'Depend upon it,' Nell said ruefully, 'the place will be shabby and damp.'

'And when did such things trouble you, Nell Newcome?' said Chad, giving her an absent kiss; they were dressing for the journey. Chad was to ride Rajah, Aisgill having given his reluctant consent, but, as Chad had said, the beast deserved some reward for having been so patient in his dressage exercises, and for having also given them four new foals, one of which looked likely to rival his father in beauty, wickedness and power.

'You'll be careful with him,' Aisgill had said the previous day.

'As with my life,' Chad had replied truthfully.

Aisgill had given him a queer look. 'I thought that the lady had run mad when she decided to marry you,' he said bluntly, 'but now. . .' And he shrugged his shoulders. 'Now I think she could have done worse. Much worse,' he added as an afterthought, watching Chad's face change when Nell came into the yard, dressed as magnificently as she always was these days; flyaway Nell Tallboys had vanished for good. Mrs Newcome was a fashion-plate.

Breakfast over, and both dressed for the journey, the coach and other baggage gone the previous day, the train they were taking with them assembled on the sweep before the beautiful façade, Vulcan's successor, Pluto, was brought round for Nell, and two lads escorted Rajah, who would still only behave himself for Chad.

Nell felt quite sentimental. It was the first time that she had gone out into the great world as a married woman. They had all decided that the stay at Penny's Hall must be done in style, Nottinghamshire society entertained, Nottingham itself visited for a few days, a boat trip to be taken up the Trent, Colwick Hall and the Musters visited, and all to be done in the intervals of looking at the coal pits there, examining the books and quizzing the obviously lax agent, before deciding whether to keep him.

'Time to go,' Chad announced, taking Nell's arm, and they walked out of the front door, through lines of servants assembled to see them off; impossible to do anything these days, thought Nell, amused, without

Henson making a pantomime of it, as though determined to show that although Nell Tallboys had married a nobody she was still the greatest lady in the North.

And finally they were on the steps, more of her people assembled, the Privy Council standing in the doorway, the train, all on horseback, patiently awaiting her — at least the men were patient, their mounts less so.

Nell was already up when the first intimation of trouble occurred. A horse and rider, foam flying in all directions from the mad speed of travel, flew through the great arch at the end of the sweep, and came to a stop before them all.

It was Ulric Tallboys. His face was alternately ashen and scarlet, his expression wild in the extreme. He advanced on Nell and on Chad, who was holding Rajah, a lad controlling the stallion on his other side.

His voice was high, furious, and he had a pistol in his hand, pulled from the holster on his saddle as he dismounted. 'So, it's true, then. You've done for me, married this piece of scum,' and he waved the pistol dangerously at Chad.

Nell, controlling her fright and unease, tried to stare him down. 'What the devil do you think you're doing, Ulric? Put that pistol away, at once. And yes, I've married Mr Newcome, as I suppose you've just heard. You received my letter?'

'Received your letter?' raved Ulric, waving the pistol at Chad, who had moved towards him. 'Keep back, I tell you, or I'll drop you where you stand. Yes, I read your letter, and you've ruined me, you bitch. I only went to Ireland to avoid a debtor's prison. The Jews and the bailiffs were after me already when it looked as though we were not to marry, and now that you have married this piece of dirt I'm like to be in a debtor's prison all my life, thanks to you. Well, I'm not having it, Nell, be damned to all of you.'

He waved the pistol again, and those around Nell, fearful for her, were afraid to do anything that might cause him to shoot her.

'Damn you,' he shrieked, 'it was only that clod you've married who saved you from death when he killed my man. Be damned to him, what have I to lose now? He shall have his reward.' And to Nell's horror he finally stopped waving the pistol, brought it up and fired at Chad, as Chad, careless of what Rajah might do if he loosed him, made for Ulric's throat, fearful that it was Nell for whom the bullet was intended.

This diversionary tactic almost certainly saved his life, since the bullet creased his skull as he lowered his head to charge, instead of taking him in the breast, but it dropped him to the ground, and Ulric, realising that he had failed, and that Nemesis was on him in the shape of Nell's people, suddenly horrified into sense by what he had done, made for Rajah in the hope of mounting him, and escaping on him.

Nell's scream of shock and horror as she saw Chad fall was lost in Rajah's snortings and whinnyings at the sight of Chad brought low, and the feel of Ulric's clumsy hands as he tried to climb into his saddle — he had already broken free from the lad.

Rajah tossed Ulric from him, and, turning, rearing, trampled him beneath his iron hoofs, transforming him into bloody rags on the ground, before flinging back his head, narrowly missing the prostrate Chad, to bolt down the drive, disappearing through the archway at the end.

Nell had already dismounted from a disturbed Pluto — all the horses present were distressed by the sudden shot — to fall on her hands and knees beside

Chad, who she feared had been killed by the man whose maimed body lay a few yards away from that of his victim. Aisgill dropped down on Chad's other side, Henson began giving frantic orders. The sudden nature of the tragedy had shocked them all, but action now followed paralysis.

She was sobbing, wailing, all her normal stoicism gone, cradling Chad's head, regardless of the blood running down his face and covering her hands, regardless of Aisgill saying, 'Come, Nell,' all ladyships forgotten, 'you must let us examine him,' for she knew only one thing: Chad might be dead, and what then did life hold for her, the reason for it being gone?

Guy and Jackson had kept up a good pace on the way north, for Jackson was fearful that Chad might already have left. He had no clear idea when exactly Chad was to go from Campions, only knew that he was working out his notice.

Guy was quite unlike his brother, in looks as well as manner, but Jackson found him a congenial companion, although a little *distrait*; his thoughts were with his brother whom he hoped to meet at journey's end.

And what then? He had asked Jackson his opinion of Shad's loss of memory, and how likely he was to regain it. Jackson had shaken his head. He had met such cases before, and they were all different, he said. Some got their memory back after a time, some never. Some, having retrieved it, forgot what had happened in the interval; others didn't. 'And no one knows why, or how,' he said. 'You meet some strange things in my line of work, Mr Guy — I mean Mr Shadwell.'

'Mr Guy,' said Guy, smiling. He liked the man, there was a bluff honesty about him, liked him the more because he seemed to respect Chad — who might be Shad.

And at last they passed into the Riding, where the land was wild and rough, like its people, Jackson said, and they were making for Campions, the great house on the edge of the moors, of which Guy had often heard and never seen, like the legendary Nell Tallboys, Countess of Malplaquet, its eccentric owner.

The the house was suddenly before them, in the distance, glowing in the watery sunlight of a late March day, at the end of a suddenly improved road — the Countess's doing, Jackson said; she had improved everything to do with her estate since she had inherited.

The works of past Earls of Malplaquet were everywhere, follies, stone bridges, triumphal arches leading to nowhere, until they could see the final great arch through which they must drive in order to reach the front of the house.

But a quarter of a mile from the arch their driver, nicknamed Pompey — another of Shad's old soldiers, now working at Clermont House, and brought along to share in the driving — said suddenly, 'Here's a fine to-do,' and tried to pull off the road, as a huge black stallion galloped past them, narrowly missing the carriage, foaming and bounding, so that it almost seemed that fire might be coming from his nostrils, finally leaving the road behind them, and running on to the moor.

. 'Rajah!' exclaimed Jackson, turning to stare. 'Now what the devil's up? Drive on, man,' and so Pompey did, through the giant arch, and there in front of them on the sweep before the Corinthian columns and the flight of steps up to them was a scene like, as Jackson said later, something in a Drury Lane spectacle.

Groups of people were milling about. A dead man was lying on the ground, broken and bloody, his head at an odd angle. Another man lay on the ground being attended to, a woman was being comforted by a middle-aged man in gamekeeper's clothes, another man in a fine gentleman's suit was shouting orders, before himself bending down to the man on the ground, who was wearing, Guy saw, a fine suit of riding clothes, and beautiful boots.

He had thick black hair in loose ringlets, was big. . . and Guy gave a hoarse shout. 'Stop, Pompey, stop,' and, on Pompey's doing so, hurled himself from the carriage to run to the group about the prostrate man, ignoring shouts and attempts to push him away by the man in the fine suit.

'Who the devil are you, sir?' the gentleman demanded, to have Guy hurl at him,

'Oh, to Hades with you, sir,' and then, 'It's you, Shad, at last,' to the man on the ground who had begun to stir, as though Guy's voice had been some sort of signal, recalling him to his old life.

Nell, Aisgill's arms around her, as though she were a girl again, began to recover herself. Nell Newcome must be as brave as Nell Tallboys had been. She was in the act of moving away from Aisgill to question Henson about Chad's condition, but as he straightened up, shouting for a servant to go fetch Dr Ramsden at once, she saw the new actors, as Jackson would have called them, arrive on the scene.

Astonished, she saw a tall fair young man, shouting something incomprehensible, hurl himself at poor Chad, who, assisted again by Henson, had begun to stir, driving away her first fears that Ulric had killed him immediately.

For Ulric she felt nothing. Later, the horror of his death would strike her, to visit her occasionally in nightmares, even though he had brought his death on himself by attempting to kill Chad, but now her only concern was her husband, and why the strange young man should throw himself at Chad, and how it was that he knew the name which Campions had given him, for Shad, to her ears, had come out as Chad.

To her infinite relief she saw Chad, blood still running down his face, try to rise, said hoarsely to Aisgill, 'Oh, thank God, he's not dead,' to hear Aisgill answer briskly,

'I told you so, my lady.'

And to her astonishment and horror she watched Chad's gaze pass over her unknowingly, and heard him ask the young man in a puzzled voice, 'Guy, where the devil am I? And what are you doing here? I thought myself in Spain when I woke up. Where's Vinnie?'

Nell was suddenly frantic at this non-recognition, the more so as Chad, ignoring her, attempted to stand, the young man, Guy — and who was he? — helping him most lovingly, an expression of acute concern on his face.

And Jackson was there, too, dismounting from the carriage, his sardonic gaze hard on them all, like a sphinx who knew all the answers, and, if he did, she, Nell Newcome, wished he would supply them.

Countess Nell at her proudest, she questioned the young man fiercely, 'Who are you, sir? And how do you know Chad?' while Henson, who had uncharacteristically been struck dumb by this strange turn of events, recovered his self-possession, and also roared at the stranger.

'Come, sir, who the devil are you?' and, pointing at

Chad, 'And who the devil's he, since you seem to know him?'

Behind them, Jackson, the only one of all of them to realise that Chad had his memory back, watched and waited.

Chad, now held upright between Aisgill and Guy, stared at Nell, said thickly, and to Nell's consternation, 'Who are you, madam, and how did I get here? I thought——' for as he had recovered consciousness he had been a guerrilla in Spain again '—I thought I was in the mountains, but then how could you be in Spain, Guy? And who are all these people? What am I doing here?' and he looked dazedly about him, wondering who the handsome woman was who stared at him so poignantly, two great tears running down her face, as the truth hit her, to bring her almost to her knees again.

Chad had got his memory back, and did not know her!

'Who am I?' said Guy, loosening his grip on his brother a little—he had been holding him as though he feared to lose him again if he were not careful—and at last answering the questions posed by Henson and the woman, who he had suddenly realised must be Nell Tallboys, and, if so, report had lied cruelly about her looks, for what a magnificent specimen she was, even in her grief. 'Why, I am Guy Shadwell, Lord Clermont's youngest son, and this——' but he was interrupted by his brother.

'Enough, Guy, enough. It must be for me to. . .confess who I am.'

Even before Guy had begun to speak, the sight of Nell moving towards him, arms outstretched, murmuring his name—for Chad sounded like Shad to him—saying brokenly, 'Oh, Chad, never say that you have forgotten me,' a look of such love and concern on her poor face, had caused something to move in Shad's head, and he remembered everything — would that he could not!

He knew that Vinnie, poor Vinnie, was seven months dead, knew why he had left London, knew of the attack, knew why he had been found wandering on the moor, knew of his service at Campions, knew why the rifle, and the dead man who had carried it, were familiar to him, knew, to his piercing horror, that he truly loved and had married the woman before him, who would not, could not now love him once she knew who he was — Charles Halstead who had defamed her — but he, and not Guy, must speak the unpalatable truth, even though it destroyed him, for the truth was all Shad had ever possessed, and he had lived by it all his life.

His face a mask of agony, he said, 'I have remembered everything. I am — God forgive me, my dearest Nell, for what I said of you, before I knew you — Charles Shadwell, Viscount Halstead; I was set on by footpads, my poor sergeant Vinnie was killed, and I was stripped and left for dead, to be saved by you and become your servant. . .'

The effort of thought, of speech, was too great for his failing senses. Shad — Chad — welcomed oblivion to give him surcease from pain and shame, and fell gratefully forward into the dark again, unconscious at the feet of the most noble lady, Nell Newcome, Countess of Malplaquet, Viscountess Wroxton, Baroness Sheveborough, all in her own right, whom he had mortally and publicly insulted seven months ago, and who he had loved with a passion beyond reason from the first moment he had seen her, and to whom he was now married.

CHAPTER NINETEEN

'You married him!' Guy's voice was almost incredulous.

'Yes,' said Nell shyly. She and Guy were in her private drawing-room, Chad's and her possessions all about them. The chessboard was set up, the backgammon board waiting to be set up, Nell's canvas work on an upright stand, books everywhere, the Campions stud book among them, the room left as it was for them to return to — everything bearing witness to their happy and useful life together.

Shad had been carried to the great bed, unconscious, their journey postponed. He was not in any danger, Dr Ramsden said, but when he had surfaced for a moment and had spoken it was plain that he was greatly confused and shocked. The strain of discovering who he was, and what had happened over the last seven months, coupled with the wound, even though it was not severe — a gash similar to the one which had helped to cause his loss of memory — had been too much for even the strong man that he was to accept easily.

He had been given laudanum to make him sleep soundly. Nell's doctor was a great believer in sleep, and now Guy was talking to Nell, and finding her quite unlike the lady of legend, in speech as well as appearance.

'Well, I'm not surprised that you did marry him,' he said slowly, 'even if, forgive me, it does seem a trifle odd, for you to marry your secretary, but Shad's such a splendid fellow.'

'Yes, he is, isn't he?' said Nell simply.

Guy hesitated, and Nell looked at him affectionately. If he thought Chad—Shad—a splendid fellow, Nell thought that Guy was a chip off the same block.

'You mustn't take any notice of the bet,' he said finally. Nell saw that Guy knew that he was on danger-ous ground, and spoke to reassure him.

Even since Chad had told her that he was Viscount Halstead, who had publicly shamed her, her mind had been in a turmoil. Her first thoughts were angry, for Lord Halstead seemed to have nothing to do with Chad Newcome, her husband whom she loved beyond life, so that when she had thought that he was dead she had understood for a moment why some widows threw themselves on funeral pyres, committed suicide.

But to reconcile Chad Newcome and Charles Halstead, that was difficult. Whenever she thought of Halstead, either now, or in the past, she was consumed with a fierce anger. But what had that to do with Chad? He was so unlike what she had assumed Charles Halstead to be from what she had heard of him. But then, wasn't she quite different from the Nell Tallboys of gossip? Her mind went round and round.

'But why?' she said, at last. 'Why did he—who you say rarely drank, get so blind drunk that he spoke of me as he did? A man who, all the time he was here, was abstemious, respected women, never troubled the female servants—why, I even had to propose to him myself in order. . .' she paused, said defiantly '. . .to get him into my bed—whereas he bet that he could have me without marriage. *That* I do not understand.'

'Well,' said Guy, 'it's like this, you see. When I was a little lad, and Shad was barely twenty—he had just joined the army, not that he wanted to be a soldier at first; he went to Oxford at fifteen, wished to be a scholar there, but Faa... Father...said no, the second son always went into the army — he met Isabella French, and fell madly in love with her.'

He stopped again, and Nell wondered what was coming, he looked so miserable. She said gently, 'You needn't tell me, if it makes you unhappy.'

'Oh, I have to tell you,' said Guy earnestly. 'He married her, you see, against Father's wishes, and Father was right — not that he knew what Isabella was; it was just that he never liked Shad for some reason, always wanted to thwart him.'

He went on. 'Well, at first the marriage seemed to be happy. She was a pretty little dark thing, not a bit like you. All Shad's women, not that there were that many,' he hastened to reassure her, 'were little. And at first they were very happy. But Shad's duties kept him away a lot, and she...couldn't live without him...it was a kind of sickness, Shad said, and she...well, she gave herself to anyone who would have her when he was away, particularly to Shad's best friend, Harvey Black, who couldn't seem to resist her.

'In the end, Shad found out; he arrived home one day to find her in bed with Harvey, and then it all came out — about him and the other men. What was worse, he fought a duel with Harvey, and then, when Harvey shot at him and missed, Shad deloped, fired into the air — he didn't want to kill him — but Harvey was ashamed of his betrayal of Shad, swore and insisted that the duel be a proper one, Shad must fire at him. They fired again, and Shad wounded him so badly that Harvey died six months later from it. You can imagine what that did to Shad.

'And then, to make it all worse, Isabella was found to

be pregnant, and the baby couldn't be Shad's. But he
stuck with her, until she died in childbirth. Yes, I know,
Nell,' he said gently, on seeing her horrified face, and
hearing her murmur,

'Poor Chad.'

'Yes, I know it's a horrid story, couldn't be worse.
After that, he barely looked at women seriously, until
last year he met Julia Merton, another little thing, and
the whole rotten business began again.

'It turned out that Julia was Jack Broughton's mistress, and was marrying Shad for convenience. It all
came out when Shad found her with him—you can
imagine what *that* did to him after the business with
Isabella, and that was why on the day he found out he
drank himself stupid, went to Watier's and made that
awful bet about you; your cousin Bobus was boasting
about your—inaccessibility, and that worked him up.
Father was badgering him to marry you, into the
bargain. I know he shouldn't have done it, but you can
see why.'

Yes, Nell could see why. She walked to the window,
looked out over the moors, and thought of a young and
chivalrous Shad, his life in ruins—and then for it to
happen again!

'Not Shad's fault,' said Guy, 'that he picked wrong
'uns; his misfortune. I suppose they picked him because
he was so good and steady at bottom. Everyone envied
him Isabella and Julia. It was only afterwards people
realised that they were both lightskirts at heart.'

Nell thought of how she had tempted him, and flushed
at the memory—and then of how he had held off. He
had been good and steady with her, too, and that was
partly why, in the end, she had been so wild to
marry him.

'He quarrelled with Faa over it,' Guy said, 'and that was when he drove north, to be attacked and lose his memory. Was he happy here?' he asked.

'Yes,' answered Nell, 'very happy. We were both happy.' She thought of their mutual joy, of the badinage which had passed between them, as well as the passion, of their shared pleasure in the horses, in their books, and the running of Campions. 'Yes,' she repeated, 'very happy.'

'I'm glad,' said Guy fervently. 'He's never been really happy, except perhaps when he was in the army, doing his duty—Shad's great on duty—and then he had to give that up when our elder brother Frederick died. And Father wasn't even grateful when Shad cleared up the mess Frederick had made of running the estates.' And then he added thoughtfully, 'Perhaps he was happy because he no longer carried the burden of the memories of Isabella, Julia and Faa's dislike,' unknowingly echoing what Jackson had said to Chad Newcome earlier.

He didn't tell Nell the truth about his eldest brother, but Nell knew from his manner that he had not loved Frederick as he plainly loved Shad.

'One good thing about all this—apart from Shad meeting you, that is—is that Faa's wild to make up to Shad for mistreating him all his life. Wants to be reconciled. I can't wait to tell him. Shad always loved Faa—God knows why, he was never fair to him.'

Nell walked over to Guy, and kissed him on the cheek. 'A present for my new brother,' she said. 'I've never had a brother, and now I've inherited a good one. Welcome to Campions, Guy.'

She was amused and touched at his response. 'Oh, you're a good 'un, Nell. Not a bit like they said you were. And so handsome, too. Whatever was all the gossip about. . .?' He stopped, flushing at what he had almost said.

'That I was plain, you mean?' she said, laughing at him, looking more vital than ever. 'Well, I know I'm no beauty.'

'Nonsense,' said Guy sturdily. 'You're the finest woman I've ever met, and I really envy Shad. You won't be hard on him when he's himself again, will you?' he said anxiously. 'I know Shad. He'll be worrying himself sick over the bet.'

Talking to Guy, listening to him about Shad, and not only the sad story he had told her, but the way in which his face lit up when he spoke of his brother, his unselfish joy that he was alive, when his death would have meant Guy's advancement, touched Nell, told her that her choice of a husband, made blindly, and against all conventional common sense, was a good one.

'No,' she said. 'No. I won't hate him and reproach him. Why, Guy, let me tell you the sad truth about myself. I believe I told my uncle that nothing in the world would induce me to marry Charles Halstead, and then when I met him I couldn't wait to do so, married him in defiance of the whole world!

'You have *no idea* how relieved Henson, my agent, is that Chad is a nobleman in disguise. He had been repressing his misgivings since the wedding-day, and now he's cock-a-hoop. I told him an hour ago that Chad is still Chad, even though he's Shad, but he'll have none of it.'

'Henson's your grand gentleman ordering everyone about?' asked Guy ingenuously, amusing Nell again.

'Yes, that's Henson. He liked Chad, but not as Malplaquet's master. I can't wait to see him bowing and scraping to Chad—"Yes, my lord, no, my lord". His universe will be an orderly one again.'

She was suddenly happy Nell Newcome again. Yes, she would tease Chad a little about the disgraceful bet, but be sure to let him know very soon that it was only teasing, that nothing he had said and done in his old life could wipe out what they had come to mean to one another since they had first met.

'And I must write to Faa,' said Guy. 'Jackson can take the letter back to London with him. And he's cock-a-hoop, too. All his mysteries solved, and he was right about your cousin Ulric, as well.'

'Poor Ulric,' said Nell. 'I can't grieve too much for him. He did try to have me killed, but he was my cousin, and as a little boy he was a bully, yet he was, apart from Uncle Beaumont, practically the only relative I had.'

She began to giggle. 'Uncle Beaumont! What's he going to say when he learns the truth? Let me tell you of him. What an about-facer that will be!'

'No,' said Shad, bruised and broken though he felt. 'I am not staying in bed for a head wound as mild as this is, and, as for damaged nerves and restoring my system, I am not a fourteen-year-old schoolgirl afflicted with the vapours. If you don't send for my clothes I shall take you by the throat, and throttle you until you give way,' and he glared at poor Ramsden who said, dodging away as his patient looked thunder at him,

'Now, Mr Newcome, my lord, pray do not excite yourself, but you really ought to rest a little.'

'I don't intend to excite myself,' ground out Shad, 'merely give myself the satisfaction of half killing you unless you do as I wish,' and he threw back the

bedclothes and made motions at Ramsden, trying to
ignore his swimming head. The one thing that he
wanted to do was to see Nell and try to convince her of
how much he loved her, and how he regretted what he
had said of her in his drunken folly, and this fool was
keeping him from seeing her. And he was damned if he
wanted to talk to her flat on his back in bed like a. . .
mollycoddle.

Ramsden, now with his back to the door, said wearily,
'I see that there is no stopping you, my lord. Perhaps it
may be wise on my part to allow you to rise; you will
soon discover how shaky you are.'

All Shad's ill-humour, which was partly caused by
his fears about where he really stood with Nell—
ludicrous to think that as a nobody he had possessed no
such fears, but now as Charles Halstead, her equal, he
felt as queasy as a green boy every time he thought of
her—leached out of him. Shameful so to speak to a man
who was, after all, only doing his duty. All his old
charming courtesy, so well known to Campions,
returned.

'I'm sorry, sir,' he said. 'I should not have spoken so.
Do but allow me this, I beg.'

'Only if you allow me my reservations,' said Ramsden
stiffly. 'I will send for one of the footmen to bring you
your clothing, and help you to dress.'

And where was Nell? Shad thought, as he allowed the
footman to tie his cravat, grateful to allow himself to be
nannied for once, he felt so weak and worthless. Was
she so disgusted that she had married the brute who
had bet on her and maligned her that she no longer
wished to see him?

Almost he wished that his memory had not returned,
that he was still plain Chad Newcome, and then he

thought of Guy's face when he had seen him, and of his duty to his father, and the estate to which he had been born. He could not be Chad Newcome, accountable to no one but Nell who had given him life, love, herself and Campions.

He shuddered at the thought of her, at the possibility of losing her, and her love, and, when Ramsden returned to examine the bandage around his head, said abruptly, beneath his ministrations, 'And Lady Elinor, she is well, I trust.'

'I hope so,' said Ramsden drily. 'She spent most of the night at your bedside after she dined with your brother, and I suspect that she is catching up on her sleep—if she is wiser than you are, begging your pardon, my lord, about her health.'

She had sat by his bed! Perhaps after all she could forgive him. He jerked a little as the doctor's touch became painful, called, 'Come in,' to the knocker at the door.

Henson entered; a cat whose cream had proved satisfactory. 'My lord,' he said—Nell's prophecy had been correct, the world was no longer turned upside-down, and Henson was happy. 'My lord, your brother has suggested that you be asked if you can remember where you might have been attacked, and in what circumstances. It might lead us to where your sergeant's remains may be found. We have assumed that he was killed when you were attacked, as you were found on your own, no sign of a companion.'

Poor Vinnie. Here he was having the blue devils about himself, with no thought for what had happened to the faithful friend with whom he had campaigned both in and out of war.

'I think I remember,' he said slowly. 'You must

understand that I was barely conscious at the time, and everything is confused. After they killed Vinnie, they stripped me, and then sat him beside me, and later I remember falling, and after that climbing. They threw the carriage and the pair of us into a quarry, you think? Which would account for the state of my hands when I was found.'

'Most like, my lord, most like,' said Henson, his manner, previously correctly cool to poor Chad, now almost unctuous, or as unctuous as such a dry stick could be. 'There are two near Campions land; a search shall be made at once, my lord. I shall organise it,' and he turned to go.

'Henson,' asked Shad, 'tell me, is Lady Elinor up yet?'

'I heard that she was stirring, my lord, and her maid said that she had eaten a late breakfast. She slept in the guest suite, my lord. Dr Ramsden thought it best that you be left on your own, my lord.' He was gone, and painfully Shad walked out of the room himself, to find Nell, and learn how he stood with her.

Nell, seated in her drawing-room, late up for the first time in years, was debating whether or not to go and see her husband, when the door opened, and, to her astonishment, he walked in.

'Chad!' she said. 'Should you be up? I thought you still asleep. Dr Ramsden refused me entry this morning.' His face was white, with great purple smudges under his eyes, and his head bandaged, giving him the appearance of a rakish Arab, she thought.

'Lady Malplaquet,' he said, bowing, quite formal, and quite unlike his manner as Chad, so that Nell knew at once that Guy had been correct when he had said how troubled his brother would be.

'Not wise, perhaps, but I am not a great one for lying in a bed, and besides, I needed to see you.'

Oh, the poor love, how nervous he was! She longed to go over, hug him, tell him not to worry, but perhaps he deserved to suffer a little for what he had said and done in his drunken folly seven months ago, even if he had got his injury as the result of attacking Ulric when he had thought Ulric might be attacking *her*.

'My lord?' she said, as formal as he, so that suddenly, to her delight, she saw his grim aspect lighten a little.

'Oh, dear, Nell, don't you start. I've already had Henson my-lording me at every second word; you'd think that no one else had ever borne a title.'

Nell gave an un-Countesslike giggle. 'Did he so? I told Guy that he would.'

'Relieved to find me respectable, I suppose,' remarked Shad, a little morosely. 'Nell, I have so much to say to you, so much to ask you to forgive me for, that I hardly know how to begin. Isabella——'

'No need to speak to me of Isabella, or Julia Merton for that matter,' replied Nell briskly. 'I've already heard all about them from Guy, and I really do not wish to hear any more, so you may set your mind at ease over that.'

Shad hardly knew whether he was grateful to Guy or not; on balance, he thought, probably gratitude was in order. 'Now, about the other matter——'

'By other matter,' interrupted Nell sweetly, 'I suppose, Lord Halstead, you mean your bet. Now, that really does exercise me. I am not sure what you exactly wagered, so I cannot decide whether or not you won or lost. Foolish of you to refuse me in the annexe; you

would have been richer by twenty thousand pounds had
you done so. On the other hand, if the bet was suitably
vague — and only you know that, if, of course, you can
recall what you actually said; I believe you were dead
drunk at the time, most unlike you, but there it is —
then perhaps our marriage may be sufficient for you to
win it. You see what a quandary I am in. I don't know
whether to congratulate you or commiserate with you.'

At the end of this remarkable speech she had the
pleasure of seeing her husband look suitably agonised,
so added to further disconcert him, 'I understand that
we are a sorry pair. I heard that you had said that of all
people you would never marry me, while I told my dear
uncle Beaumont exactly the same thing in the same
somewhat indelicate terms about you. And here we are,
tightly joined to the very partner for whom we had
previously expressed extreme aversion. Sheridan, were
he still alive, would have found it a suitable subject for
comedy, I'm sure.'

'Nell, Nell, it is not a joke,' protested Shad. 'Here am
I trying to tell you how sorry I am for what I said. . .'
He stopped. His head was thundering away, and his
heart was doing the same thing. Had he lost her or not?
Difficult to tell when she was roasting him so preposter-
ously — but, after all, he deserved it, did he not?

'Well, I don't propose to cry over it,' said Nell
robustly, 'and it's hardly grounds for divorce, so we
seem to be destined to remain firmly attached to one
another, legally, if in no other way. I wonder if the
terms of the settlement allow me to pay your bet? If
you've lost it, that is. And will that noble conscience of
yours allow you to accept my assistance?'

'I'm hardly stumped for twenty thousand,' Shad said,
'little though I shall like paying out such a sum as the

consequence of my own folly — why are we going on in this havy-cavy manner, Nell? I came down to apologise to you, and you have done nothing but talk nonsense since I arrived. My head won't stand it,' he said plaintively.

'Well, let me relieve your deserved misery a little,' said Nell, deciding not to push the joke too far. 'Guy tells me that the bet was never properly registered; you were too foxed to sign anything, or whatever gentlemen do on such occasions, and consequently the terms of it are immaterial, and there is no chance of your winning or losing anything, and I shall not need to perjure myself by declaring that we. . .anticipated our wedding vows — you see how delicate becoming a married woman has made me; goodness knows, by the time we have our first child I shall be so proper that a College of Vestal Virgins would envy me. Why are you laughing, Chad? What are you doing?'

For, thundering head and all, Shad had given a little groan, leaned forward and pulled her from her chair where she had been sitting, looking up at him with the most provoking smile on her face as she teased him beyond endurance.

'I won't have it, Nell,' he muttered distractedly. 'I don't care how badly I behaved, or what you think of me; I love you, dammit, to distraction, and if you continue as you are doing you will be pleasured on the carpet immediately, thereby either finishing me off for good, or allowing Henson to come in and find us at work, and how he would deal with that I should like to find out, but am unlikely to do so.'

And then he had her in his arms and was kissing her wilful mocking face, until they both sank on to the sofa, where for a moment it looked as though they might end up celebrating the fact that they were husband and wife despite the possibility of being interrupted, or doing Shad's head a permanent harm.

Sanity suddenly reigned. They pulled apart, Nell rosy, Shad greyer than ever, but happier than he had thought was possible since he had finally remembered who he was on the previous afternoon.

'So, I am forgiven, Lady Malplaquet, for the wicked things I said before I knew you?'

'And I am forgiven, Lord Halstead,' she answered, suddenly serious, 'for the wicked things I said and thought about you?'

His answer was a kiss, and another saucy look from Nell when lovemaking paused for a moment. 'Well, one thing that's certain,' she said wickedly, 'is that whatever anyone else thinks of our marriage we are sure to please your father and my uncle, and that must be something to cheer about, seeing that neither of them has ever been pleased with us before!'

Shad's shout of laughter at that nearly took his poor head off.

'Oh, Nell,' he groaned, 'you really must stop, or you will have me back on my bed of pain again, and Ramsden will say, "I told you so," and I don't think I could endure that; he's displeased with me enough already.'

'Happy to think that my wishes come second to your physician's,' Nell riposted, and then, when he reached for her again, 'No, Shad, for Shad you will be from now on, I will be serious. We have a great deal to arrange as soon as you are recovered, for, whereas Lady Malplaquet marrying penniless and landless Chad was one thing, I am sure that Lord Halstead marrying the lady will provide the lawyers with work for a twelve-month.'

Shad had already thought that life as his old self was likely to be a great deal more complicated than that which he had lived since he had arrived at Campions. He thought wistfully of unencumbered Chad, who was rapidly disappearing into the past — the Chad who Aisgill had thought *might* have been a corporal, or perhaps even a sergeant, in the cavalry, but who, in reality, had been a captain, and later an aide, and a good one. Landless unknown Chad, actually Charles Shadwell, Viscount Halstead, Clermont's heir, with all that that entailed in duties, responsibilities, as well as rank and privilege.

Campions, and Aisgill, would have to come to terms with Shad, but there were already signs that Campions was happy to discover that the mistress had chosen so truly when she had given poor Chad her heart and her inheritance.

'Not yet,' he said gently, pulling her into the crook of his arm, where she fitted as though she had been designed for nothing else. 'For the moment, alone here, let us be the Countess and her secretary, duties and responsibilities forgotten.' And then, belying his own words, he started up. 'Rajah, what happened to him?'

Nell pulled him down again. 'He trotted in off the moor late last night, exhausted, like his master, but, like him, he will recover, I hope.'

'I am already recovering,' announced Shad firmly, 'and will continue to do so, provided you do not provoke me too much. A suitable deference to your lord and master would do wonderful things for me. See to it, Mrs Newcome, see to it.'

'Willingly,' murmured Nell, 'willingly, provided

always you offer a similar duty to the mistress of
Campions.'

They lay there, comfortable and settled for life, Chad
Newcome — and his Countess.

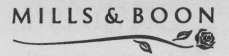

LEGACY of LOVE

Coming next month

HIDDEN FLAME
Elizabeth Bailey

England 1797

Miss Theodosia Kyte knew she only had herself to blame for her present dire circumstances, but her only alternative was, she felt, totally closed to her. So as a companion to the old tartar, Lady Merchistan, she made the best of a bad job – until Mr Benedict Beckenham arrived to visit his godmother!

Because of his scandalous background, Benedict's aim was unqualified acceptance by Society, but for that he needed to marry money, and Theda did not qualify, despite his passion for her! Impasse – until that arch manipulator Lady Merchistan put the cat among the pigeons…

ONE LOVE
Valentina Luellen

Atlanta 1864

Shanna de Lancel, though orphaned by the progress of the American Civil War, was more fortunate than most, for she had her faithful servant, her money, and the friendship of Alexander Amberville, who took them to his plantation *Wildwood*. Shanna welcomed the peace, so was all the more unprepared for the arrival of Rafe Amberville – the son and heir, but at odds with his father and brother Wayne! Only slowly did it dawn on Shanna that she was a pawn in intrigue she did not understand, but who was she to trust? Wayne – or Rafe…

LEGACY *of* LOVE

Coming next month

DEVIL WIND
Catherine Blair

France 1789

High on the cliffs overlooking the sea, Devil Wind castle
loomed dark and foreboding. This was Rochella's new home
– and she knew instantly that her husband, Lord Devlin, was
equally unhappy with their arranged marriage.

At first sight of his enchanting bride, Devlin longed to defy
his name and its burdens. For Rochella's safety, he must keep
theirs a marriage in name only. Yet, how long could he run
from the need to love her as his heart demanded? Spellbound
with desire Rochella would soon discover the dark secrets
that cast their shadow on a man who had sworn never to love.

ODESSA GOLD
Linda Shaw

USA 1897

Genny Carlyle wasn't sure she trusted Odessa Gold. The man
was an ex-convict and a gambler, and who knew what else. It
was true – she didn't really have much choice. Yet there was
something about Odessa that made her want to follow him,
no matter where he led.

Ten years in an Arizona prison had hardened Odessa against
the lure of innocent young women. So why, then, did he find
himself wanting to take on Genny Carlyle's battles and fight
them for her? With Genny, there was a bright future up
ahead, but his past was quickly closing in on them, and the
time to turn and face the darkness had finally come.

TWO
HISTORICAL
ROMANCES
&
TWO
FREE GIFTS!